# THE FORGIVEN COWBOY'S BEST FRIEND

MELODY ARCHER

# BOOK REVIEWS

*"Such a heart warming story. Many misconceptions and those who should really care & love you are the ones who hurt you the most. Throughout all the happenings their second chance comes and makes for families to reconcile with the past."*
*~Amazon Review*

*"There is no doubt that this is a beautiful love story. However, Archer does a masterful job of revealing how much one's private life affects their relationships with others. Loved the book from cover to cover."*
*Suzette ~ Amazon Reviewer*

# WANT TO READ MORE SWEET ROMANCE?

**Eliza and Daniel Stevenson's love story is waiting for you.:)**
**Grab your copy of this Free Sweet and Clean Romance!**
**Go here:** https://www.melodyarcher.com/free-book/

*"Forgiveness is a strange thing. It can sometimes be easier to forgive our enemies than our friends. It can be hardest of all to forgive people we love." Fred Rogers*

# PROLOGUE

The airplane landed with a sudden jolt on the tarmac at the International Airport in Great Falls, Montana.

Wyatt James Callahan winced at the sudden movement.

He expelled a breath and rubbed his leg as painful memories returned from this last tour of duty.

After weeks of living through physical hardship, mental anguish and waking up with nightmares, his commanding officer had without warning, let Wyatt know he was going home.

He suspected someone higher up in the chain of command might have pulled some strings.

Truth be told, he hadn't wanted to come home.

He failed his men. He failed his father's expectations. And he failed his best friend.

This time Wyatt knew he had messed up big time.

Now, he would have to face everyone who was important to him.

That was the scariest part of all.

Limping slightly as he got off the plane, he saw his brother Denver leaning against the back wall of the lobby.

His black cowboy hat sat at an angle on his long head. Seeing the familiar sight from their growing up years, a pang of homesickness swirled in his belly.

His brother looked up and spotted him. A grin turned up the corners of his mouth.

"Hey, man." Denver grabbed him and pulled him into a big bear hug.

His brother had always been one to show his affection.

Today, more than ever, he appreciated the hug.

"Good to see you, Denver." Wyatt slipped his duffel bag onto his shoulder as they waited by the luggage claim. Soon his black suitcase came around with his name written in bold red across the front.

Denver grabbed the bag before he could take it. "Got it. Let's go, little brother."

Wyatt chuckled. "Just because you're taller by one inch, doesn't change the fact that you're still my *younger* brother."

"Yeah, whatever." Denver laughed out loud as he led the way out of the airport and to the parking lot. After they set Wyatt's suitcase and bag in the back of the pickup truck, they began the windy trail home toward their family ranch.

He smiled inwardly as he thought of the place where he'd grown up most his life. Callahan Cattle Crossing. It seemed fitting that his father had named his ranch the Triple C.

"So, Dad managed to bring everyone home for Christmas this year?" Wyatt turned to his brother, increasingly feeling the need for answers.

"Yep. He insisted on everyone being together." Denver shook his head from side to side.

Wyatt's brow puckered in worry. "It makes me wonder why."

"Who knows? Maybe Dad was feeling a little nostalgic and wanted the family together again for Christmas. I mean it is his favorite time of year." Denver shrugged.

"Hmm. Maybe." Somehow Wyatt was sure it was more than that, but he didn't voice his thoughts out loud.

His shoulders stiffened as they drove up to the sprawling ten bedroom ranch house that was set between tall pine trees arching high into the sky.

For better or for worse, he was home.

Loud barks greeted him as he opened the truck door.

Two large Bernese mountain dogs barked loudly and bounded up to his side, tails wagging.

"Hey there, Jack and Jill. I've missed you two." Wyatt scratched behind their ears. "Are the two of you still competing for affection?" Jill snuggled closer, wanting to outdo her companion.

He chuckled and with one last scratch for each of them, turned and grabbed his bags from the back of the truck.

A chilly wind from the North bit into his cheeks as he walked up the steps to the front porch. Snow continued to float down from the sky, covering the ranch in a fluffy white blanket.

Wyatt stared out at the rough ranch land that stretched out for miles.

He looked at the snow covered barn and the fenced pasture that lay just beyond.

A smile turned up the corners of his mouth as he remembered the day Mack and Annie Callahan had brought him to their ranch home as a foster child.

He'd been the first child they had brought to their home. Only eight years old at the time, the Callahan ranch to him had seemed like pure Heaven compared to the broken home he'd come from.

Mack and Annie must have appreciated having him around, because in the end they adopted him. Within the next few months, they had brought home seven other boys. A passel of hurting orphaned boys between the ages of six and eight had found a new home.

Within a couple of years, they had adopted eight boys, who were proud to call themselves part of the Callahan family.

This family and ranch at the base of mountains had been the best place for Wyatt and his brothers to grow up.

And they soon grew to love their new Dad and Mom.

Since their Dad called each of them home for Christmas, Wyatt knew it must be serious. Mack Callahan was never one to make a fuss about anything.

He'd always been a tough cowboy. A man's man.

Wyatt had looked up to his Dad since he'd been adopted. Each of his sons respected him. Which was also why they did their best to return to the ranch when he called them home.

A pucker formed between his brows. What was the real reason Dad had asked each of his sons to return home?

The front door squeaked open, when he turned, he saw his brother Denver poke his head through the opening. "Wyatt? Come in from the cold. Mrs. Garrett tells me dinner's ready."

"Coming." Wyatt sighed and went up the remaining stairs and into the ranch house.

"Look who finally made it home." Sawyer walked over and gave him a quick hug. "Good to see you, man."

Wyatt grinned. "Glad to see you too." He looked around at his six brothers. "All of you." A strong sense of belonging always hit him when he came back to the ranch.

And as much as he wished Mack hadn't ordered him back home, now that he was here, he was grateful to connect with his family once again.

Each of his brothers gave him a quick hug, giving him loud greetings and ribbing him with old family jests.

Suddenly his brothers moved aside and Wyatt saw his tall, broad shouldered father step toward him.

His heart stopped for a moment and he felt as if the clock had turned back in time to when he was a small eight-year-old boy facing Mack Callahan for the first time.

Wyatt's hand shook slightly and his brows creased together. Unanswered questions flooded him. Would the prodigal son be welcomed home?

His once strong father now walked slower with a limp, his once tall and straight frame slightly bent over.

Mack Callahan's grey gaze held his for a long moment before he spoke. "You came back."

"Yes, sir. Just in time for Christmas." Wyatt stood still, his years as a soldier never far away. He swallowed and nervously waited for his father to say something.

Without warning, his Dad placed one large hand on Wyatt's shoulder and squeezed.

Mack's grey eyes misted as his steady gaze met Wyatt's. "I've missed you, son. Welcome home."

With those words, Wyatt was pulled into a bear hug by his father.

His own arms trembled as he embraced his dad.

It had been a little over four years since he'd last been home.

Tears pricked at his eyes and Wyatt blinked rapidly to stop them from escaping and running down his cheeks. He clapped his dad on the back, relieved to have been welcomed home.

He didn't deserve a welcome. He didn't deserve forgiveness. And he didn't deserve love.

Yet, from his father's tight embrace, it seemed, that's exactly what was offered.

Wyatt swallowed convulsively as his Dad stepped back, the trembling still in his arms.

His Dad grinned widely and slapped Wyatt's shoulder once more, before turning his gaze to his other sons. "Let's eat. It's time to celebrate."

"Now, just you wait a minute, Mack Callahan. My oldest son, needs a hug from his mother." His Mom walked between all his brothers, her gaze focused point-edly on him. She stood still, just staring at him for a moment, her blue eyes glistening as tears bordered her eyes.

Suddenly, a large smile appeared and she gracefully wiped a stray tear with the corner of her apron.

Wyatt walked forward and gently embraced Annie Callahan in a big hug.

When he finally released her, she was smiling from ear to ear. "Welcome home, son." She turned to look at her large family. "Now, we're ready to eat."

All seven brothers followed their Mom and Dad's slow-moving gait to the large dining room. This area of the house had been specially designed for his Mom.

Annie Callahan had asked for a large kitchen and dining room that overlooked the grassy knoll that led down to her garden area and where they could view the thousands of acres of the Triple C ranch.

Mack had done exactly that, determined to do what-ever it took to make the woman he loved happy.

For all their growing-up years, they had sat in this spot for breakfast and supper. Everything had stayed the same until last year. Now it looked like, once again there would be a need for changes. Wyatt could see that his Dad's health was failing.

"It's so good to have my sons around the table again." Mack sat at the head of the table, a slight smile hovering over his lips as his gaze reached each of his sons. Annie sat next to him on his right hand side, a smile on her face as she looked at her husband.

"Not all of your sons made it home, Dad." Dakota's

husky voice came from the other end of the long table, his low voice sounded strangled.

A tear trailed down Mack's weathered cheek and with a shaky hand he quickly wiped it away. "I know and I'm sorry for it. I miss Levi every day, son."

Wyatt looked at Dakota, seeing the anguish in his eyes at the loss of the brother that had been closest to him not only in age, but in friendship.

Dakota and Levi had a strong bond that had formed ever since Mack and Annie Callahan adopted them. They'd only been a month apart in age, each of them from a different family heritage.

Yet, even those differences — something that each of his brothers shared — didn't bother them. Instead, they had formed a bond that had been unbreakable.

Dakota hurriedly swiped a stray tear from his cheek.

"It's because we are missing one of our own that I'm even more grateful that you all are home." Mack swallowed, his grey eyes shimmering with tears as his gaze slowly swept over each one of his sons around the table.

Each of his sons were clearly moved as they remembered the brother who had died the year before during covert military operations.

Cole spoke up. "We're happy to spend the holiday with you, Dad. But you've got us worried. Why did you call us all together?"

Wyatt looked at his father, glad his brother had spoken up.

He definitely noticed as he walked through the door, that his normally powerful father — the formidable cowboy Mack Callahan — looked older and frailer. He echoed Cole's worries.

"I'll get to that. I do have something important to talk to you all about." He looked at Mrs. Garrett, who was now standing by the open kitchen door, wiping her hands on her apron. "But, we'll say grace first so Mrs. Garrett's wonderful meal doesn't get cold."

Each of them bowed their head, a tradition that had begun a string of firsts, ever since each boy had been adopted by Mack and Annie Callahan. When his Dad finished saying grace, each of them started passing the food around the table.

"Mrs. Garrett, you've outdone yourself as usual. Military food doesn't even come close to your home-cooked meals. Thank you." Wyatt smiled at the cook who had been a fixture in the Callahan household for as long as he could remember.

"Wyatt, I've missed feeding your empty stomach. Glad you're back, so I can feed you again." Mrs. Garrett winked at him, a big smile on her face as she walked around the table, double checking everyone had been served.

Wyatt noticed his Mom paid extra attention to Mack, whose hands shook a little when he tried cutting his roast beef.

Annie made quick work of cutting up the food on his plate. "I think it's tougher to cut this time. Let me do it."

"Oh, alright." Mack nodded, a grateful smile on his pale face.

As always Wyatt was grateful his Mom had found a way to help Dad without embarrassing him. She had always been a huge blessing to their family.

His brows furrowed with worry. It didn't really go away until they had finished eating and Mack started talking.

"I know you boys are wondering why I asked you home for Christmas this year." Mack wiped his mouth with the napkin, setting it down on his plate before he looked at each one of his sons. "Before I tell you why I've asked you all to come home, I want to share with you a story."

He took a sip of water before he continued. "I don't know if I ever told you boys the story of how your mother and I met, but I wanted to tell it today."

Each of his sons looked at their father, eager to hear what he had to say.

Mack looked at Annie and reached over, squeezing her hand.

"As you know, your Mom and I have been married fifty-one years." Mack Callahan paused and swallowed. Wyatt glanced at his parents, a warmth filling him at the incredible love for each other he saw reflected in their eyes.

Expelling a heavy sigh, Mack continued. "But what you might not know, is that the first time I asked her to marry me, she refused."

His father's eyes crinkled at the corners as he got caught up in memories. "We first met right here in our small town of Refuge Mountain. Back then it was a nothing more than a small town with a general store, a small church and a one room school-house."

Mack sighed at Annie and patted her hand, then turned to his sons with a faraway look in his eyes. "I still remember to this day when I first saw Annie. It was around the start of the new school year. I had just started my last year in school and into the classroom walked this girl with big brown eyes and long brown hair.

"She wore a pink ribbon in her hair that day, and it matched the pink blouse she wore. She was as pretty as a picture." He winked at his wife.

"When the teacher introduced her as a new student, I wrote down her name in my notebook, determined to memorize it so I could get to know her."

Mack chuckled. "And I got to know her. I'd walk her to school, and we'd see each other at church on Sundays. I fell in love with Annie. She said she loved me too, and so the day after I turned nineteen, I asked her father for permission to marry her."

Dad shook his head. "He refused. Said, he wasn't about to let his only daughter marry the son of a dirt-poor farmer. In short, I was told in no uncertain terms that I wasn't good enough to marry Annie."

Mack sighed heavily.

"So, you married her anyway." Denver leaned back in his chair, amusement tilting up the corners of his mouth.

Mack nodded. "I did, but it wasn't until five years later that I'd finally get my chance."

"What happened, Dad?" Wyatt remembered his Mom saying something about how she met Mack Callahan when he was younger, but now he couldn't remember the story.

"Well, I tried to talk Annie into marrying me anyway, but she told me she didn't feel right going against her Dad's wishes." Mack sighed. "I was heartbroken and angry over Annie's decision. I ended up leaving home and joining the military. I was desperate to get away."

Mack shook his head. "A year later, a letter from my mom informed me that my Annie was getting married. She married a businessman. I was heartbroken and used the pain and anger to pour myself into serving my country. I rose quickly in the ranks, reaching the rank of Major."

He expelled a breath before continuing. "Turns out, Annie was only married three years before her first husband Ted died unexpectedly. And just a few months after that Annie's father died from a heart attack, leaving Annie alone and living with her mother."

"When I returned home, the following year after I finished my tour of duty, Annie was back living with her mother in her parents' old home. She was still as beautiful as ever. I worked on my Dad's farm and bought more land and cattle to expand the ranch and I courted Annie. A few months later, Annie finally said yes to my proposal."

"I'm so happy I said yes, my love." His mom's gentle words were followed by a loving smile for their Dad.

Wyatt could see that his brothers were moved as he was, by their Dad's romance with their Mom.

"Yours and Mom's love story was one for the books, Dad." Wyatt spoke up and took a sip of water.

"Yes, it was." Mack ran a shaky hand through his silver hair, his gaze unwavering as he looked on each of his sons. "There's a reason I wanted to share our story with you all today." He hesitated a moment. "Our story is about second chances in life and in love."

Wyatt squirmed a little in his chair as he thought about the one love of his life that he'd lost forever.

Why was Dad bringing this up now?

Mack set his elbows on the dinner table and steepled his fingers as his gaze focused on each of his sons. "What better time to talk about second chances, than with all of you boys gathered around my table at Christmas? It's the season of hope, miracles and love."

Wyatt could see his other six brothers moving restlessly in their chairs. He was glad he wasn't the only one who found all of Dad's talk of love and second chances uncomfortable. He figured he didn't need the reminder of the love of his life that he'd lost.

He sure hoped Dad would make his point soon. All this talk of love and marriage was making him squirm.

Mack swallowed emotion before he continued. "Your Mother and I have had a long talk. She understands each of her sons better than anyone. We know each of you has lost a woman you once loved. Our fondest wish is that each of our sons would get their second chance at love, just like we did."

Mack grinned, first at his wife, then at each of his sons. "That's why I'm going to do whatever it takes, to see each of my seven sons find brides they love."

Wyatt's belly tightened and his shoulders tensed. There was a look of determination in his father's eyes as he leaned back in his chair.

The satisfied smile his dad wore on his wrinkled face was a look he remembered all too well.

What exactly was Mack Callahan plotting this time?

# CHAPTER ONE

yatt

A SHARP CRACK of thunder in the sky above shook the large group of mourners who stood solemnly at the graveside.

Sudden flashes of lightning raced across the darkened sky, lighting up the two large bells that hung side-by-side on the Bell tower of the Community Church in their small town of Refuge Mountain along the base of the mountains in northern Montana.

Wyatt James Callahan stood motionless as he watched multiple bursts of light brighten the Church Bells against the blackened sky.

The bells reminded him of all those things he used to count on in his life: *hope, miracles and love.*

Now, years later, he couldn't lay claim to any of those gifts for himself.

Wyatt was convinced he didn't deserve good in his life. *At least not anymore.*

He'd hurt too many people. He'd made too many mistakes. He'd done too much wrong.

To his way of thinking, some things he'd done didn't deserve forgiveness.

His gaze lowered from the Church Bells in the background, to the casket sinking deep into the ground.

Today he mourned the death of a good friend.

Tom was someone he'd grown up with here in Refuge Mountain.

This was the second funeral Wyatt had stood by in the last three days.

Their Dad, Mack Callahan, had passed away a few days ago, and it had shaken him and his family to the core. His mom and six brothers had stood silently by Dad's graveside as his body was placed in the earth.

Besides his brother Levi's passing, a couple of years ago, burying Mack Callahan had been one of the most difficult losses he'd experienced.

It had been unexpected and heartbreaking.

Last year at Christmas his dad never let on that he was dying. Wyatt shouldn't have been surprised. It was like his father to be stoic and muscle his way through whatever hand life dealt him.

Wyatt really missed him.

It had been a huge loss for each of Mack Callahan's sons to lose their father's solid and steady presence.

Wyatt wasn't looking forward to a future without his Dad in his life.

But he wasn't going to think about that today.

Today he was here to honor a friend who lost his life.

Sergeant Tom Hart's sudden death, under Wyatt's military command two weeks ago in combination with his own injuries, had been the reason he'd come home a little earlier than planned.

Facing the small group of mourners, he stood straight and tall, his body tense. He was dressed in full Captain uniform out of respect for his friend, who had died in their last combat mission.

Wyatt pulled his mouth into a tight line and stared at the newly covered grave. His hand shook as memories haunted him of that day. He clenched his hand into a fist, keeping it at his side to stop the shaking.

He should be the one buried today, instead of his friend.

It was his fault Sergeant Hart had died.

He knew of at least one other person mourning Tom's death who would agree.

Abby Hart.

Wyatt turned, using his full six-foot-three inch height to find her. As she stood next to the grave, her black hat shielded the beautiful face he knew so well. Her mother and sister were on one side, and Tom's mom — Abby's mother-in-law — on her other side.

Abby was well and truly safeguarded.

She was protected from the likes of him.

Despite the annoyed glances he received from some

older Refuge Mountain residents, Wyatt continued to let his gaze rest on her.

It had been so long since he'd seen her last. It seemed like a lifetime ago. He was hungry for a glimpse of her and now that he saw her again; he was drinking his fill.

His brows crumpled in worry. He couldn't help but notice how fragile she looked.

A form fitting black dress hugged her slender figure.

Abby wasn't eating properly. He remembered from years ago, she didn't eat when she was stressed or overwhelmed.

Her jaw clamped tight when she saw him watching her.

Wyatt was certain she was upset with him. She wasn't going to listen to what he had to say. Not today, and maybe not ever.

There was so much he needed to tell her.

He wanted to say he was sorry for not meeting her at their special place all those years ago. He wanted to tell her he was sorry for leaving town so abruptly. He wanted to tell her how truly sorry he was about her husband's death.

There was too much unspoken history between them.

Abby's green eyes stared at him for a moment longer. Her lips pressed shut as if forcing herself not to make a sound.

Wyatt met the unflinching accusation in her gaze, as if it was his due. He deserved every bit of hatred and contempt she threw at him. And yet, despite knowing that, he couldn't stop himself from longing for her forgiveness, anyway.

He missed the easy-going friendship he'd had with her. He missed their late night talks. He missed everything about her.

Abby had been his best friend.

He yearned for what they once were together.

Wyatt sighed in frustration. What was he thinking? She was someone else's wife — his good friend Tom Hart's wife — er, widow.

*You need to leave her alone. Haven't you already caused Abby enough pain? Already, she can't stand the sight of you. Just let it be.*

As if to prove his inner thoughts true, Abby quickly turned to stare straight ahead, but not before Wyatt noticed that her green eyes had darkened to match the angry thunderclouds in the sky above.

Wyatt swallowed and expelled a frustrated breath before returning his gaze to the Pastor, who was speaking a final blessing.

Knots formed in his belly.

He didn't want it to be this difficult between them.

Yet, he didn't see any other way. And he didn't know if things would ever get better between them.

Impatient, he expelled a breath as the graveside service ended.

He waited patiently for the mourners to walk away from the graveside, back to their waiting vehicles.

Thunder cracked loudly in the air above once again. Most people hurried, eager to get away from the threatening sounds of rain.

He stood motionless as people walked by him.

Two gray haired ladies turned to look at him. The

Peabody twins. Gretchen and Gertrude Peabody were the oldest residents of Refuge Mountain and very vocal about all things — or people — they approved of or disapproved.

Their father, George Peabody, had owned the first General Store in Refuge Mountain and the twins still operated the store to this day.

Both of them tossed him a disapproving glare as they passed by.

It was obvious the twins had long memories of his wild younger days. He was convinced that their attitudes reflected those of the rest of the folks in their small town.

He sighed heavily, relieved when they moved on.

Wyatt wished he could talk to Abby.

As he saw Abby walk away from the grave, he saw another woman with strawberry blonde hair, wearing a dark grey dress embracing Abby. He'd remembered Abby's best friend Sierra Baxter from her High School days. He was thankful Abby had family and friends that supported her during this difficult time.

It wasn't long before Abby's friends and family had left her side to talk with others who had come to show their respects for her late husband.

For the moment, it seemed she was without protectors by her side.

Without hesitating, Wyatt's long legged stride took him to her side.

She looked up and gasped at his unexpected appearance at her side.

With one hand, he removed his service cap and fingered it between both of his hands before nodding to her. Her large green eyes, simply stared at him as if unsure of what to say.

Wyatt forced himself to speak before he lost his nerve. "I'm real sorry for your loss, Abby."

He swallowed nervously, shifting the cap in his hand. "Tom was a good man."

Abby's eyes brimmed over with tears, weaving a path down her cheeks. How he wished he could capture her tears with his thumb and hold her gently in his arms. But of course, she would never allow that. At least not anymore.

Abby looked up at him, her lips quivering as if she was about to say something, when Abby's older sister stepped between them.

"Can't you see she's been through enough?" Hadley's short dark brown hair bounced as she lifted her chin, her brown eyes narrowed and dark with challenge. "Stay away from her. You've hurt my sister one too many times, Wyatt Callahan. I'm not going to give you the chance to do it again."

With one last accusing look, Hadley grabbed Abby's arm and hurried her away from him.

Wyatt expelled a breath. Hadley wasn't wrong. He had hurt Abby.

He stood motionless for a moment, watching the sisters walk away. Guilt and remorse flooded him once again and he turned on his heel and walked stoically toward his truck.

His hands were still shaking as he turned the truck onto the road that led back to the Triple C Ranch.

He berated himself all the way back home. *Why does*

*your brain turn to mush whenever Abby is nearby? You've got to stop trying to talk to her. She's not for you. She might have been the woman you loved years ago, but she'll never be yours again. Just accept it.*

Wyatt tried to convince himself of that truth. But, for some reason his heart didn't want to agree.

But this time he was determined that his heart wouldn't have a say in the matter.

This time around, he would stay away from the only woman he'd ever loved.

*❧*

"I CAN'T BELIEVE you let that man speak to you." Hadley finished pouring tea into Abby's teacup and set the teapot down on the hot plate with a huff.

Ever since the graveside service to bury her husband five days ago, Abby's sister had either called or texted everyday.

Each time Abby talked with her sister, Hadley prattled on and on about how terrible it was that Wyatt Callahan had come back to Refuge Mountain.

Today, her mother and Hadley had shown up at the ranch for lunch. Her mother said she was concerned about Abby now that Tom was gone.

Abby sighed in frustration at her sister's constant meddling. "Wyatt didn't do anything other than voice his condolences, Hadley. Just leave it be."

Helen Meadows, Abby's mom, poured more tea into her cup, shaking her head and sighing.

"What?" Abby could tell by her mother's body movements that there was something she disapproved of.

After a small sip of tea, her mother slowly set her cup down before returning her gaze to her youngest daughter. "I think your sister is right, Abigail."

Her mother always used her full name when she was upset with her.

It was a little annoying.

"You mustn't do anything to ruin your good name. In my opinion, getting overly friendly with the man who once asked your father for your hand in marriage isn't a good idea. Especially considering the fact that you just lost your husband." Her mother sipped her tea, looking pointedly over the rim of her teacup at Abby. "I mean, what will people think?"

A flash of heat rose from her belly, shooting up to her chest and inflating until she was sure she would burst. She expelled a long, slow breath, counting backwards from ten.

"Mom and Hadley, I am grateful for your concern." Abby sighed heavily, still trying to regain control of her temper. "But I am well aware of how people in this small town gossip. But, as an adult woman, I am fully capable of choosing who I want to talk to or spend time with."

"But Abby, surely you see the wisdom in avoiding a man like Wyatt Callahan. Your father, when he was alive, didn't want you associating with him as you well know. And now that your husband Tom is gone, you must continue to do everything you can to uphold and respect the prominent Hart family name in this community." Her mother persisted in offering her advice.

Abby coughed and nearly choked on the tea she'd just swallowed. The absurdity of her mother's words made her want to laugh out loud. Instead, she grabbed a napkin from beside her plate and coughed once more. She could feel bile rising into her throat from the churning in her belly.

There were so many secrets and lies in their own family that had been hidden away, hoping the world wouldn't find them out. And her mother was worried about Abby's reputation if she got too close to Wyatt Callahan?

It was ridiculous.

"Excuse me for a moment. I need some water." Abby stood to her feet, hurried into the kitchen and grabbed a glass.

Turning on the water faucet, she held the glass with shaking hands. Closing her eyes, she breathed out slowly. Taking a drink of water, she tried desperately to get rid of the acidic taste in her mouth.

How could her mother still hold her father's decisions regarding relationships or marriage as something she should heed to?

Did she think Abby didn't remember the bruises on her mom's face the day after their father spent the evening in town? Wasn't it enough, that the one time she'd tried to stop one of his drunken rages, she received a broken arm for her efforts?

She understood that her mother wanted to respect her Dad's memory. Yet, it bothered Abby that her mother continued to bring up the fact that her father hadn't thought Wyatt Callahan was good enough for her —

wasn't good enough for their imperfect family.

Yet in the end she had given in to her parent's wishes. She'd married Tom Hart.

The Hart family owned a lot of businesses in their small town of Refuge Mountain and surrounding area. She married into that prominent family, which was probably the one thing she had finally done right, that had finally pleased her parents.

However, she'd only been married one month before she learned her new husband had his own set of problems.

Problems she'd lived with as Tom's wife for five long years.

Her husband's addiction had almost ended their marriage.

She hadn't told a soul, but she still lived with the consequences of her husband's bad choices today.

Maybe she had been doomed from the beginning.

Swallowing back the rest of the water, she set the glass down and walked back to the dining room.

Sitting down at the table, Abby sighed, looking first to Hadley and then to her Mother.

"Thank you for your advice, Mom and for yours Hadley. I will think about what you've said." Abby swallowed before continuing.

"Thank you for being here for me today and for your help. But, I really need to go take care of my horses. The weather has changed and I see a storm is on the way, so I need to make sure they're okay. I'm sure you'll want to get home before this driveway turns to mud."

Abby set her chin with a new determination. She

didn't want to offend her family, but she desperately needed space to figure out her own life.

Her mother and sister looked at her as if she were a puzzle they were trying to figure out.

Finally Hadley sighed. "Well, we certainly don't want to be stuck here on the ranch in this rainstorm. I was so happy when you and Tom bought Dad and Mom's ranch. Living in town has been so nice and clean, without the worries of ranch life. How you can stand living here is beyond me, Abby."

Hadley stood to her feet and picked up the purse she had slung over the back of the chair. Her sister had always been real fussy about how she liked things. They had never understood each other. "Coming mom? We should probably get home before the weather turns worse."

As Abby digested her sister's words, awareness dawned on her about the real difference between them.

Abby loved the ranch, because it could remove her from untrustworthy people and gave her the freedom to work all day with animals. Horses, dogs and cats were animals that she loved and they loved her back unconditionally.

Understanding her pets was far easier than understanding people.

Her mom stood to her feet and Abby walked them both to the door. "Abby, I hope you'll listen to my advice." Her mother slipped on her coat, before glancing in Abby's direction. She sighed. "I only want the best for you."

"I know you do." Abby didn't want to talk about it anymore. Whatever she said would likely start another disagreement, so she simply kissed her Mom's cheek and hugged them both. "Love you. See you both later."

Abby watched from the kitchen window as they drove off the ranch yard. As she watched them drive away, she was thankful that so far her family or none of her friends from town had learned the desperate state the ranch was really in.

Now that Tom was gone, she really hoped she wouldn't learn of more unpaid debts.

Her finances were hemorrhaging at the seams. She was doing her best to pay off debts, but she could only manage a small amount every month.

Her biggest worry however, was that in all likelihood she was going to lose the ranch.

The letter from the bank and her visit with the mortgage lender last week confirmed her worst fears: If she didn't pay the rest of what was owed, the bank would foreclose by the last day of December.

Fear and anger knotted in her belly.

She didn't have any idea how she was going to save the ranch. All her life, this ranch had been the one place she felt she belonged. How could she lose it now?

Fear and anger warred inside her. She was afraid to lose the one thing that meant the world to her. She was angry at Tom for dying and leaving her alone in the first place.

Guilt consumed her as these thoughts filled her mind. *Abby, how can you be angry at your husband because he passed away? You can't hold onto this. It wasn't Tom's fault he died.*

Abby shook her head, trying to dispel the angry narrative going round and round in her head.

For today, she had to look reality square in the face. Her husband was gone, and she needed to fix her money problems before the bank took her ranch.

Worry gnawed at her as she thought of the upcoming meeting she had with her husband's attorney.

Abby wasn't looking forward to meeting with Tom's lawyer in a few days. Would she learn more terrible news?

In the past year, she'd needed to take on extra work, just to cover all the bills.

Abby closed her eyes. She wished with all her heart that she could have one moment of peace, away from the constant pressure of bills, lack of money and expectations of family.

Turning her head, she stopped at the framed picture of her and Tom at their wedding five years ago. A single tear slipped down her cheek.

Now that her husband had passed away, she was well and truly alone. *Why did you have to leave me, Tom? I'm trying hard not to be angry at you right now. And I don't mind admitting I'm scared. I really don't know if I can manage everything on my own.*

She walked over and touched the framed wedding portrait, running one finger over her husband's handsome features. *Ours might have been a turbulent marriage, but I still loved you in my own way.*

She kissed the tip of a finger and pressed it to the face of her husband in the photo. More tears fell down her cheeks. Angrily, she wiped them away. *You will not live in fear, Abigail Meadows Hart. What's done is done. Now is the time that you must choose courage in spite of your fear.*

The loud splatter of rain against the window, the crack

of lightning and thunder and the powerful whinny of horses brought her back to the task at hand.

Abby straightened her shoulders and hurried to the porch to slip on her raincoat and gumboots. She had work to do.

As she ran across the yard to the barn, the stormy weather hit so hard that she could barely see. Heavy rain poured down in sheets and she was dripping wet by the time she opened the sliding barn doors.

Only one horse was in the stall. The other horse was somewhere in the pasture.

Closing the front doors behind her, Abby hurried to the back of the barn and opened the door wide enough so she could see if her horse was nearby.

On normal days, they stood under the feed shelter in the middle of the pasture. She hurried toward the shelter but her horse wasn't there.

Abby went back to the barn and gave Blackie his feed, deep in thought. What she needed to do was find the missing horse.

Stocking, her beloved mare, was missing.

Worried, Abby called out. "Stocking, come home."

She called and whistled for her horse a few times, worried when she didn't hear an answering whinny. She whistled once again.

The piercing sound was so loud it could've split the air, yet there was no response. And still no sign of her horse.

Her brows creased together, anxious over what might have happened. With a new determination born of passion for her horse, she hurried over to the black gelding who had been kept dry and rested in the barn.

Slipping a bridle over his neck, Abby led him out of the stall and toward the back barn doors.

She wasn't looking forward to being out in the rain, but she was desperate to find her horse. Stocking needed to be back home where she belonged.

Pulling open the sliding doors, she was just about to slide onto Blackie, when she heard the clopping of horse hooves coming closer. She peered outside and saw two horses walking toward the barn. One was her horse, and the other was Wyatt's large coffee colored quarter horse.

Walking between the horses was Wyatt Callahan.

He had a half smile on his face as he stared at her. "Looking for something?"

His tall form with well muscled shoulders and arms were what first attracted her to him when she was a teenager. He looked tough, lean, and sinewy.

Wyatt was as rugged as the jagged mountains behind her ranch.

He'd always done so much for his brothers and parents. She had always wondered if his broad shoulders ever tired of the troubles he carried.

As a teenager, Abby saw how busy he was with responsibilities like attending college and helping care for the Callahan cattle and horses. But he'd started making time for her, too.

Then he'd begun teaching her how to train her horse. Sometimes they would race, and other times she would help Wyatt and his brothers round up their cattle. Abby remembered it had been impossible to resist her handsome next door neighbor.

So she spent a lot of time with him and grew to love

him. Their age difference didn't bother her. Wyatt had been twenty-four when she was eighteen, but they understood each other.

Then, just when Abby was convinced he would marry her, Wyatt left town without a word.

She'd been so angry. First angry and then desperately sad and lonely without him.

This week had been the first time in seven years that she'd laid eyes on him.

Looking at Wyatt now, he was still as confident, big and powerful as ever. The small crow's feet, she noticed by his eyes, only made him more handsome.

His gray eyes, shadowed slightly under his cowboy hat, studied her with a curious and probing intensity. She felt as if his gaze saw into her very soul.

Abby blinked, lightheaded at the intensity of his gaze.

Though her heart shuddered away in her ears like a runaway horse, she stood perfectly still and met his eyes with an unwavering stare.

Heat suddenly crept up her neck to her cheeks and the anger she'd held in for so many years at what she saw as Wyatt's betrayal flooded to the surface.

She pushed aside all thoughts of attraction, as she remembered how he abandoned her years ago.

"I was just about to search for Stocking." Her words were short and crisp and knots twisted in her belly. "Where did you find her?"

Anger simmered beneath the surface of her words.

Wyatt expelled a breath, emphasizing the muscles clenched along his jawline. "I was out with my men rounding up the cattle, when we saw your mare having a bit of trouble. I headed over and helped her get unstuck from an overgrown bush she'd got herself caught in."

He ran a practiced hand down her horse's lame foreleg. "Stocking's been limping a little. She has a few scars, but with some care she should be back to normal in a week or two."

Abby's eyes grew big with concern as she saw the dried blood on her mare's leg. She bent down and looked closer at the gash. Her stomach knotted in worry for the one horse who had been with her since childhood.

"She'll be okay Abby." Wyatt whispered her name and a strong hand squeezed her shoulder gently.

Tingles spread quickly from her shoulder to her whole body at his touch. A familiar ache rose in her belly and spread upwards to her heart.

Memories of Wyatt's unwavering friendship, gentle embrace and passionate kisses flitted across her mind right at that moment and she jerked away as if scalded.

She could feel a softening in her heart towards him as she remembered what they had.

But she couldn't let that happen. She couldn't let herself fall for him again.

Standing to her feet suddenly, she straightened her shoulders and cleared her throat. "I know she'll be fine. I'll see to it." Abby tried her best to sound confident and cringed as her voice trembled.

Wyatt nodded with a taut jerk of his head. "I know you will, Abby. But, I'll be back to check on Stocking if it's all the same to you." He wasn't asking, he was stating a fact. "Right now, your mare needs to be fed and brushed down and kept warm for the night."

Wyatt took over and led her horse to the last remaining stall in the barn. Irritation snaked like a coil from Abby's belly, running up and down her arms. He had always been so confident, knowing what was best and taking the action necessary to see it done.

This was her horse. She should be the one making the decisions.

*Abby, stop it. Wyatt knows way more about how to heal your horse than you do. For once, just leave it be.*

She watched as he led the horse into the stall. Abby was thankful she'd had the foresight to add fresh straw to this stall. This wasn't the usual stall for Stocking, but it didn't matter.

Abby brought warm water and offered him the clean cloth.

Wyatt took the wet cloth and wiped her mare's wounded leg. After it was clean, he reached into his pocket and pulled out a healing salve. She remembered he always carried different ointments and salves in case of animal injuries. It looked like he hadn't changed.

Abby ran her hand gently down Stocking's neck to calm her while Wyatt cleaned and added salve to the wound. She remembered he had always been good at helping animals heal.

Most likely his passion to help animals heal was one of the big reasons he went to Veterinary College. It was what he was doing when she was still in High School. Back then, Wyatt had always taken the time to check out their horses and the fifty head of cattle her father had on their five hundred acres.

Now he was back.

It looked like she would be in Wyatt's debt once again for taking care of her horse.

Wyatt stood to his feet and patted Stocking's neck. "Stocking will be right as rain in no time, won't you, old gal?" He turned and looked lazily at Abby through half-closed lids. "Your mare just needs a week or so to heal and then she'll be ready to play and have fun like she did before."

Abby heard the double meaning in his words. Heat rose to her cheeks. Yes, like her horse, she needed healing. But she wouldn't be playing anytime soon, and certainly not with her handsome neighbor.

Wyatt's grey eyes clung to hers as if analyzing her reaction.

"We'll see." A momentary look of discomfort crossed her face.

She couldn't miss the promise as well as the unspoken pain that glowed in his grey eyes.

Her breath caught for a moment, and she swallowed quickly.

Abby's eyes glued to his, she stood motionless as a wave of longing for the love they once had, hit her belly.

As quick as lightning, she lowered her thick brown lashes. There was no way she was going to let Wyatt know she was vulnerable to him. Not this time.

Wyatt's lips were tight with strain for a moment before a familiar mask of cool indifference descended once again.

Several long strides took him quickly to the gate, and she raised her eyes. He turned to look at her, with one hand on the doorway of the stall.

The tensing of his jaw betrayed his frustration before he spoke. "I'll talk to you in the morning."

He touched a finger to his cowboy hat and nodded once before he walked away.

Abby warmed at the gesture, so reminiscent of the gentleman cowboy from her childhood.

She expelled a breath, frustrated for letting herself harbor any warm feelings for him at all. She reminded herself that those carefree, fun days were long gone.

It was too late for dreams of a true family. It was too late for them. It was too late for love.

She'd do well to remember that from here on out.

# CHAPTER TWO

yatt

"How is Abby's bay mare doing?" Denver set down his coffee cup and looked across the table at Wyatt. "I saw that horse limping when you took her back to the Meadow's ranch."

"Yeah, she was limping all right. I cleaned her leg and added a healing salve last night, but I told Abby I'd be back to check on her horse this morning." Wyatt finished the rest of his coffee cup and set it down. "Which reminds me, I need to get going."

Wyatt pushed back his chair and stood to his feet, his thoughts already on seeing his beautiful neighbor again. He started walking toward the door, when his Mom spoke up.

"Don't forget to be back home by eleven this morning,

son." Annie Callahan spoke in a gentle voice, but her eyes still held a haunted look ever since her husband's death. "Your Dad's lawyer, Tobias McCrae, said he'd be stopping by for the reading of the will."

His Mom's gaze went around the table to include all seven sons who were seated there. She looked back at Wyatt. "Mr. McCrae said it's important that we're all here, including Mrs. Garrett, her granddaughter Cassie and old Sam."

Wyatt listened from the doorway. He wasn't surprised that Dad's old lawyer asked for those people who had worked on the ranch the longest to be there for the reading of the will. Mack had always been generous to workers who had worked and faithfully served at the Triple C ranch.

"I'll be back in time, Mom." Wyatt nodded quickly before turning and leaving swiftly.

As he walked to the barn, his thoughts were focused on seeing Abby again.

Seeing her last night had been like giving a glimpse of a seven course meal to a starving man. Even with dirt smudges on her face and her auburn hair tied back in a braid, she was as beautiful as ever.

However, he could tell from the way she responded to his nearness, Abby was as skittish as a filly that had been abused one too many times by her handler.

The momentary fear he'd seen in her eyes before she'd suddenly stood to her feet and backed away, had shaken him to the core. Her normally clear green eyes looked haunted.

Abby was afraid.

What was she scared of — or maybe the better question was who?

He was determined to do whatever it took to protect Abby.

Only problem with that was his beautiful neighbor wanted to be as far away from him as possible. He'd need to convince her somehow, that she needed him.

Soon, he was galloping his large horse across the field. His gelding was a quarter horse cross with a Belgian draft horse and stood a little over seventeen hands high.

Wyatt had named him Goliath, which seemed fitting.

He loved riding across the fields in this early part of the morning.

The mountains on the west side of Callahan ranch land stretched for miles, and a little farther north was the Meadows ranch land. He corrected himself. That land belonged to Abby Hart now.

He had just begun to get used to the fact that Abby was married, when Tom Hart joined his military unit three years ago.

When he'd first arrived, Wyatt had been happy Tom had been placed in a different unit. He didn't want to have to communicate with the husband of the woman he loved day after day. It was much too difficult.

But then, unexpectedly, Tom Hart had been placed under Wyatt's command.

Instead of seeing Tom Hart as a good friend from years ago, Wyatt saw him as the man who had stolen the woman he loved.

Wyatt realized he hadn't understood what it meant to

be heartbroken until the first time Tom received a package from home.

He still remembered the deep pain that fisted in his belly. Abby Meadows Hart was writing letters and sending loving care packages to her husband... a man other than him.

The next day, Wyatt began working out and training extra hard whenever he was off duty. He'd found another way to channel all his pent up frustration and heartbreak.

Wyatt trained his men hard and when they went on different missions it showed. They worked together in harmony like a finely tuned string quartet. The day that Sergeant Tom Hart was killed it had shocked everyone, but Wyatt most of all.

Tom had been a really good friend. Wyatt had known him since the Hart family had moved to their small town of Refuge Mountain when Tom was a freshman in High School. Tom was a year younger than Wyatt, but they had become good friends. They had been sort of like the three Musketeers that included Tom, Wyatt and Abby.

Tom worked at his Dad's restaurant franchise with his Dad and younger brother Will. Later on, when Tom's Dad was elected Mayor of their small town, Tom had become very busy but still found time to sneak away for some fun.

Wyatt and Abby both worked hard on their family ranches, but when the three of them could get away they would go hiking, horseback riding or fishing.

Memories of time spent with both Tom and Abby at their favorite fishing spot along the creek brought a smile to his face. Those years when they were teenagers were happy ones.

He had grown close to Tom Hart and grieved for the good friend he'd lost.

Yet, as much as he'd enjoyed Tom's friendship, the companionship Wyatt missed and longed for most, was that of Abby Meadows Hart.

Memories flooded his thoughts as he skirted around the fence line near the mountain that brought him on to Abby's land.

One of the first times Wyatt had seen his pretty young neighbor, was when she was ten years of age, riding her horse along the side of the mountain on Callahan land. She had lost her way and had crossed from her Dad's property and onto Triple C ranch land.

Even back then, she had attracted his attention as she rode her horse towards him, her thick auburn braids flying in the wind.

After that first time seeing her riding, every spring and summer, he met up with Abby riding her horse.

He'd thought of her only as a cute kid until the summer she turned sixteen. He'd been away, taking college courses to earn his Veterinary degree when he'd come home as usual to help his Dad and brothers on the ranch.

She was chasing a few stray cows to bring them back home, when her horse went limp. Wyatt had watched as Abby got off her horse holding tightly to the reins and running a hand along her forelegs trying to see what was the matter.

The corners of his mouth turned up at the vivid memory.

*"Your horse stuck, Abby?"* Wyatt rode his horse to the base of

the mountain, bypassing the fence line to enter Meadows ranch land.

She turned to him, her auburn hair out of braids for the first time hanging down her back. Her slim figure, had turned womanly with curves in all the right places. He couldn't help but notice the change in her since he'd seen her the year before.

As he approached her, Wyatt felt uncomfortable with his new awareness of Abby as a woman. He'd forced himself to focus on her face rather than her figure.

"Yeah, Stocking won't budge. I'm supposed to get these last cows into the pasture nearest the barn, but I don't know why my horse isn't moving." Abby sighed, looking up at him, her beautiful green eyes asking for his help.

Wyatt, at that moment, knew he was in trouble. He was attracted to Abby. In many ways he had been shocked by this new revelation.

It made him nervous around her, even though he did his best to remain indifferent. His emotions screamed the opposite, but Wyatt disciplined himself to treat her like he would a little sister.

He had always been more like an older brother to her.

"Your mare might have caught some rocks in one of her hooves." Wyatt got off his horse and walked over to Abby. He remembered checking her mare's hooves and found one of them with rocks, which he quickly dug out. Handling horses was something he was used to doing.

Once he finished his task, however, he turned to Abby. She was so close to him and her nearness made him edgy.

"Thanks so much, Wyatt." Her big green eyes had looked at him, a grateful shimmer in their depths. "You got me out of trouble again. You're the best." Impulsively, she had thrown her *arms around his neck. He wrapped his arms around her waist, pulling her close.*

*Holding Abby close, he enjoyed the scent of her. Wildflowers and cinnamon.*

*But he only held her a moment, before he untangled her arms from around his neck.*

*He had stepped away and caught a glimpse of hurt in Abby's large green eyes.*

*Wyatt experienced a pang of regret, but realized Abby didn't understand. He was far older than her, and yet what he felt for her was more than simple brotherly affection.*

*She was young and innocent, and he needed to keep his distance.*

*"I'm happy to help, Abby. Stocking should be fine now." He spoke before he walked quickly back to his horse.*

*He slipped onto his gelding, and touching his fingers to his cowboy hat, nodded at her before he galloped away.*

Thinking back to that day now, Wyatt wondered if Abby remembered that day as vividly as he did.

Finally, two summers later, after Abby turned eighteen, Wyatt had spent a lot of time with her. By the end of that summer he'd told her he loved her and asked her to marry him.

Abby had said yes, but that they could only marry if their relationship had her mother and father's blessing.

But her father had turned him down flat. He'd said Wyatt wasn't good enough for his daughter. Her father told him not to see his daughter again.

So he'd hurried home and stayed up late that night writing a long letter to Abby. He told her how much he loved her, but that her father didn't want her to marry him.

He asked Abby to wait for him for a year. Maybe by then he would be able to prove to her father he was worthy of Abby. Maybe receiving his Veterinary degree would be a step in the right direction.

In the letter, he'd asked Abby to wait for him. He would come back. He asked her to write to him and he would write her back.

But Wyatt never heard from Abby again. There had been no letters from Abby. Wyatt had finished his Veterinary degree and had returned home determined to talk to Abby, only to find out she was engaged to be married to Tom Hart.

It was a devastating blow.

He remembered clearly one day as he'd been riding the range; he saw Abby from a distance. She was kissing Tom Hart.

A jealous anger had consumed Wyatt. Later on he'd packed up his bags, determined to put as much distance between him and Abby as he possibly could.

The next morning, after a tearful goodbye from his Mom and a gruff one from his Dad, Wyatt went to catch a flight.

He ended up in boot camp and quickly advanced up the ranks to Captain. He was busy enough that he barely had time to think about Abby. That was just the way he wanted it.

Wyatt had been away from home for two years before he went back home for a brief visit at Christmas.

His family didn't talk about Abby, and Wyatt didn't ask. He preferred it that way.

So, the next summer when Tom Hart showed up and later on was transferred to his military unit, Wyatt was in shock. But he was also angry that Sergeant Hart was placed under his command.

It seemed the worst kind of cruelty to have the reminder of Abby's rejection of his love every day. It had proven to be the hardest thing Wyatt had ever done to remain indifferent and not be harsher on Tom than his other team members.

But, he'd done it.

Sergeant Tom Hart had become one of the most valued members of his team until one day he was unexpectedly shot and killed during a secret military mission.

Wyatt had been Tom's commanding officer and had felt like it was his fault that Abby's husband died.

Now here he was, back at Abby's ranch once again.

Except this time, Wyatt didn't have any hopeful ambitions of earning Abby's love. Not this time. He knew that would hold true even more when she found out the truth about his part in her husband's death.

No, this time Wyatt decided he was only here to pay a debt to his friend Tom Hart and to take care of his widow. He decided to help heal her animals and do whatever else needed to be done to see to it that Mrs. Abby Hart was taken care of and protected.

He'd do it, even if being so close to her and not claiming her as his own, would be one of the hardest things he'd ever done.

Wyatt owed her that much, at least.

He reached Abby's barn and took off Goliath's bridle and tied a long rope to his horse's halter, so he'd stay near the barn. Wyatt wasn't sure how long it would take with Abby's horse.

Wyatt stepped into the barn, only to hear voices. One was Abby's and another was a much deeper voice he didn't recognize.

He didn't like to eavesdrop, but since his goal was to protect her, he felt it was his duty to listen in.

"Abby, I'm sorry to hear about the loss of your husband. Tom was a good man." A deep baritone voice continued. "I want you to know I'm willing to help with whatever needs doing."

"That's very kind of you, Reno." Abby's weary voice responded, her voice sounding labored. "Right now, I'm fine. But I'll keep that in mind."

"It's not just kindness, Abby. I want to get to know you better. In fact, I was thinking we could go to a movie Saturday night. You know, to take your mind off of troubling things. What do you say?" Wyatt recognized the coaxing voice of Abby's neighbor, Reno Blackwell.

"Thanks for asking Reno, but I don't think I'm ready for a new relationship. And likely won't be for some time. Sorry, but no, I won't be going with you to see a movie. I'll be staying close to home." Abby's voice sounded tired and sad.

"Oh, come on, Abby. You need to have some fun too." Reno persisted.

Abby's low sigh was filled with misery and Wyatt suddenly realized he'd heard enough.

Anger coursed through his veins as he entered the barn and approached Reno, his jaw set in determination.

He glanced once at Abby, whose brows bunched together in worry at his approach.

"I believe the lady already told you no, Reno." Wyatt came to stand beside Abby and directly across from Reno. With his arms folded, he stood there motionless while he waited.

"Stay out of it, Callahan." The terse words flew quickly from Reno's lips. "I was talking to Abby here." Reno stared at Wyatt, his face pinched in that bulldog stance he'd had ever since they were together in middle school.

Wyatt's lips twitched for a moment as memories surfaced. "This whole situation seems very familiar. I seem to recall a time when I had to stop you from bullying another girl in middle school. This is getting tiresome, Reno."

"I was not bullying. I was asking Abby nicely." Reno folded his arms across his chest. "Besides, I don't see how it's any business of yours?"

Wyatt grunted and leveled his cold stare at Reno. "Now that Abby's husband is no longer here, I'm seeing to it that Abby's taken care of and protected from unwanted advances from men like you. Now I would advise you to leave peaceably, or do I need to insist?"

Reno stood there for a moment, a stubborn refusal in his cold grey eyes. "I'll leave, Callahan. But, you'll regret your meddlesome ways someday, I swear it!" He voice was low with anger as he hurriedly shoved his cowboy hat on his head. Nodding quickly at Abby, he stomped out of the barn.

Wyatt could hear Reno's loud voice and his whip urging his horse into a gallop as he rode away.

"Has Reno been around your ranch lately, bothering you?" Wyatt's gaze searched Abby's green eyes. She lowered her lashes, avoiding his gaze and flicked a speck of dirt from her jeans.

The way Abby looked away from him, told him everything he needed to know.

Wyatt walked slowly to where she leaned up against the door to Stocking's stall.

"Hey, Abby. Please, look at me." Placing one hand on the wooden stall beside her head, he gently cupped her chin with the other and searched her upturned face. Her long brown lashes slowly uncovered large green eyes that moved up to look at him.

For a moment, the green eyes that met his own were misty and wistful.

"I just want you to know, I will do everything in my power to protect you, Abby. Especially from your bothersome neighbor." He whispered and without thinking, Wyatt stepped closer and gently ran the back of his fingers over the soft curve of her cheek.

His finger followed her jawline down to her full lips, lightly grazing them. Tingles of warmth shot up his arm and his pulse raced as thoughts of pressing his mouth against Abby's strawberry lips surged through him.

At her slight gasp, Wyatt pulled his hand away quickly. Even now, seven years later, Abby still had the ability to make him crazy with longing for her sweet kisses.

Memories washed over him of the passionate kisses

they'd shared that day seven years ago when Abby agreed to be his wife. It had been heaven to hold her in his arms.

No, he wasn't going to think about that.

"I promise to do all I can to keep you safe." He whispered and stepped away from the lure of the red haired beauty, with a renewed determination to keep his distance from her.

THE SKIN on Abby's cheek tingled and her lips still trembled from the gentle touch of Wyatt Callahan's fingers.

Just being close to her former best friend — caused a shiver of awareness to run up and down her spine.

Releasing a sigh, she was grateful he'd stepped away from her. Even now, Wyatt stood much too close for comfort.

She couldn't help but admire how well, his broad shoulders and muscled arms filled out that western shirt he wore. His brown hair, curled slightly above the collar, giving him a playful look.

Abby's fingers twitched, as she remembered the softness of his hair the day he'd kissed her when she'd agreed to his proposal.

But then just as suddenly, Wyatt left.

And she'd married Tom Hart instead.

Anger burned in her afresh as she thought again of how Wyatt had left her all alone.

Now that he was back, it didn't change the fact that she

was still angry at him. Abby didn't want him to be near her.

Her voice shook with anger and her words flew out. "You don't have to worry about me, Wyatt. I can take care of myself. I have for years." Abby clenched her jaw to kill the sob in her throat.

She had to prove to Wyatt that she was immune to him. She had to prove to herself that she was immune to this man who had caused her so much heartache.

"I know you can take care of yourself. But with men like Reno Blackwell and probably others hanging around you, now that Tom's gone, I don't want to leave you alone without some sort of protection." Wyatt's words were carefully modulated, his tone cool and even.

"Why does it matter to you, Wyatt? Isn't leaving what you do best?" The words flew out of her mouth before she could stop them.

He stiffened as though she had struck him.

He clenched his mouth tighter while they stared at each other across a sudden deafening silence.

Seeing his pale face, Abby's conscience suddenly struck her. She shouldn't have lashed out at him like that.

"Someday soon we'll need to talk about what happened seven years ago, Abby." Wyatt's deep voice shook a little, but his tone remained calm. Abby fought to control her swirling emotions.

He went on. "But, today's not that day. I need to check on your horse and then I'm expected back at the ranch." Wyatt sighed heavily, and she heard a deep anguish in his voice.

For a moment, she glimpsed that haunted look on his

face, but it was soon replaced with a look of cool detachment.

Abby swallowed hard and bit back tears. There had been too many years of hurt, anger and loneliness.

Now that Wyatt was back home, he was getting the brunt of it all.

Abby turned to open the door to her mare's stall. Feeling guilt for tearing into him, she conceded. "Maybe we'll talk. But for right now, I do appreciate you taking a look at my horse."

Wyatt nodded and walked inside. It didn't take him long to examine her mare's wounded foreleg.

"Her leg is healing well." He wiped his hands on a clean cloth and looked over at her. "I'd say a week of healing and rest for Stocking, and she'll be ready to ride again."

Abby swallowed. "That is good news. Thank you."

She blinked back tears quickly, hoping Wyatt wouldn't notice.

Her reaction made her aware that Stocking meant more to her than she realized. Her horse was the one animal who hadn't left her, when she'd lost everyone else that she loved.

As she walked Wyatt to the barn door, she waited as he slid on the back of his horse.

"I'll be back later this week to check on your mare, Abby. See you later." Wyatt nodded and touched his finger to the tip of his cowboy hat in one fluid motion before turning his horse around and galloping away.

As she watched the dust fly up after him, Abby expelled a long, heavy sigh.

Her sense of loss was raw and fresh. Not only had her

husband Tom just died and her father before that, but now Wyatt had returned home. How was she to handle her former fiancé back in her life? How was she to endure the constant reminder of losing him?

A heaviness entered her chest reminding her that the only things she had left were the festering sores of an aching heart.

❧

WYATT FINISHED RUBBING down his gelding and set him loose in the pasture behind the barn.

He looked at the beautiful view of the pasture and fields that spread out until they reached the base of the mountain.

Calling this ranch home was a far cry from where he would've ended up if Mack and Annie Callahan hadn't adopted him.

His gaze moved to the massive blue sky behind the mountain and his heart filled with gratefulness for all he'd been given.

Walking toward the ranch house, he was reminded again of Abby Hart. As much as he was determined not to think of her, Abby continued to come to the forefront of his thoughts.

Pain squeezed his heart as he remembered Abby's words from this morning. *Isn't leaving what you do best?* Her green eyes had sparked with the cold anger of betrayal.

He had hurt her years ago, and he was sorry about that. He regretted it more than she knew. And yet, Abby had also hurt him when she hadn't responded to his letters. They would need to talk about what happened between them years ago.

It wasn't doing either of them any good to leave things unsaid between them.

As he stepped into the house, he could hear the sound of his brothers' subdued voices coming from the great room. Wyatt stepped into the large room and was met by Mrs. Garrett.

"Let me get you a hot drink, Wyatt. Coffee?" Mrs. Garrett smiled up at him.

Wyatt nodded. "That would be great, Mrs. Garrett. Thanks." As their cook bustled away, Wyatt looked around the room. Mr. McCrae sat on one of the leather couches nearest the fireplace, talking with his Mom. Her face brightened when she saw him and waved for him to come to join them.

Wyatt sighed. He really wasn't looking forward to the reading of the will. In the past year, Dad had mentioned he planned on dividing their thousands of acres ranch land in seven ways for each of his sons.

So this formal reading of the will almost seemed like a waste of time.

But he would endure it to make his Mom happy.

He walked between the sofas where his brothers sat as they talked with each other.

Reaching his mom, he sat beside her and kissed her on the cheek.

His mom squeezed his hand. "Good. I'm glad you're back, Wyatt. You remember your father's lawyer, Mr. McCrae?"

"Of course." Wyatt got up from his seat and shook the older man's hand. "Good to see you again, sir."

"And you, Wyatt. It's been a few years since I saw you last. You're back from your tour of duty then?"

"Yes, but I'm not on active duty any longer. I'm home to stay." Wyatt explained.

"Good, good. How's ranch life treating you?"

"I can't complain. I've got more than enough animals to care for but it's work I've always liked, so it's all good." Wyatt explained more details of how they planned to make the ranch more environmentally friendly. Mr. McCrae listened with interest.

It wasn't long before Mrs. Garrett returned and handed Wyatt a coffee.

"Do you want another cup of coffee, Mr. McCrae?" Mrs. Garrett was used to serving all sorts of visitors that showed up at different times to the ranch.

Their cook and also the person they relied on to let them know what work was being done each day in and around the ranch house. Her granddaughter Cassie had come to live and work with Mrs. Garrett quite a few years ago. It was good that she had a helper.

"No thanks, Mrs. Garrett. I think I'll get started on the reading of the will, since it looks like everyone is here." Mr. McCrae looked around the room. Wyatt followed his gaze and noticed that old Sam had also arrived.

Sam sat by the chessboard table, twisting his cowboy hat in his wrinkled brown hands. Old Sam was a long time friend of Mack's.

They had served together. Sam had saved Mack's life

years ago, getting him to safety in time for the doctors to heal him.

Mack Callahan asked Sam if he wanted to live on the ranch with him. He told him they could be cowboys together, and Sam had been excited about it. He never married, but had a brother who lived in Virginia whom he visited every year.

Mack's lawyer cleared his throat. Everyone in the room turned to listen to what he had to say.

"As you all know, we're all here for the reading of the last will and testament of Mack Callahan." Mr. McCrae's took papers out of his briefcase before he continued talking. "Now then, a few weeks ago was the last time I had the pleasure of talking with Mack Callahan. Only a few days later he passed away."

The room was silent, everyone wrapped in their own feelings of loss.

"Mack made a few slight changes to his will before he passed away. I'll go through those changes in a minute. But first, I want to read what Mack Callahan had to say to all of you."

Mr. McCrae perched his reading glasses on the top of his nose and held the handwritten letter in his slightly shaky hands. "If you're listening to this, it means I've gone to my reward. You have all been such an important part of my life and in my own way I've loved everyone of you. I was blessed to live my life with family and friends that meant the most to me in the world. Thank you all for that."

Dad's lawyer took a deep breath, before reading on. "Now, as Tobias McCrae has most likely told you, I've made a few small changes to the will. But as I see it, those changes are only in your favor. To my lifelong friend Sam Ford, I leave you that fifty-acre plot of land by the creek you've had your eye on for years along with fifty thousand dollars. Now you can finally put your feet up and enjoy a good rest. You've earned it my friend."

Wyatt looked over at Sam, who blew his nose into his handkerchief. It appeared that Mack had known just what to give his friend.

"To our ranch organizer and favorite cook, Mrs. Garrett. I give you this deed to a house I own in Refuge Mountain and fifty thousand dollars. When you're ready to retire, you'll be able to put your feet up and watch more of those sunsets you love. You've earned it. And as for Cassie, I'm giving you that Bay mare you've worked with since she was a filly. You've done well by that horse, and it's time she was yours."

Wyatt grinned at the smile on Mrs. Garrett's face and of happy surprise and the wide-eyed grin of her granddaughter Cassie. It was just like Mack to be generous with those who had faithfully worked on the ranch for years.

Dad's old lawyer looked over at his mom as he continued. "To my beloved Annie. I couldn't have asked the good Lord for a better best friend and wife than you've been these fifty-one years."

"To you dear heart, I leave the ranch house and the thousand acres of land where the homestead sits. To you I also leave the income from all of my rentals, but the income from the other investments and the manufacturing company in our small town of Refuge Mountain goes to our seven sons. I hope you enjoy time with our sons and with the new brides they will bring into our family. I love you, my darling."

Wyatt reached over and slipped an arm around his Mom's shoulders. Tears ran unheeded down her cheeks and Wyatt handed her a handkerchief he kept in his pocket.

"Thank you, son. I don't know why I never have one of these when I need it." His mom turned to him with a shaky smile before she wiped away her tears.

"It'll be alright, Mom. Are you doing okay?"

Annie Callahan squeezed her son's hand. "I am good. I'm just sad that your Dad is gone. He was larger than life and I loved him. I think it's finally sinking in how much I will miss him."

"I'm sorry, Mom. I hope you know all of your sons will do what we can to help you and be there for you. Whatever you need." Wyatt squeezed his Mom's hand, his smile warm.

"Wyatt, I know you will. You are all such wonderful sons. Dad and I have been so proud of each of you." She patted the top of his hand. "Never fear, I will be fine. If there's anything your father has taught us all, is to love each other and work together, especially through difficult times. Our family will be fine as long as we're together."

Wyatt nodded and his smile got bigger. "We will stick together, Mom. I promise."

Annie smiled and squeezed his hand as Mack's lawyer continued to read the will.

"To my seven sons, your Mom and I are so thankful to have each of you in our lives. We couldn't have asked for better sons than all of you, and I want you to know how proud I am of each of you."

The lawyer continued. "To the seven of you, I give the ranch land divided up seven ways. This works out to around ten thousand acres for each of you. As your Dad, I've watched you as you grew up and worked with the horses, the cattle and the land. I know you each love this ranch and I know you'll do right by it."

Mr. McCrae took a deep breath and continued reading. "However, there is one request I have. I don't want my sons to work this land and continue to live their life alone. You're each older now, but you still haven't married. So, I'm asking each of you to make good on the promise you made to your mom and I, a few years ago."

He hesitated before he went on. "You promised that when you found the woman you loved, you would marry her by the end of that year. All I'm asking is that each of you marry by Christmas in the same year you find the woman you love. Annie and I married on Christmas Eve many years ago, which is why Christmas, is such a special time of year for us. Your Mom and I had our second chance, and I've always been grateful for that."

"Now, it's your turn. I want each of you boys to have your second chance with the woman you love. I've written a letter to each of you with details on a task I'm asking of you."

Dad's lawyer paused and peered over his glasses at each of them before continuing. "If you follow through on what I ask you to do, and Mr. McCrae agrees that it's been done, each one of you will also be given money to begin building that dream that your mother and I know means so much to you. I love each of you and I know you'll choose wisely. I wish each of you; my sons and your brides; all the happiness in the world. Love, Dad."

The old lawyer, folded up the letter from Mack Callahan and looked at the family gathered there.

Wyatt expelled a breath, irritated over the new changes to his father's will.

He heard his brothers shifting in their seats, many of them sighing in exasperation.

Dad's lawyer reached into his briefcase and took out a stack of envelopes.

"Here's the letters your father wrote each of you." Mr. McCrae walked over to Wyatt and each of his six brothers and handed each of them an envelope.

Wyatt rubbed the back of his neck, attempting to ease the growing tension.

It was just like Mack Callahan to have one last trick up his sleeve.

He shuffled the envelope in his hand.

Wyatt had a strange feeling that whatever his father wrote in this letter, was going to be something he wasn't prepared to do.

After Mr. McCrae left and the family had lunch together, Wyatt went to his bedroom. He was thankful his room was located in the farthest corner of the west wing of their sprawling ranch house.

He needed to be able to read his letter in private.

His hands trembled slightly as he opened the envelope and held the letter in his hand.

Mack Callahan's familiar bold handwriting seemed to leap off the page as he read.

*For my oldest son, Wyatt. Your mother and I were so excited the day we found you in that foster home, years ago. It was a long time ago, but to my mind it's still as real as if it happened yesterday.*

*You were covered in bruises on your arms and legs, and you had scars and burn marks on your arms and hands.*

*At just seven years old, you had a worldly wisdom that no child that age should understand. Even though your eyes held fear that day, you still agreed to let us take you to our home.*

*You became our son, and you bore the Callahan name with respect and pride. Your mother and I have often thought of that first year when you and your six brothers came into our family. Each of you boys brought us great joy, and we've loved the honor of being your parents.*

*As our oldest son, many times throughout your childhood and even these last few years as an adult, you have shown a kind of servant leadership.*

*I know your brothers have often looked up to you and followed your example. So what I've decided to ask of you, will be another way of serving others.*

*Wyatt, I'm asking that despite the differences you've had with Abby Meadows Hart in the past, that you make it a priority to help Abby out at her ranch for six months.*

*Show up to help her every day. Help her with taking care of her horses, cattle, dogs and fix things up around the ranch and anything else that needs fixing.*

*Since I learned that Abby lost her husband, she's been heavy on my heart, as have you, son. I knew I needed to make changes to this will. I believe she will have a tough time trying to make a go of that ranch.*

*I have reason to believe Abby hasn't had it easy with her*

*parents or with her husband and in-laws. But that's where you come in. I believe you could make a big difference and help Abby turn things around on that ranch. This could also give you the time needed to heal some old wounds between the two of you.*

*Who knows, but maybe helping Abby will bring the two of you together? It's possible that the two of you might fall in love once again.*

*It would be your second chance at a happy life with the woman you loved years ago, much like I had with your mother. Besides, a Christmas wedding would be the perfect way to end the year.*

*I know what I'm asking of you Wyatt is an unexpected and difficult task, but I know you will soldier on through.*

*You're a fine man, son. You're tough from all that you've endured, but I know inside you beats the heart of a compassionate and caring man.*

*If you agree to help Abby for six months — and Mr. McCrae agrees that you have — then you will receive ten million dollars and a share (along with your six brothers) in the Callahan Manufacturing Company in Refuge Mountain.*

*The amount of money from both, should give you a good start on funding that dream you've been passionate to begin.*

*I wish I could be a fly on the wall to watch you marry and live your dreams, but the Doc says that my time on this earth is short. I'll be cheering you on from up above. Remember, I'm proud of you, son. I love you, Dad.*

Tears coursed down Wyatt's cheeks.

The letter in his hand shook as he reread it.

He really wanted that money to fund the dream to help children from broken homes.

He'd had that dream for years, inspired by his own

painful experiences. But Mack was asking him to find ways to help Abby and be close by her side every day, for all of six months. That was a big commitment.

And what had his Dad wrote about the two of them falling in love?

There was no way. Abby hated him for leaving all those years ago. She would never forgive him.

Mack had his head in the clouds if he thought Abby would give him the time of day.

But maybe he could find ways to help Abby. It was something he'd thought of even as he flew home.

He wondered if he could help her out somehow. Maybe he could do more than help with her animals. He'd have to think on it.

He realized it was the very least he could do.

He owed Abby. There were a lot of mistakes he needed to make up for.

Wyatt decided he would serve Abby and help her out on the ranch as much as he could.

But as for falling in love, that wasn't going to happen.

# CHAPTER THREE

bby

ABBY POURED hot coffee into her favorite mug and went to sit by the kitchen table.

Her orange and brown tabby cat, seeing her mistress relaxing, quickly saw an opportunity and jumped on her lap.

"Buttercup, you scared me." Abby sighed and stroked the back of her cat's back, absently with one hand while she sipped her coffee with the other.

"You always keep me company when I need it most." She scratched her cat behind the ears and was rewarded with deep purring sounds.

Abby looked out the window by the kitchen table where she had a view to the back yard and her fields beyond.

The red and orange hue of dawn was just beginning to peek over the mountain range where her ranch land ended. She yawned once again, letting out a sigh.

"I've been up bright and early so many mornings and still I don't have much to show for all the work I've been doing." In her frustration, she swallowed the brown beverage quickly, burning her tongue. "Ouch."

She had two horses to train this morning before she was supposed to meet with Tom's lawyer.

Abby fingered through the pile of bills on the table. She had paid only half of them this month, and she still had the largest credit card bill staring at her, unpaid.

All her savings were gone as well as the large emergency fund she had kept on hand.

It had been six weeks since the graveside service, and things were definitely not getting better. If anything, they were getting worse.

Since Tom had... no, she wasn't going to think about the bad memories anymore. It wouldn't do her any good to think negative thoughts about the husband she had just buried.

Instead, she needed to take care of her responsibilities.

Abby combed her fingers through the thick fur on her cat's tummy. "Well Buttercup, it looks like I'll need to put another advertisement in the newspapers to teach students horse riding lessons, or perhaps I could see if any ranchers are looking for a horse trainer. But, I have my doubts that the older crowd of ranchers around here would want a woman horse trainer."

"But, I've got to do something. If I don't try something, I won't have the money I need, to pay the bills and

I'll lose the only home I've ever known and loved." Abby sighed.

A tear slipped down one cheek. Angrily Abby wiped it away. She wasn't going to turn into a blubbering mess, simply because she had some terrible circumstances to deal with.

Somehow, there had to be a solution. She was determined to find it.

She finished the rest of her coffee, picked up her cat and hugged her quickly before setting Buttercup on her feet.

She opened a can of her cat's favorite tuna dish, then scooped it into the cat dish and refilled her water bowl. "Buttercup, here's your food. I'm going out to the barn, the chores won't get done on their own."

Opening the back kitchen door, she whistled for her golden retriever. "Lassie, there you are. Did you think I forgot about you?" Abby patted his head, enjoying his thick fur for a moment.

She poured dog food into her dog's bowl and added fresh water into his other bowl. "You can keep me company in the barn when you're finished."

Hurrying across the yard to the barn, she breathed deeply of the fresh spring air. Seeing the green leaves and green grass in the spring, reminded her of new beginnings.

Sadly, she didn't think there would be any sort of new beginning for her. She'd be lucky enough to stay afloat in the storm that her finances were going through at the moment.

Strangely enough, Wyatt Callahan had continued to

stop by almost every day in the past few weeks. He checked on the health of her mare, her other horse, and her cattle. Sometimes she only caught glimpses of him, other times he said a quick hello.

Sometimes she looked into the pasture and caught Wyatt staring at her, but when he saw her looking at him, he quickly turned back to his work.

Abby was so confused.

On one hand, she was grateful for all his help because she really needed it, but on the other hand, having her ex-fiancé nearby every day was difficult emotionally.

Abby was more attracted to him than she could explain, but loving a man meant getting hurt again.

She'd already done that twice and refused to fall in love again.

For the rest of the morning, she worked hard training two horses that nearby ranchers had brought over to her ranch.

One was a two-year-old purebred Morgan mare, and the other was a two-year-old Quarter horse mare.

She had trained two other horses for these ranchers before, and they seemed to trust her ability. However, there were many other ranchers in the area who didn't bring their horses to her for training.

Abby wasn't sure why. Of course, she had heard from the small town gossip vine, that the older ranchers wouldn't ask a woman to train their horses. They were too set in the old ways of doing things.

But Abby didn't believe that was true for every rancher in these parts.

Most likely, the older ranchers just needed to see for

themselves the great results she got from horses that she trained.

Sometimes it seemed like no matter what she did, she was fighting an uphill battle. If it wasn't one thing, it was the other.

First she struggled with her finances, next she was struggling to ward off unwanted would-be suitors like Reno, and then before she knew it she was trying to convince other ranchers in the area that she was actually good at training horses.

Abby sighed as she led the Morgan mare into her stall. As she brushed down both horses and saw to it they were fed, she thought about the upcoming meeting with Tom's lawyer.

Knots formed in her belly just thinking about it.

She hurried to shower and change, and then drove her old green pickup into their small town of Refuge Mountain.

Driving down main street, Abby knew her old green pickup was as familiar to the small town's residents as they were to her. Maybe she'd get a chance to talk to her best friend Sierra Baxter, who worked as a waitress at their town's local coffee shop, *The Little Bean Cafe.*

She parked at the coffee shop as it was only a short walk to Mr. Ian Brown's law office. She decided she would visit with her friend later, as by then she might need a bracing drink to help her get through the rest of the day.

Abby got out of her truck and pulled the jade green cardigan sweater closer. She hurried across the street and opened the door to the law offices of Morris and Brown.

Stepping inside the office, she froze.

Sitting there in the waiting room were Tom's parents, James and Martha Hart. Beside them, sat Tom's younger brother, Will Hart. She should have remembered that in coming to hear the reading of Tom's will, meant she would see her late husband's family.

Abby braced herself, forcing a smile. She had never had a very good relationship with them. She had tried to be helpful and kind to Tom's mother and father when they were first married.

But, by their critical words and actions, they gave the impression that they never wanted her there.

So in the end, Abby had never felt like she was part of their family when interacting with either of Tom's parents.

She forced a small smile, hoping that with Tom's passing his parents would finally accept her.

Mrs. Hart flashed her a look of disdain. "Finally, you've arrived. I was beginning to wonder if attending the reading of my son's will, was important to you at all." Her mother-in-law huffed, her voice heavy with sarcasm.

The shock of her words felt like a hundred knives stabbing her belly. She didn't know why Tom's mother seemed to hate her, but it had been like this since the day Abby married her son.

Still, Abby struggled to maintain an even, soothing tone with her mother-in-law. Her father-in-law just nodded at her, without a word said between them.

Abby sat down straight backed on the waiting room chair with her hands balled into a tight fist hidden in the folds of her sweater.

She replied hurriedly. "Good morning, Mr. and Mrs. Hart. Good morning, Will."

A door opened and out strode Tom's lawyer, Ian Brown. Abby had never been more grateful for the interruption.

"Mr. and Mrs. Hart and Will good to see you. Abby, I'm glad you're here. Please follow me." Mr. Brown led the way down the hall and into a large office. The lawyer waved to a leather sofa and three armchairs.

Abby waited until her in-laws were seated on the sofa before she sat down in the armchair. She turned to Ian Brown, Tom's lawyer.

After the lawyer's assistant offered them each coffee, Mr. Brown began to speak.

"First of all, I wanted to let each of you know that I'm sorry for your loss. Tom Hart was a good man. He'll be greatly missed of course by all of you, his family, but also by folks here in our small town." The lawyer glanced at each of them and then shuffled through his papers and finding the correct ones, he held them in both hands.

"Tom came to me to have the paperwork drawn up for his will, just before he left on his first military tour three years ago. He wanted to make sure his affairs were in order before he left the country." Mr. Brown looked at each of them solemnly.

Abby swallowed hard and bit back tears.

Without warning, sobs split the air. Abby turned to see her husband's mother weeping out loud, rocking back and forth.

Her husband handed her a handkerchief, but didn't put his arm around her or hold her hand. Instead, Tom's brother Will leaned close to his mom and squeezed her hand to soothe her.

Even though Abby's heart ached with her own loss, she felt sorry for Tom's mother. Seeing the way James Hart kept his emotional and physical distance from his wife, gave her an epiphany in that moment.

In Abby's mind, it explained why there had been so many times Tom kept his distance from her and didn't know how to have a meaningful relationship with his wife.

Was the emotional neglect Tom's mother experienced from her husband, the reason she was mean to Abby ever since she married Tom? Abby didn't know, but in that moment she felt a rare spark of compassion for her mother-in-law that she'd never had before.

After a long while, Martha Hart's sobs softened into small sniffles.

The lawyer took a deep breath and began to explain how Tom wanted things in his will. "I leave all my worldly goods to my wife, Abby Meadows Hart. This includes the ranch, the old farm truck and all those things obtained in the marriage, except for a few items that I have specified herein."

He went on. "I give my favorite trail motorbike to my brother Will along with an album of treasured boyhood photos. To my parents James and Martha Hart, I leave old childhood photo albums along with my baseball bat and glove. I didn't have much, but I hope you know how much I loved you all. Love, Tom."

Abby sat for a moment in silence, thinking about her late husband's will.

Mr. Brown bundled up the paperwork and placed it into the folder. "That is Tom Hart's last will and testament. Does anyone have any questions?"

Abby shook her head silently. "No."

"Will or Mr. and Mrs. Hart?" Ian Brown questioned.

Will Hart shook his head. "I'm good. Tom's wishes seem clearly spelled out. I don't have any questions."

Without warning, James Hart's eyes darkened like angry thunderclouds as he looked at the lawyer and then at her.

Abby unconsciously jerked back in her chair, and an unwelcome blush stained her cheeks at the stern look he gave her.

Her father-in-law was a portly man whose cheeks suddenly were puffy with red streaks from his displeasure. "Well, it's not clear at all to me." James Hart looked at his youngest son, who sighed heavily and sank back in his chair.

Tom's father looked at Abby. "How come she gets everything, but I don't get the ten thousand dollars that my son Tom owed me? Where in my son's will is it spelled out that I will receive the money he owes me?"

Mr. Brown took a deep breath and began to speak. "Well, Tom didn't have enough money leftover…"

Martha Hart interrupted and pointed at Abby, her cold eyes sniping and lashing as much as her words did. "Of course our dear son Tom didn't have money."

Mrs. Hart's eyes flashed in anger. "It's easy enough to guess where your money has gone, James. We can see for ourselves. I am convinced your son's wife has spent the money owed you, on that eye-sore of a ranch and those ridiculous horses of hers."

Abby went numb, staring at her in-laws with increasing shock and anger. Blood began to pound in her temples and her face grew hot with humiliation at their insinuation that she was the reason Tom didn't have the money that he'd borrowed from his father.

Her heart hammered in her chest, her breathing ragged from the accusations. Abby willed herself to calm down.

She reminded herself, they didn't know all the terrible secrets she'd kept out of respect for her late husband. If Tom's parents found out, they would be the ones embarrassed and humiliated.

But she had more honor than to spend her time talking against her deceased husband. She had more self-respect.

"As I was saying, your son's will did not mention any extra finances, only the one property — the ranch — which was willed to his wife, Abby." The lawyer's voice sounded a little strained as he spoke. She could tell Mr. Brown was trying to diffuse the sparks of anger in the room.

Abby felt the nauseating sinking of despair. She couldn't believe that Tom's parents would speak to her like that. The insults were barbed and hurtful. Both of their gazes held accusation and blame.

She looked at Tom's brother, Will. She could only see the grief that lingered in his eyes. She knew Will Hart had never been one to rock the boat, instead he had always gone along with his parents' plans.

Abby's gaze shifted back to the lawyer who was wiping the perspiration from his forehead with a handkerchief.

A shudder sifted through her body, and the swell of pain was beyond tears. She didn't want to leave anything undone from her late husband's will.

Her heart squeezed in anguish as she realized what she needed to do.

She spoke quickly before she could change her mind. "If you give me six months, I will pay you back the ten thousand dollars my husband owed you." Abby spoke with quiet and firm resolve in her voice.

Her father-in-law's eyes narrowed for a moment as he looked at her. He nodded. "That would be the decent thing to do."

His lack of appreciation stunned Abby. Even a little acknowledgement or a thank you would've gone a long way towards establishing a better relationship between them.

"Of course." Abby didn't say much because if she did, she was afraid she would ruin the thin layer of peace between them.

Instead, Abby turned to the lawyer. "Are we done here?"

"Yes, I believe we have finished." Mr. Brown nodded, a look of concern in his eyes. Abby was sure he knew the state of her finances through his close association with her late husband. But she also trusted the lawyer to honor his confidentiality agreement with Tom.

She wasn't about to let her parent in-laws know about her worries or fears.

Somehow she would make it through on her own.

Abby was shrivelling on the inside, but through sheer force of will she smiled. Nodding to everyone, she spoke quickly. "Alright then, I need to get back to my chores. Thank you, Mr. Brown, for your time. See you all later."

She hurried out of the lawyer's office, ran to her truck and sat on the driver's seat, her body trembling in frustration and anguish. Abby's fingers fisted around the steering wheel, her knuckles turning white as her grip tightened.

A loud knock on the truck's window surprised her. She turned to see Sierra standing there.

Rolling down the driver's side window, Abby stared at her best friend with eyes brimming over in tears of frustration.

"Abby, what's wrong? What happened?" Her brows wrinkled together in worry as Sierra's blue eyes met her own.

She clamped her lips to imprison a sob that threatened to escape. She quickly wiped at a lone tear that escaped down one cheek. "I just met with Tom's lawyer. His parents and brother were also there for the reading of Tom's will."

"Oh. I'm sorry, Abby. I'm sure that was an awful experience." Sierra reached over and squeezed her hand, her blue eyes full of compassion. More than anyone else, she trusted her best friend to keep confidential the stressful and often terrible things she shared about her life.

They had spent many hours sharing their joys, fears and troubles with each other over the years. Abby trusted Sierra with her life.

"It was." Abby closed her eyes for a moment and sighed. "My mother-in-law has a way of putting me in my place, that makes me feel like I'm the worst person in the world. But, I really should be used to that."

Another tear slid down her cheek. Angrily she wiped it away, desperately not wanting to give into a moment of weakness.

Sierra rubbed her hand lightly along her arm. "I don't think that's something you should be used to. But I've been learning a hard truth about life and relationships. It's funny — in a sad way — how those people whom we love and respect the most are also the same folks we need to forgive the most."

Abby nodded, pain squeezing her heart at the truth of her friend's words. "Yeah, that sounds about right."

She didn't want to think about that right now. "That's why I've decided to do my best to keep my distance from my late husband's parents. For now, it seems like the safer choice."

"I'm sorry they've been so hard on you. Well, at least today's meeting is over."

"The meeting with the lawyer might be over, but there's still a new problem I have to figure out an answer to."

Sierra creased her brows together in worry. "What's that?"

"It turns out that my late husband owed his father ten thousand dollars. Now, my father-in-law wants me to return the money Tom owed him. I promised I'd get it to him." Abby gave a choked, desperate laugh. "Problem is, not only do I already have a large debt, but I'm barely getting by each month as it is."

"Tom didn't leave you anything in the will?"

Abby sighed heavily. "Just the ranch. And I'm grateful for that, but it's also heavily mortgaged. I'm really worried, Sierra. I honestly don't know how I'm going to manage everything."

Her friend sighed and crinkled her brows, something she always did when she was deep in thought. Abby turned to look at her. "There has to be some way to get you through this. Could you sell some cows to get the money you need?"

"I've sold most of them already, but you're right. I need to sell the last few cows." Abby nodded woodenly to herself. She bit her lip, the harsh reality she was now facing filled her mind with shadows and her heart with terror. "I'll need to sell my horses as well."

Her heart swelled with pain at the realization.

"Abby look at me." She looked at Sierra through the mist of tears that clouded her eyes. "It may not come to that. I know how important your horses are to you."

"I can't see any other way." Abby replied in a low, tormented voice. Her horses were the one constant in her life. They had always been there for her, when people in her life let her down.

She swallowed and took a deep breath, wiping her eyes one last time.

"Sometimes life has pleasant surprises. There might be another way to get the money you need. I believe your courage and determination will see you through this, Abby. You've always had that in spades." Her friend's words were the light brush of hope that she needed.

Abby clenched her jaw and nodded quickly. "I hope you're right. Thanks Sierra."

"Anytime you need to talk, I'm here, okay?" Sierra looked over at the coffee shop. A line of customers had formed outside the shop. "But, it looks like right now I need to get back to work. I'll call you later."

Abby watched as her friend hurried back to the coffee shop.

Closing her eyes, she rested her head on the steering wheel. A heavy sigh escaped her lips.

Thoughts of selling her animals tore at her heart. She could sell the remaining cows she had, but she would have to keep at least one horse. Ranchers around these parts would lose all respect for a horse trainer who didn't have a horse.

It looked like she was stuck between a rock and a hard place.

In the end, she knew she must do what needed to be done to save the ranch and pay back her father-in-law.

Swallowing the sob in her throat, she hurried to start the truck engine and then drove down the street and out of town.

Tears flowed the whole way home and she couldn't stop her hands from shaking.

Abby's thoughts were filled with what she had promised Tom's father she would do. How was she supposed to find ten thousand dollars in six months?

Driving up the dirt lane that led to her ranch yard, she parked near the barn and sat there a moment, her belly in tight knots.

It was the very thing she dreaded. She would have to sell Blackie and she'd have to sell her quarter horse, Stocking.

She would have to sell the few cattle she had left. Her herd would be empty at that point. But she needed to do it. That was the only way she could find the money before six months were up.

The pain in her heart became a sick, fiery gnawing as she thought of selling her beloved horses.

Abby hurried into the barn and opened the door to Stocking's stall. She gave her mare an apple, knowing how much she liked the treat. Patting Stocking's neck, she suddenly burst into tears.

"I have to give you up." Her tears fell down her cheeks, landing on her mare's neck. Her mare nuzzled her gently before going back to eating the bits of hay.

The pain in Abby's heart became unbearable. The one animal she wanted to keep, she would need to give up.

All her life she'd had to give up people or things that she loved.

Her mare had been the one companion that had always been there for her. Her father had let her keep Stocking when she was born. He said the mare was too damaged to do him much good.

As a filly, her horse was born with birth trauma, which the veterinarian had told her Dad might cause girth and flank sensitivity even when her mare was full grown.

Her Dad didn't want to have to deal with that, so Abby worked with Stocking. And it took years of gentle handing to teach her mare to trust, but finally Abby had been able to put on a saddle and ride her.

Her mother and sister had always thought that her attachment to her horse was really strange. Growing up her mother encouraged Hadley's longing to be with friends and couldn't understand why Abby would rather ride her horse or spend time with her beloved animals.

But at school, Abby had only a couple of friends. Sierra was one of them, and she just accepted her as she was. When Abby would come to school with bruises on her arms and around her back, Sierra was patient with her and helped her get better. It was so different from some of the other girls in school, who just teased her because she didn't dress in fancy clothes.

During her years at Refuge Mountain High School, Abby remembered Tiffany Leggier, who came from a from a well-to-do family. Tiffany was always dressed in the latest clothes and always had one or two guys that she was stringing along.

They teased Abby for being so backwards. Tiffany and the popular girls she hung around with, told her she wasn't normal with her quiet ways and with the fact that she spent most of her time with farm animals.

But being with animals was the one place Abby found unconditional love. She never knew when her Dad's temper would erupt.

As she entered the teenage years, she realized his bursts of anger usually occurred after he came home from the bar, stumbling through the house loudly in a drunken stupor.

Deep sobs racked her insides as she remembered. Placing her head against her knees, she cried for all the years of pain and heartache.

She sobbed until she was exhausted.

All of a sudden, a gentle hand squeezed her shoulder.

She looked up, surprised to see Wyatt kneeling on the hay covered floor of the stall.

"Abby honey, tell me what's wrong." The heartrending tenderness in his gaze, along with the affectionate name he called her, was her undoing.

Tears blinded her eyes and choked her voice.

Wyatt sat against the stall beside her and put his arm around her. She leaned into him with her head on his shoulder, grateful for his comfort. He held her there for a long time, just letting her cry.

His arms felt strong and protective. Abby could have stayed there forever.

Finally, after a long while, her tears subsided and were replaced with soft hiccups.

"Abby, please talk to me. Why the tears?" Wyatt leaned over and cupped her chin with one hand so he could see her eyes. "Are you sad about losing Tom?"

"No." Abby stopped herself. Where had that thought come from? She was sure that wasn't what she meant to say. "What I meant to say is, I am sad about losing Tom, but that's not why I'm crying today."

"You can tell me." It was Wyatt's soft words and the gentle way he held her that caused her to spill what was in her heart.

"I was just at the lawyer's office with Tom's parents and his brother Will. Mr. Brown went over Tom's last will and testament." Abby shuddered as she could still hear Martha Hart's sarcastic and accusatory comments ringing in her ears.

"What's wrong?" Wyatt's dark eyes, like his deep voice, were warm and filled with concern.

"I just learned that I'm deeper in debt than I realized."
Abby's voice broke, and she swallowed a sob. She didn't
want to tell Wyatt Callahan that her husband died, owing
a lot of money to his father. "I'm already in over my head
as it is."

"I take it the news wasn't good at the lawyer's office?"

Abby shook her head as her brows puckered together
in worry.

"Just so I can get a clearer picture of things, how many
horses are you training right now?" Wyatt's concerned
eyes searched hers.

Abby wiped stray tears from her cheeks. She didn't
really like talking about her finances, but she also knew
she could trust Wyatt not to tell anyone.

She swallowed and explained. "Two horses. I don't
have much experience at horse training, although I do
love it. I think that's why horse owners around here aren't
willing to hire me. So no, I don't have as much income
from that as I need to cover ranch expenses and pay off
the extra debt."

"Abby, I've seen you work with horses and how you
train them. You're good." Wyatt's grey eyes stared into her
own, confident and steady. His words had a way of
making her almost believe him. "What I don't understand
is why you'd doubt yourself?"

A shaky hand tucked a loose tendril behind her ear.
She tried to push back the raw sores from memories that
haunted her. "My dad always said working with horses for
me, would always be a hobby. He said I should try doing
something serious like teaching, like other women my
age. So that's why I started teaching children to ride." A

soft, brittle laugh emerged as she tried to hide the pain in her heart.

"Abby, I don't know why your father would tell you that. All I know, from what I see, is that you have a real gift for working with horses. They listen to you and do what you ask of them. Any rancher would be lucky to have you train their horses."

She nodded and quickly blinked back tears that pricked the back of her eyelids. "Thanks for saying that, Wyatt. That means a lot."

"It's just the truth." Wyatt was silent for a minute. He looked away for a moment before he turned back to her, his eyes bright and his jaw set in that determined way of his.

"We'll figure out a way around this." He paused for a moment and then smiled. "You know what? I have four horses that are almost two years of age and ready to be trained. Two mares and two stallions. I'd like you to train them."

Her brows scrunched together, not sure she liked this sudden solution. "Are you offering this job because you feel sorry for me?" She didn't want anyone — but especially not Wyatt Callahan — to feel sorry for her. She was determined to stand on her own two feet.

"Not at all. I've been too busy dealing with problems with our cattle and trying to sort through the paperwork my Dad left behind, that training the horses has skipped my mind. But, it needs to be done." Wyatt turned to her once again, a slow smile forming on his face. "So, I'm asking you. Abby, will you train four horses that desperately need your help?"

Wyatt's slow smile had always been his best feature, and unconsciously the walls around her heart melted a little more. Even though she was still angry with this man for what happened years ago, she wasn't about to turn away a job opportunity that she desperately needed.

She wasn't about to look a gift horse in the mouth.

"I will." She thought about the size of her small barn. "I don't have enough space to take in four more horses. Will it be alright with you if I train at your place?"

"Yes, that would be good."

"When do you want me to start?"

"Tomorrow morning too soon?"

Abby thought of her much slower schedule at the moment and realized she had a bunch of time. "That'll work."

"Good. I'll make sure the training area is ready for you tomorrow."

"Thanks. I look forward to it." She looked up to see Wyatt's intense gave as it travelled over her face and searched her eyes.

His gravelly voice whispered. "Me too."

Abby's heart jolted, and her pulse pounded at the intensity of their attraction. He was so disturbing to her in every way. And it was something that had lasted for years. When she married Tom, she had done all she could to push memories of Wyatt out of her mind.

But, now Tom was gone.

Wyatt was here sitting beside her, and she couldn't deny the immediate and total attraction she felt towards him.

Ever since Wyatt had returned home weeks ago, she'd

dreamed of being held within his embrace. She'd dreamed of his kisses.

It didn't help that every time she saw him, that pull was even stronger.

Wyatt's gaze studied her with a curious intensity. When his eyes moved down to stare at her lips they darkened with an unknown emotion.

His arm around her shoulder tightened, pulling her closer. One large hand cupped her jaw and there was no mistaking his intentions.

Her heart rate accelerated and tingles spread down to her belly.

Wyatt leaned his head down, his gaze resting on her lips.

Her mind told her to resist his kisses, but her body refused to listen.

Abby slipped her hands around his neck and a warm tingling spread over her lips as she anticipated his kiss. She remembered Wyatt's passionate kisses from years ago.

Once again, she was cocooned in the circle of his arms and anticipating the touch of his lips on hers.

Suddenly, she heard a loud bark and repeated scratching on the outside of the wooden stall door.

Abby pulled away at the sound.

Without warning, she'd been rudely awakened from a deep slumber.

Abby looked up at Wyatt, wide-eyed, while her heart fluttered wildly in her breast. She fought back from the overwhelming need to be held in his arms.

Instead, she moved away and Wyatt let his arm fall to his side.

Wyatt expelled a breath, frustration evident on his face.

"That's Lassie." Abby stood to her feet, needing space between them. "I'll go check on him."

Wyatt ran a hand through his hair, his mouth bent downward in a grimace. "I gathered that. Couldn't your dog have a better sense of timing?"

A shaky smile was her only response.

Abby couldn't respond. What was she doing allowing herself to get close to him again?

She hurried to the door of the stall.

Wyatt stood up and followed her, his long strides easily catching up to her.

She opened the door and, Wyatt followed her out, latching the door behind him.

Nervously, Abby patted her dog on the head, before looking up at Wyatt. His eyes still held the smoldering flame she'd seen before.

She tried her best to ignore it. She couldn't allow herself to fall again for the same man who had abandoned her all those years ago. He'd taken her heart with him. Now, she simply couldn't trust him with it again.

Abby squared her shoulders and forced a crisp tone in her voice. "Well, I should finish my chores. I will see you tomorrow."

Heat stained her neck and flew up to her cheeks as she stared at him.

Wyatt leaned close, his gaze as soft as a caress. "I definitely look forward to it."

His whispered words were warm against her hair, shifting the auburn tendrils against her cheek.

Abby's gaze was glued to his full mouth, which formed a slow smile, filled with anticipation that made her heart race.

She quickly averted her gaze and stepped back.

He touched the tip of his cowboy hat with his fingers, and with a nod walked away.

She stared after him until she couldn't see him anymore in the distance.

Her whole body still hummed with the dizzying current from being near this man that stirred her senses.

While she was grateful that he had four horses for her to train, Abby wondered how she would manage to work on Wyatt's ranch.

Already, he was wreaking havoc on her senses.

She would just have to only focus on training the horses and not think about Wyatt Callahan.

# CHAPTER FOUR

yatt

"WHAT HAS you smiling so much, this morning, Wyatt?" Denver Callahan poured more coffee into his cup and grinned at his brother.

Wyatt shook his head, as he buttered his toast. "And what's wrong with smiling in the morning?"

"Nothing, except you hardly ever do it, especially not in the morning." Dakota growled from his place at the far end of the breakfast table.

"Well, maybe I'm turning over a new leaf."

"Yeah, it's not as simple as that. It's a girl." Sawyer spoke up and chuckled, looking at all of his brothers at the table.

Wyatt expelled a breath as his brothers teased him. "Maybe. I'll never tell."

He finished his toast and drank the rest of his coffee, so he could leave his brother's never-ending teasing. "I'll see you all outside. We'll talk about what needs to be done for the day."

"Sure, brother. We'll be there soon." Denver called out.

Just as Wyatt was about to go out the door, his mother followed and called his name. "Wyatt, I just wanted to let you know I'm having a few ladies over for tea today. I just don't want you to be surprised when a large number of vehicles show up here later this morning."

"Thanks for letting me know. Have a good time with your friends, Mom." Wyatt leaned over, kissed her cheek and winked at her before leaving the house. Whistling, he walked to the barn, Jack and Jill at his heels.

"Hey you two. You're looking happy." Wyatt scratched the thick fur behind their ears. "That must mean Cassie's already fed you this morning. Well, come along. You can keep the cattle in line today."

As he walked to the barn, he thought of those few precious moments he'd had with Abby last night. Holding her in his arms and gazing into her big green eyes had been his undoing.

The scent of wildflowers, clung to her as he held her close. His heart rate had pounded in his ears as he bent to kiss her sweet strawberry red lips and then they were interrupted by the dog.

Wyatt grimaced in frustration at the memory as he walked into the training area near the barn.

Somewhere deep inside him, there was a longing to get closer to Abby. He hoped they would, especially since they would be working together in close quarters for the foreseeable future.

Yet, he reminded himself that he wasn't looking to fall in love. Except for when he was adopted by Mack and Annie Callahan, he'd only ever experienced pain and rejection by people he loved.

Since he came home, seeing Abby again reminded him of her rejection of him. Maybe it's not what she intended all those years ago, but it's what he'd felt.

He'd been trying to help her every day like his Dad asked, but still keep his distance. Conflicted inside, he battled his true desire to hold her close. It's why he didn't say much when he checked on her horses or cattle. He had been trying to guard his heart.

But last night as he held Abby in his arms again, reminders of the love they once shared came back. Those times spent together, riding the range, or fishing together, or looking for stray calves, were all sweet memories to him.

However, if Abby's chilly tone when he left last night was any indication of her feelings, he would need to move slowly.

It seemed like she was sending him mixed signals. Was it possible she was feeling as mixed up as he was?

Well, he wasn't going to worry about that right now.

He had a lot of work to get done today and thinking about his beautiful neighbor wasn't helping him get it done.

He opened the gate to the training area and walked around the newly built riding area his Dad had built a few years ago.

The whole area used the soft black earth that was good for the horses' hooves. The riding area was about a half acre long and about half as wide. There was a lot of room for horse training and riding here.

His Dad had always been training the next new horse in this fenced in area. Wyatt remembered the first time he rode his first horse. It had been in this fenced in area, which at the time had been a lot smaller.

He was newly adopted by Mack and Annie, and his new Dad wanted to go easy on the new boy from the city as he adapted to ranch life.

His Dad needn't have worried as Wyatt loved it at the ranch. Even those handful of times he was bucked off a horse in the beginning, hadn't stopped his love of riding horses or ranching.

This was the first real home where he had been truly accepted and loved for who he was. This was the one place where he belonged.

He loved it when the people he cared about recognized the ranch for the haven it was.

Wyatt's gaze swept over the fenced in training area, looking forward to when Abby would come to train the horses today.

Last night's almost kiss with his beautiful neighbor had frustrated him.

He couldn't sleep until late at night, thinking of Abby. He realized he was more attracted to her now than he'd been years ago.

Now that he'd asked her to train his horses, it meant they would be in close quarters almost daily for quite a few months, at least. He remembered his Dad's letter to him, asking him to serve and take care of Abby for at least six months.

Thinking back to last night, Wyatt realized his Dad's last request was only granting him the opportunity to become close to Abby... which was something he'd dreamed of for years.

Yet, the hardest part of seeing her at the ranch every day, was the possibility that he'd fall crazy in love with her once again only to face her rejection like last time.

Well, he wasn't going to dwell on it. It was time to get to work.

The ranch wouldn't run itself. He needed to get the day's work organized. Wyatt was determined to make the Triple C even better in the coming years than it had been before his dad died.

He watched as his six brothers walked across the large ranch yard, joking and jostling each other. He was thankful to have grown up with them.

They couldn't have been more different, but somehow when they became part of the Callahan family their differences seemed to fade away.

They'd learned to appreciate each other for their unique gifts, abilities, and individual personalities.

Mack and Annie Callahan had both taught their sons how to do that. And Wyatt was grateful.

Denver called out. "We're over here, Wyatt. I'm glad you have decided to keep the ranch work organized. Since you know all that's going on around the ranch, tell us what our jobs for today should be."

"Or maybe, we could just take the day off?" Dakota was always up for some type of fun.

Wyatt grinned. "Sorry, no time off this week. There's too much that needs doing. I've given a few of our ranch hands the job of fixing the fences in the South part of the pasture, closer to the mountain range today."

He went on. "As I was riding yesterday, I saw some spots in the Southwest pasture where the fences seem to be down. Sawyer and Cole, if you could take care of fixing those that would be helpful."

"Sure, man. We've got it." Cole and Sawyer headed toward the large garage where they stored their ATVs. It was easier to travel around their near seventy-five thousand acre ranch land and carry the tools they needed with the four wheelers.

Wyatt checked the list he'd made on his smartphone. "And the cattle need checking. I made the rounds yesterday, but Dakota, if you and Hunter could check on the cattle in the Northwest pasture that would be great. Zane and Denver same goes for the Northeast pasture, if you could check on the cattle there, that would be great. You know what to look for."

After his brothers left, Wyatt looked at the weekly schedule and saw that the farrier was coming tomorrow to shoe the horses.

Some of their horses were in desperate need of having their hooves looked at and fixed. With their forty five head of horses, and ten thousand, one hundred and fifty head of cattle, the Triple C ranch was a big project that took a lot of work.

However, it was a job that Wyatt loved. He was glad to be home. It made him happy to be back with his family and working with the animals he loved.

At the sound of hoof beats, he turned his head only to see Abby riding her horse across Callahan pasture land. Soon, she reached the large ranch yard.

Walking her horse near the training area, she saw Wyatt and quickly got off her horse.

"Good morning, Wyatt." Abby nodded to him as she slipped the knotted reins over her horse's neck.

Wyatt eyed her under the shadow of his cowboy hat, appreciating the pretty picture she made. Abby wore her usual jeans and a long-sleeved western shirt. Two thick auburn braids hung past her shoulders to her slim waist, giving her that innocent girl-next-door appeal he loved so much.

Her dark brown cowboy hat with her well worn brown leather cowboy boots completed the enticing picture she made.

"Wyatt?" Abby put one hand on her hip, a sure sign she was exasperated with him. "Where do you want me to put Stocking while I'm working?"

Heat rose in his cheeks as he realized she'd already asked him once, and he'd been too busy staring at her to listen to what she had to say.

"Sorry. Ah, lets put your mare in one of the extra stalls in the barn." Wyatt led her to the barn and opened one of the stall doors while Abby led her horse inside.

Wyatt took the saddle off while Abby took off Stocking's bridle. Finding the mare water and feed, he carried both to the stall so Abby's horse was taken care of.

"Thanks, Wyatt. Appreciate it." Abby whispered something to her mare before she followed him out of the stall.

Wyatt walked to the stalls on the other side of the barn

where they kept the eighteen-month to two-year-old mares and stallions.

"Here are the four horses I was thinking we could start training." Wyatt pointed at each of them in their stalls. "I think for today we'll start with our two-year-old quarter horse, whom we've named Mustang. He's been restless lately and could use a good workout."

"Sure. Let's do it."

Wyatt attached the lead rope to the horse's halter. He had halter-broke this one, but hadn't got any further than that.

Abby walked beside Wyatt as he led the large colt to the training area near the barn. He opened the wooden gate to the training area, and Abby followed, closing the gate behind her.

"I just started to put the halter on him about two weeks ago. Mustang's been getting used to the halter and the rope, but he's only in the beginning stages." Wyatt handed the rope to her. "He's all yours."

Abby took the rope from his outstretched hand and as her soft skin touched his, a jolt of electricity flowed from his hand and up his arm. He let his hand linger, enjoying the softness of her skin.

"Thanks, Wyatt. I'll go slow with him."

"First lesson, is to teach this colt to trust his handler, right?" Wyatt had seen her train horses before and liked how Abby moved slowly with each young horse as she taught them to trust.

"Yep. But, trust sometimes takes longer than we'd like. It all depends on the horse." She spoke casually, but there was a pensive shimmer in the shadow of her eyes.

He didn't miss the double meaning in her words. She wasn't only taking about the horse, but of them learning to trust each other.

"Well then, it's a good thing we can take all the time we need." Wyatt peered at her intently, and despite her closed expression, he sensed her vulnerability.

Abby nodded, and a small smile turned up the corners of her mouth. She gripped the rope tightly, patting the neck of the two-year-old colt with gentle hands as she spoke in a gentle whisper. "Yes, that is good." She continued to pat the horse's neck. "Well, I'll get started then."

Wyatt nodded, watching as with slow movements, she directed the horse toward the center of the training area.

ABBY'S SKIN tingled from the touch of Wyatt's hand on hers.

Each time she saw him, the pull of attraction was stronger. She felt like a breathless girl of eighteen again, and it scared her. She didn't know how to put a stop to these feelings.

She began training as she normally did. Moving the rope ever so slowly, so the horse could see it on his right and left side, she began to work with him to get him used to watching the movement without becoming skittish. The restless two-year-old colt flinched a little.

Speaking in soft tones to the horse, she tried to calm him. "It's okay. You'll get used to me and this rope."

Abby loved the way Mustang's ears perked up and the

intelligence she saw in his big brown eyes. As she touched the rope gently to the colt's forelegs, it curved a little around one leg.

She remembered learning years ago from Mack Callahan, that when you're training a young horse, continue to add pressure and then loosen it.

Pressure and release.

Give and take.

This constant back-and-forth movement caused the horse to become familiar with the natural rhythm that went with having a rider on his back.

She continued to work with Mustang to get him used to the rope around his forelegs and hind legs. Once she was confident that the colt was getting more comfortable with the look and feel of the rope, Abby threw it gently around his neck.

Mustang jerked his head up and backed away, unsure about the idea of something strange around his neck.

"It's all right. You're doing great. Just a few more minutes and we'll be done training for the day." Abby walked closer to the colt and turned the rope so that it went around the horse's flanks, which caused him to turn in a circle. He responded quickly, turning in a circle. When she redirected the rope to the other side, the colt followed again.

"You're done for today, Mustang. You're an amazing horse and incredibly smart." Abby rubbed a hand along his neck and the horse jerked his head up and down, as if in full agreement.

She grinned as she led him to the gate.

Wyatt was still standing there, watching her.

Her face heated a little as she realized he must have been standing there watching her the whole time. When she started training a horse, usually, she was so focused on the training, that everything else faded away.

"You have a natural way with him, Abby." Wyatt opened the gate as she led the colt out of the training area.

He walked beside her and patted Mustang's neck. "He's the most skittish horse out of the bunch of two-year-olds in our stables, so you've already accomplished more in one day than I have in a few weeks. I'm impressed."

The sincerity in Wyatt's voice, flooded her with warmth. It meant a lot to hear this man — a cowboy with great horse skills — praise her own horse training abilities.

"Thank you Wyatt. That means a lot coming from you." Abby's eyes moved up to his and flushed at the glint of admiration in his gray eyes.

Flustered from his steady gaze, her words tumbled out hurriedly. "Tomorrow, I'll work him more with the rope and we'll start him soon with a bareback pad. It won't be long and he'll be ready for that."

"Sounds good, Abby." As they reached the barn, the high pitched sound of a woman's voice reached into her ears.

A pretty blonde woman walked around the corner of the barn, not stopping until she reached them. "Wyatt Callahan, there you are."

"Tiffany, hello. What can I do for you?"

"Well, I don't quite know, but there might be something." Her laugh tinkled as it spilled from her lips. Abby tried not to grimace at the flirty sound that came from this woman.

Tiffany Leggier, was dressed to the nines, in a slimming skirt and high heels with a body hugging short sleeved blouse that seemed to reveal more than it hid.

"Tiffany, you remember Abby Hart, don't you?" Wyatt looked over at Abby, his low voice even and controlled.

"Of course. Hello Abby. I'm surprised to see you here. I was convinced that with the recent loss of your husband, I wouldn't be seeing you much about town or hereabouts. But, it seems I was wrong." Tiffany's fake laugh spilled over again.

"Well, the horses still need to be trained. So here I am." Abby took a deep breath, forcing a calm tone. For some reason she couldn't pinpoint, why Tiffany's tinkling voice and high pitched laugh, irritated her. "But, I do need to start training the next horse, so I'll just take Mustang into the barn and feed him and rub him down."

Wyatt's brows creased together, but he nodded. "Thank you, Abby. I'll be there shortly."

As Abby walked away, she could hear Tiffany's flirty voice speaking to Wyatt. "Wyatt, why must you always be so busy? I have an idea that will help you relax. Refuge Mountain's annual Fall Festival and Barn dance is on Saturday. Were you planning on joining in the fun?"

"Can't say I've given it much thought." Wyatt's voice had the same determined control as he replied.

"Well, if you didn't have plans, I thought maybe we could go together Wyatt. It would be fun. What do you say?"

Abby had reached the open barn door, as she overheard Tiffany ask Wyatt for a date. She shook her head and expelled a breath.

For some reason, a burning sensation rose in her chest as she turned to see Tiffany sidle up closer to Wyatt. Abby, thought of all the years in High School, when Tiffany had dated all the boys and had even tried to take Wyatt from Abby when their relationship had become more serious.

A twinge of frustration rose up inside her, but she forced it down. Abby told herself, she was just feeling irritated with Tiffany for interrupting her horse training day, but that wasn't completely true.

She was jealous, plain and simple.

Jealous of Tiffany for capturing Wyatt's attention.

Her emotions didn't make sense to her own mind.

Abby was aware that Wyatt had shown interest in her since he returned, but she had been cool towards him over and over again.

Maybe she was a bit like the young horses she trained.

Skittish and afraid of anything new or strange.

Maybe in her case, she feared being rejected by love all over again.

The colt beside her shook his head mirroring the annoyance she felt. Abby stepped into the barn, happy to be away from having to watch Wyatt and one of his girlfriends.

She led the horse into his stall and rubbed him down good.

Abby had just finished feeding and watering Mustang, when she heard the stall door open. Wyatt stepped in. "How is he?"

"Mustang is good. I'll start training the mare next, if

that's all right by you?" Abby opened the stall door and Wyatt followed her into the middle aisle of the large barn.

"Sure, that's fine." She started to move forward, when Wyatt lightly touched her arm.

His touch sent sparks flying up her arm again.

"What is it?"

"I need to tell you something. I did something you might not appreciate." Wyatt had that charming boyish look in his gray eyes, the same one she'd always had a tough time resisting.

Abby put her hands on her hips, and her eyes narrowed slightly. A wave of apprehension swept through her as she waited for him to explain.

"When Tiffany asked me to take her to the annual Fall Festival and Barn dance, I told her I already had a date."

Abby sighed and simply nodded. "Okay."

"I said I was taking you."

Abby stared wordlessly at him, her heart pounding. "But... why?"

Shocked by his declaration, she could only stare at him.

"Because I really didn't want to show up at the dance with Tiffany on my arm. She could talk the hind leg off my fastest horse." Wyatt grimaced while Abby giggled softly at the picture that emerged in her mind at his description.

But that didn't explain things.

Abby sobered and looked at him, irritated that he'd gone ahead and decided she was going to the dance with him without even asking her.

"Why did you tell Tiffany you were taking me to the

dance?" Her cool tone was evidence enough that she was not amused.

Wyatt's eyes darkened and the intensity of his gaze made her vaguely confused. He stepped closer even though she felt impaled by his steady gaze.

Reaching out on hand, he slid his fingers along one of her long braids and studied it a moment, before peering at her intently.

"Abby, need you ask?" He low voice was as soft as a caress. "I've waited seven years to dance with you again. I hope you'll say yes." His steady gaze bore into her in silent expectation.

She fidgeted with her hands and shoved them into her jeans pocket. While her insides fluttered with excitement at his words, her mind argued that this wasn't a good idea.

Abby shook her head and blurted out a lame excuse. "I hadn't really planned on going to this year's Fall Festival."

She sighed and looked away from Wyatt, toward the horse stalls. There was no question, she would much rather stay home and be with her animals instead of spending an evening with the folks in their small town.

"Abby, I know you had a very difficult year with losing Tom alongside the other difficulties you've gone through." He cupped her chin tenderly in his warm hand. "But honey, I really think you should be at the Fall Festival."

His tender voice caused her to come undone on the inside. She bit her lip to hold herself back from crying. Despite her efforts to hold it back, a lone tear made its way down one cheek.

Turning her head away from him, she swallowed back

a wave of tumultuous emotions that threatened to undo her.

Sucking in a deep breath, her soft voice determined.

"I can't think of any good reason why I should go. It'll just be the same thing. A bunch of folks from town gossiping about me, just like usual." She quickly wiped a tear away before turning to look back at him.

His brows drew together in an angry frown before he set his jaw with determination.

"All the more reason for you to be there, to show the gossipers that they can't beat you down. And if you need reasons to go, I've got three that come to mind." Wyatt's other hand found her braid and toyed with it.

"The first reason is that people need to see that you're okay. Some of those folks are your friends and think the world of you. It would set them at ease to see you face to face, to see for themselves that you're okay. And the ones that don't appreciate you, they'll see you as a determined woman who won't let gossip hold her back from living her life." The corners of Wyatt's mouth turned up at this.

"The second reason you should be there, is that it would benefit you to mingle with other ranchers in the area. Some of those families will be at Refuge Mountain's Fall Festival. You'd have a chance to talk to them and learn if any ranchers need a good horse trainer." She nodded at this, realizing it was probably a good idea.

"I suppose that's true." She realized he hadn't finished. "And the third reason?"

Wyatt stepped a little closer. "The third reason is the most important. I believe this will be good for us both.

You need to kick back and relax a little, and I believe I'm the man to show you how."

He sent her a smile that sent her pulse racing.

Abby hesitated, torn by conflicting emotions. She wasn't sure if going to the dance with him was a good idea. But he had made some good points. Maybe going to their small town's annual fall event would be a good idea.

Being with Wyatt at the dance simultaneously thrilled and frightened her, but maybe by going, it would settle all the small town gossipers who were talking about her. Maybe it was the right thing to do after all.

Abby expelled a breath. "All right, I'll go with you, Wyatt. But I think it's better if we don't look at this as a date. We're simply two neighbors going together to the Fall Festival."

Wyatt leaned close, his voice tender, almost a murmur. "I think it would be a lot more fun as a date, but we can do this your way."

Her cheeks heated at his warm teasing, and she offered him a hesitant smile. She nodded and offered him a noncommittal smile. "Okay, then."

Tingles of awareness burst in her belly, and nervously she took a step back. Thoughts of him getting closer aroused old fears and uncertainties. She swallowed hard, trying to manage an answer.

"Well, I should be getting back to work." Abby's emotions were tumbling around like a Ferris wheel on high speed.

She needed to get back to some place safe. Some place where she was away from Wyatt and this crazy attraction, he stirred in her. She needed to get back to some place she could work with horses.

The roguish grin Wyatt gave her, made her blush.

She forced her lips to part in a curved, stiff smile.

Then hurriedly, she turned and walked towards the stall of the next horse she was training that day.

Abby was determined to prove to Wyatt that she had no intention of permitting herself to fall for his many charms.

## CHAPTER FIVE

 yatt

WYATT STEPPED out of the horse barn, his mind still on his beautiful neighbor.

He drew in a slow, steady smile at the thought of taking Abby to the dance. She'd told him she didn't want it to be a date, but in his mind since he was taking her to the Fall Festival that meant he was responsible for taking care of her.

He would do his best to protect Abby and help her have fun. He guessed that for most people that might seem like an old fashioned idea, but that was the way he saw it.

Wyatt's mouth curved into an unconscious smile as he thought of spending the evening with Abby.

A sudden rumbling sound brought him out of his

musing, and he turned his head. He saw dust flying up and his brothers coming towards him on their four wheelers.

Dakota and soon Hunter barrelled toward him and stopped their ATVs right in front of him, screeching dust up as they did.

Wyatt stopped and stared at his brothers, his hands on his hips and a pucker forming between his brows. "How come you two are in such an all fired up hurry? Where's the fire?"

"No fire. But you'll be happy we hurried just the same. Just wait until you hear what we have to tell you." Hunter slipped the helmet off his head and shook his wavy blond hair as he got off the four wheeler.

Wyatt patiently waited as his gaze roamed between his two brothers.

An oddly primitive warning sounded in his brain. "So what did you find?"

Dakota got off the ATV and walked toward Wyatt. His brother's blue eyes were sharp and assessing an advantage Dakota had with the half Sioux blood running through his veins. "I'm getting to that. We were in the Northwest pasture checking on the cattle, when I had a feeling to count the head of cattle. Sure enough, we discovered fifty head have gone missing."

"What?" Wyatt rubbed one hand on the back of his neck. Knots formed in his belly as he thought about what could have happened to their cattle. Missing? Since dad had passed away, they'd hadn't experienced that sort of trouble. The responsibility of taking proper care of his father's ranch weighed heavily on his shoulders.

"Did you do another head count, to double check?"

"Yes. And it was fifty head of cattle that are missing. We're sure of it." Hunter came to stand beside Dakota as he spoke.

The silence between them grew tight with tension.

"Well, it goes without saying, that's a big problem. Did you see any unusual tracks along the fence line?" Wyatt asked, hoping to understand what happened to the missing cattle.

"Yeah, the two of us drove along the fence line. That's the other bad news." Dakota's expression darkened with an unreadable emotion. "The fence has been cut in a clean line from top to bottom. And to answer your next question, I saw some new truck tire tracks on the other side."

"Hmm, so we might be dealing with a modern day cattle rustler." Wyatt's eyes narrowed as an anger sparked inside him. "Who would do this? Have we made any enemies lately? Or did Dad have some folks who were mad at him, or angry enough to steal his cattle?"

Dakota shook his head in that silent way of his.

"I don't think so, not as far as I can remember, anyway." Hunter ran a couple fingers along his chin thoughtfully. "As for the seven of us, I don't think there's folks in these parts who would want to steal our cattle out from under us."

Wyatt shook his head silently as he thought about it, and he couldn't come up with any answers.

"Well, it looks like I'll need to take this matter to the sheriff. Maybe he can figure out who did this. Meanwhile, we'll need to go out and fix that fence line."

"We pieced the fence line together for now. But we'll head back out and string up some new wire along that place where the fence was cut." Hunter picked up his helmet as he spoke. "I'll just grab what we need from the shed. Be right back, Dakota."

"Sure thing, bro. Thanks." Dakota looked at Wyatt, his eyes glinting like hardened steel. "Don't worry. We'll figure out who did this brother. No one harms our cattle and gets away with it."

Wyatt reached out a hand, clapping Dakota on the shoulder. "Thanks, Dakota. With you working on it, using your tracking skills and keen eye for details, we're sure to figure out where the missing cattle went."

Soon, his brothers drove away in their ATVs with all the tools they needed to get the fence line fixed.

Wyatt walked to the ranch house, deep in thought. He hurried in through the back door of the ranch house that led to a back office. The back office was where he did most of his calling or had meetings with his ranch hands.

He made a phone call, knowing this needed to be dealt with as soon as possible. As soon as he finished talking with the Sheriff, he felt better. Sheriff Hank Turnbull didn't like to leave any stone unturned. So, with his assurance that he'd be looking into it, Wyatt breathed a sigh of relief.

Next, he called one of his ranch foreman on his two-way radio. "Carlson, could you ask around and see if there are three ranch hands who would be willing to take a night shift babysitting some cattle tonight?"

"Sure, boss." The radio crackled a little on the other side, and he heard muffled voices in the background. "Slim, Lennie and I can do it. Where did you want us?"

"If you could watch the cattle in the Northwest

pasture, that would be great." Wyatt hesitated before continuing. "And Carlson? I think we should let the boys know, we'll need them to do this for the next week or so, just until we can get a few things figured out."

"Problems boss?"

"Yeah, there's fifty head missing. So, if you take turns keeping watch during the night, hopefully there won't be any more problems."

"Sure, boss."

"Thanks, Carlson." Wyatt turned off his two-way radio and sighed heavily.

He really didn't need this newest problem. But somehow they would get to the bottom of it.

Wyatt walked quietly up the stairs and in through the back door of the kitchen.

He saw a batch of Mrs. Garrett's homemade cookies on the counter and grabbed one.

Mrs. Garrett swatted his hand with a spatula. "Seems, I still have to watch out for cookie snatchers, even after all these years." She clucked at him, but the smile on her face told him she was teasing.

"I can't help it, Mrs. Garrett. You make the best cookies in the state." Wyatt grinned, popping it into his mouth. Their cook's fresh chocolate chip cookies were irresistible.

"Well, I don't know if I should believe your flattering words. You're likely just hungry young man. Supper will be soon, so one cookie is all you get." She kept a firm eye on him and he grinned.

"You sure run a tight ship, Mrs. Garrett."

She grinned. "You know I do."

"All right. As much as I want another, I won't nab anymore." Wyatt started to walk away to shower and change, but turned quickly to ask. "Have Mom's guests left?"

Mrs. Garrett sighed, shaking her head. "Yes, your mom's friends have left. But you know Wyatt, you can't avoid women forever. Someday, you'll need to open up your heart enough to love and marry one of those women you keep avoiding."

Her granddaughter giggled as she placed the cookies in their container. Cassie grinned at her grandmother's plain speaking.

The corners of Wyatt's mouth turned up. He'd always enjoyed their verbal sparring. "You're right as usual Mrs. Garrett. But you'll be happy to know that I'm not trying to avoid all women. For instance, I like being in the kitchen with you and Cassie."

"Oh, get on with you Wyatt Callahan and your fast talking ways." Mrs. Garrett shooed him out of the kitchen, waving a tea towel at him.

Wyatt chuckled and hurried away, a big grin on his face as he heard Cassie's giggle in the background.

After quickly showering and changing he went to the dining room, to see his mom and brothers already seated.

Wyatt walked to the head of the table where his mom was seated and kissed her on the cheek.

Seeing dark circles beginning to show under her eyes, Wyatt squeezed her hand. "You feeling okay, Mom? You look a little tired today."

"I am a little tired, Wyatt. I think having the tea and lunch today took more out of me today than I realized.

But we really had fun, so it was worth it." His mom smiled tiredly at him and squeezed his hand.

"Well, maybe for the rest of the day you should just put your feet up tonight and relax." Wyatt gave his mom a gentle smile filled with concern.

Annie Callahan nodded. "I think I'll do that. Thank you, son, for always looking out for me."

"Of course. I've got to take care of my best girl." Wyatt patted his Mom's hand.

He sat in his usual chair among his six brothers, a thoughtful smile on his face.

Mrs. Garrett and Cassie placed the roast beef, potatoes and gravy on the table and were soon sitting with them ready to eat. His mom said thanks for the meal and then just as quickly the food was passed around.

Mom started talking about what happened in her day. "I had a nice luncheon today with some lovely ladies from Refuge Mountain today."

"That's great, Mom." Zane spoke up. "It's nice to see you smiling."

"Thanks, Zane. It was a wonderful day." His mom was thoughtful for a moment before she spoke again with a twinkle in her eyes. "Did I mention that some of the ladies that came to the house today, are single?"

"Aww... Mom." Cole expelled a heavy sigh.

"I'm sorry, son. I promise not to tease you anymore... at least not today." Their mom winked at her youngest son, giving him the fun smile she'd shown each of her sons, and they had come to appreciate.

Wyatt grinned and most of his brother's laughed out

loud at their youngest brothers displeasure at the mention of dating a woman.

Although in all honesty, Wyatt could understand how Cole felt.

He had avoided relationships ever since his engagement to Abby had been broken. He'd been heartbroken when her father said he would no longer allow Wyatt to date his daughter.

But the fact that she didn't respond to his letters or his texts had been like a festering wound that hadn't fully healed.

Wyatt hoped that maybe at the Fall Festival, when they spent time together, there would be time for them to have a talk about what happened years ago.

Determination rose up inside him, somehow, some way, he would break down the walls that guarded Abby's heart.

&

ABBY BRUSHED down Stocking and set her out in the pasture for the day, along with Blackie.

As she worked outside this morning, she'd been a little disappointed to see a cloudless blue sky.

Most days that would have been perfect weather, but she was looking for some excuse to tell Wyatt why she couldn't go with him to the Fall Festival and dance.

Looked like she wouldn't be able to use poor weather as an excuse to stay at home.

Double checking to make sure everything was in order in the barn, she ran to the house.

Looking at her wristwatch, she realized that she only had a little time to get ready before Wyatt would arrive.

She hurried into the shower and washed her hair, thankful to be clean once more. Towelling herself dry, she slipped on her housecoat while she combed through her long auburn hair.

She hurried to put on makeup.

Then, grabbing her hair dryer, she dried her hair a little more, so it wouldn't be completely wet when she put it up.

With a quick look at her reflection in the floor length mirror, she could see no tangles in her waist length auburn wavy hair. That was good, it meant she didn't have to take the time to brush through it again.

Looking through her closet she pulled out her long A-line wine red colored skirt that flowed out from the knees in layered flounces.

The black lacing down the side of the skirt gave the outfit a real western appeal. Searching again, she found an emerald green colored short- sleeved linen blouse she had bought last year. She decided it would be a nice comple-ment to the skirt.

After laying the clothes on the bed, she picked up her brush, trying to decide how to do her hair.

Suddenly, the doorbell rang.

Her heart accelerated as she realized Wyatt had arrived. Looking at her watch, she realized he was right on time and that it had taken her longer to get ready than she planned.

Feeling scattered, she hurried down the hallway to the

front door, deciding he would just have to wait until she was dressed.

Opening the door, she spluttered. "I'm almost ready. You can come in and wait if you want."

Abby stood there with the door open, but Wyatt was motionless. She didn't miss his obvious examination as his gaze swept her from head to toe, before coming back to look her in the eyes.

"Don't worry. I was about to get dressed and put my hair up in a bun or something." Abby spoke in a hurry, knowing she was late.

Wyatt stepped inside, but stopped in front of her. Abby looked up, only to see him eyeing her with appreciation.

His hand ranched out, and his fingers trailed through her long hair that reached to her waist.

Wyatt's voice was gruff as he whispered. "Don't put your hair up, Abby. I can't remember the last time I saw it hanging loose like that." He lifted a strand of her hair and touched the silken strands to his cheek. "You are beautiful, just the way you are right now."

His nearness made her senses spin and his words wrapped around her like a warm blanket.

She felt the electricity of his touch as his fingers wound their way through her hair.

He stood so close, she could feel the heat from his body.

Some part of her wanted him to kiss her. If she were honest with herself, she had wanted him to kiss her since the first day he started showing up on her ranch to help her.

He was so handsome in his black jeans, navy blue

western shirt and cowboy hat that her breath caught in her throat.

Her heart thumped erratically as she looked into his eyes.

His gray eyes darkened as he searched her face, and his gaze moved to her lips.

No, she couldn't let this happen. She couldn't let him kiss her right now. She wasn't ready.

Abby cleared her throat, pretending that he didn't affect her. At the sound, Wyatt stepped back.

"I need to get dressed for the festival." Abby whispered.

Wyatt set his face into his normal detached and cool expression.

"I'll wait here." Wyatt whispered and stepped farther back to let her pass.

Abby hurried to her bedroom, and closing the door behind her, leaned her head against it. She sighed heavily and gave herself a stern lecture. *Abby, you can't let yourself be affected by this man. Besides, this isn't a date. This is just two neighbors going to the Fall Festival together.*

As she slipped into the skirt and blouse, she reminded herself of that.

As soon as she was dressed she looked in the mirror again. Her green eyes were big and round in her oval face, with a few sprinkles of freckles across her nose and cheeks.

While she brushed her long hair intending to put it up, Wyatt's words came back to her. *Don't put your hair up, Abby. I can't remember the last time I saw it hanging loose like that. You are beautiful, just the way you are right now.*

Abby felt her pulse pounding in her throat at the memory.

She stood motionless, staring at her reflection.

Well, maybe for today, she could let her hair hang loose. She told herself it wasn't to please Wyatt, but rather because she hadn't worn it that way in a long time.

Maybe it was a sign that like her hair, as a woman she was being freed from the restrictions that had confined her for years.

Tomorrow would be soon enough for everything — including her hair — to return to normal.

Abby slipped on her dark brown leather cowboy boots and walked to where Wyatt waited.

He whistled as soon as he saw her. "Every cowboy there will want to switch places with me, Abby. You're gorgeous." His whispered words sent her heart racing again.

She blushed fiercely at his compliment and spoke with a hesitant smile. "Thanks, Wyatt. You spruce up quite well yourself." Abby was rewarded with Wyatt's slow smile. It reminded her of those many warm summer evenings they had spent together years ago.

They had often ridden horses together, gone fishing, or sat together on the porch swing on the large wrap around deck at Wyatt's parent's ranch house.

A shiver ran through her body. She shook her head to banish the memories.

Turning, her gaze met Wyatt's. He grinned.

"Ready to go?"

Abby nodded. "Let me grab a sweater, just in case the weather gets cold." She reached over to the coat tree in the corner and grabbed an open front black cardigan sweater that she hung over her arm. "All right. Let's go."

"After you, my lady." Wyatt nodded as he held the door open. He repeated the action when they reached his truck. Abby was reminded once again of one of the many reasons she had been attracted to him years ago.

He was a gentleman through and through.

She felt protected and cared for when she was with him.

As he got into the driver's seat, he started the truck and then for a long moment his gaze roved and lazily appraised her.

Something intense flared in his eyes as his gaze searched hers.

He was so disturbing to her in every way. Her heart jolted and her pulse pounded.

She was grateful the drive to Refuge Mountain wasn't a long one.

Being this close to Wyatt Callahan was doing strange things to her heart.

Abby worried that, too much time spent alone with her handsome neighbor would pull her further into his invisible web of attraction from which she'd never escape.

# CHAPTER SIX

bby

FEAR GNAWED AWAY at Abby's confidence as they arrived at the Agriculture complex at the edge of their small town.

So many people from town and nearby ranchers had joined in the festival.

Wyatt parked the truck and walked around to open her door. She gave him a small smile and nervously wiped her hands on her skirt before she accepted his hand to steady her as she stepped out of the truck.

"Shall we?"

Abby nodded and walked by Wyatt's side towards the canvas tents that were lined up in a U shape outside the complex.

"I see the Peabody twins are busy collecting this year's pies for the pie baking contest. There's Mrs. Garrett with hers." Wyatt nodded toward one of the tents where two gray haired ladies were collecting pies. There were so many that the assorted pies sat near the edges of the table.

"I'm glad your cook entered the contest. She makes the best apple pies." Abby still remembered all the treats she had when she used to stop by Wyatt's place.

"That she does."

Abby noticed Father Tim and Reverend Jon standing together in conversation near the pie table.

Father Tim's white hair shone like a halo around his head. The friendship he showed to the young Reverend Jon was inspiring to see.

Abby had always thought the two of them were a good example of how to continue to have a deep friendship, even when there were some differences of opinion.

Father Tim spotted them first. "Hello Mrs. Hart and Wyatt Callahan. How are you both today?" He walked over and shook first her hand and then Wyatt's.

Abby stammered and awkwardly cleared her throat. "I'm well, Father Tim. Keeping busy as ever."

"Well, that is good news. You've been in my prayers ever since your Tom passed away." Father Tim's gentle tones filled with concern nearly had her in tears.

An unfamiliar warmth filled her belly at his concern. She nodded. "Thank you, Father Tim. That is truly appreciated."

"And Wyatt, how is your family doing since your Dad passed away?" Father Tim reached out and squeezed Wyatt's shoulder, his searching pale green eyes not missing a thing.

Wyatt's voice shook slightly as he spoke. "We're doing

well as can be expected, Father Tim. Losing Dad left a big hole in my Mom's life as well as that of my brothers and I."

Father Tim sighed heavily. "I'm sorry for your loss. Losing a loved one is never easy. Mack Callahan's passing has been felt deeply by your family and also among our ranchers and folks in our small town of Refuge Mountain."

"He was a man who stood by his convictions and was a great example of how to serve your neighbor. We had some good talks over the years. He will be missed."

Wyatt nodded and spoke in a subdued voice. "I appreciate your kind words, Father Tim."

"Just saying the truth as I see it, son." His eyes sparkled with joy. "Well, I hope you enjoy the Fall Festival. It looks to be a promising day." Father Tim said as he eyed the apple pies on the table and winked before walking away, Reverend Jon by his side.

"I like those two." Wyatt chuckled and looked at Abby and held out his hand. "Shall we continue?"

Abby nodded and placed her hand in his, glancing up with a small smile.

They continued walking along the wide pathway that left a lot of walking room, between the canvas tents the vendors had set up.

Abby breathed deeply of the brisk and cool air that traced her skin. She wrapped her cardigan around her body, to help ward off a chill. She spotted a vendor who was serving hot drinks.

"Should we grab some hot apple cider?" Abby nodded toward the shopkeepers. They waited until he had served other customers, before handing them their drinks.

Wyatt took a sip and with hooded eyes looked over the rim of his cup, staring at her. "Hmm, perfect."

Abby shivered at the hint of appreciation in his gaze. She didn't miss the double meaning in his words, and her pulse pounded.

Heat crept up her neck to her cheeks and she lowered her gaze, doing her best to ignore the tiny glow that rippled over her skin at his compliment.

A slender, delicate thread of friendship had started to develop between them again, something she never thought would happen. There was an unspoken truce between them.

She didn't want to ruin their easy companionship by unearthing past wounds or by encouraging the growing attraction between them. She simply wanted to enjoy the day together with Wyatt.

Instead, she turned and took a sip, doing her best to focus on light topics, like her hot drink. "It's delicious. It's been so long since I had hot apple cider."

"Then I believe we need to see to it that you enjoy yourself more often. I'm willing if you are."

Her cheeks heated at Wyatt's flirtation. Somewhere deep inside, she was frustrated that he still had the ability to make her blush. She turned slightly to look at the people around them.

She saw two young boys approach Wyatt. Walking beside them was an older lady who tried to slow them down.

"Mr. Callahan, you're here."

"I am. Good to see you Joey and you too Tony." Wyatt

lightly ruffled the hair on their heads and grinned at them. "Are you having fun?"

"Yes, we are." Joey smiled and turned quickly to his brother before looking up at Wyatt. "But we'd have more fun if you taught us how to ride horses at your ranch."

Both boys wore a hopeful expression on their faces as they looked up at Wyatt. Wyatt bent down and sat on his haunches to speak to them face to face. "Well, I'd like that too. We can work it out if Mrs. Beaseley is agreeable to the idea?"

Wyatt looked up at the older woman who sighed, almost as if the two boys were wearing her out with all their energy. Abby could see that these two young boys had energy to spare.

Before the older woman could respond, the boys turned to her, a pleading expression on their faces. "Please, can we go to Mr. Callahan's ranch to ride horses?"

"Boys, I'm sure Mr. Callahan is much too busy to teach you." Mrs. Beaseley looked at Abby and then at Wyatt, uncertainty on her features.

The crestfallen look on each of the boys' faces, grabbed at Abby's heart.

"I have time, Mrs. Beaseley. I could make time in my schedule twice a week to teach the boys horse riding, if you're okay with that?" Wyatt smiled at the older lady, and she nodded quickly.

"All right, I suppose that would work. But you boys will have to behave yourselves and mind Mr. Callahan." Mrs. Beaseley spoke sternly to the two boys, who both nodded vigorously.

Abby could tell they would do almost anything to get

their chance to ride horses. She smiled as she remembered a similar excitement when she was younger.

"Good. I'll let you know of my schedule and choose some days that work for me and we can adjust our schedules, Mrs. Beaseley." Wyatt nodded to the older woman before grinning at the boys. "I look forward to seeing you boys again."

"Yay. We can't wait. Thanks, Mr. Callahan." Joey gave him an impromptu hug and his brother did the same.

"You're welcome, boys. See you soon." Wyatt waved as they walked away.

"That was nice of you. Where did you meet those boys?" Abby's curiosity got the better of her. Most of the time, she'd seen Wyatt Callahan as serious and formidable, but seeing this softer side of him with those boys was a revelation.

Wyatt hesitated a moment before he spoke. "I met them at the community center here in town. They were asking for a few adults to mentor some of the youth, and I decided to sign up. Mrs. Beaseley is a foster parent to four children, the two youngest being Joey and Tony."

Abby stared wordlessly at him for a moment, trying to figure him out. "And here I thought you were a lone cowboy, focused only on ranching and taking care of animals."

"Well, to be honest, that was my intention." He turned to look at her and grimaced.

Abby was curious, seeing the change on his face. "What made you change your mind?"

Wyatt sighed. "Retiring from the Military — along with Dad's passing — started me thinking. I asked myself what I was doing to help anyone else? The answer was basically nothing. So I began to think about how I could change that. Joey and Tony seemed like a good way to start."

"Are you helping those boys because you were in the foster system when you were a child?" Ceaseless questions hammered at Abby. Somewhere deep inside, she wanted to unravel the mystery of this man.

Wyatt chuckled. "You sure are full of questions."

"I guess I'm just curious about you."

He simply nodded. "Maybe. They're good kids and if I can give them a hand up, I feel like I should." Wyatt grabbed her hand, his gaze meeting hers, a shuttered look in his eyes. "But I think that's enough questions for now. Let's continue enjoying the sights, shall we?"

Abby could tell Wyatt was sidestepping her questions.

"All right." She agreed with a disappointed sigh. There was so much about Wyatt Callahan that was unknown. But she was determined to gather all the missing pieces of the puzzle until she had the full picture.

They walked side by side, looking at more crafts that folks from their small town were selling. Abby's mind was on what Wyatt had told her, wishing he had told her more about what happened in his childhood.

Abby stopped to enjoy some older women weaving on a loom, when she looked up and saw her sister and Mom walking toward them.

She braced herself for the criticism that was sure to come from her sister's lips.

"Enjoying your day, sister?" Hadley's gaze swept over

Abby and then turned to Wyatt and back to her again, a heavy dose of disapproval in her tone.

Her sister seemed to take some sort of satisfaction in showing her displeasure towards Abby's actions and decisions.

She experienced criticism from her older sister throughout their growing up years, but for some reason, in the past few months it had only gotten worse.

Abby straightened her shoulders and struggled to maintain an uneven, conciliatory tone as she responded. "Yes, I am very much enjoying my day. Nice to see you, Hadley and Mom. You remember Wyatt Callahan."

Abby turned to look at Wyatt and saw him clench his mouth tighter. It looked like she wasn't the only one who didn't appreciate Hadley's disparaging comments.

"Of course. Hello, Wyatt." Abby's mom at least knew how to keep a civil tongue in her head most of the time, despite her disapproval of Abby's choices.

Hadley's mouth thinned with displeasure. "Yes. Hello Wyatt."

Wyatt's eyebrow quirked upward as he responded in even tones. "Mrs. Meadows, good to see you. And Hadley, I hope you're keeping well." Wyatt shook both of their hands, a small smile lifting the corners of his mouth.

"Your family is well?" Abby's mother nodded curtly, keeping her conversation polite, even though by the coolness of her tone of voice Abby could tell she was displeased.

"My family is well enough, thanks for asking. How about you, Mrs. Meadows?"

"We're fine. Along with my daughters, we are still

mourning our most recent loss of Abby's husband, Tom." Mrs. Meadows looked pointedly between Abby and Wyatt.

Knowing her mother as well as she did, Abby could tell by a single look that her mother wasn't pleased that her youngest daughter was with Wyatt in public, here at their small town's Fall Festival.

"I understand. Tom's passing was a great loss for your family, the Hart family, as well as his many friends in Refuge Mountain. He will be missed." Wyatt nodded soberly.

Her mother nodded, but Hadley turned her hard, cold-eyed smile toward Wyatt. "But not by you, I would imagine."

Abby gasped. "Hadley, what a terrible thing to say." She looked over at Wyatt. His face was paler than usual, his expression one of pained tolerance.

A knot formed in her belly, as anger at her sister's insensitivity grew. "I think you're letting your tongue run away on you again. I'll have you know that my late husband Tom considered Wyatt a good friend."

Her mother stiffened in astonishment at Abby's stern words.

Hadley, on the other hand, retorted in cold sarcasm as she stared at Abby.

"That might be true. But I still don't believe any respectable widow should be flaunting her newest love interest to the entire town, so soon after her husband's death." Hadley stared at her with cold eyes a moment longer, before she turned to their mother, slipping her hand in hers.

"Let's go, Mother."

Mrs. Meadows' features held anxiety mixed with concern as she looked at Abby. "Yes, Hadley. See you later, Abigail dear."

Abby shook her head in shock as she watched her mother and sister walk away.

She swallowed hard and bit back tears.

There was a sourness in the pit of her stomach. Her own mother and sister judged and condemned her as guilty without even the benefit of hearing or trying to understand her side of the story.

They had also hurt Wyatt.

"I'm so sorry. My sister had no right to talk to you like that. I don't understand why she's so angry." Abby spoke softly and turned to look at the man beside her.

Wyatt turned toward her, and his face remained motionless and detached as his gray eyes looked into her own.

"She's being a protective older sister."

Abby shook her head. "Maybe that's part of it, but insulting both of us? No, there must be something else going on."

Abby dropped her lashes quickly to hide the hurt that was eating her inside.

She desperately wanted to leave.

Turning, she began to plan the best route to avoid running into any more people they knew, but that idea was stopped when she spotted Tom's parents, James and Martha Hart walking nearby.

Abby grimaced. Her hand gripped the plastic cup

tighter with every step her parents-in-law made, before they stopped in front of them.

Wyatt turned and nodded, his fingers touching the tip of his cowboy hat.

Martha Hart's eyes narrowed as her gaze fell on Abby, then at Wyatt.

Abby sensed a storm brewing and trying to hold it off, she spoke first.

"Good afternoon, Mrs. Hart. Mr. Hart. It's good to see you." Abby's voice cracked with nervousness as it usually did whenever she encountered Tom's parents.

Mrs. Hart huffed loudly. She looked like she was about to speak, when Wyatt interrupted suddenly.

"It's nice to see you both. Sorry, we can't stop to talk. We've got someplace to be." Wyatt spoke quickly and nodded. Grabbing Abby's hand, he pulled her to his side protectively.

"Yes, we must go." Abby nodded, breathing a relieved sigh. She followed Wyatt, trying to keep up with his long strides.

As they walked away, Abby overheard Mrs. Hart speak to her husband in a voice loud enough for people around them to overhear. "Well, I never. Tom's not six months in the grave and already Abby is running around with Wyatt Callahan."

"I believe my mother-in-law is angry with me." Abby's heart constricted inside her chest, aware of the truth of her words.

Deep inside, she always had this feeling that she wasn't good enough whenever she was around her dead husband's parents. She hurried beside Wyatt. "Where are we going? You said we had someplace we needed to be."

They reached the parking lot and Wyatt pulled her to where he'd parked his truck in the shade of some trees.

Wyatt turned to Abby, his jaw set in anger. "We do have someplace to be. Any place that's away from that woman." Opening the truck door, he tossed her tapestry bag inside.

"I told you it was a bad idea for me to show up today." Abby reached a shaky hand to push hair behind her ear.

Wyatt cupped her chin in his hand. "Abby, listen to me. It's not you that shouldn't be here. It's Martha Hart, who shouldn't be saying all those mean things about you or about the fact that you're here today with me."

Abby sighed heavily. "I'm just so tired of never doing the right thing or never being good enough in her eyes." A tear slipped down Abby's cheek and she shivered as she fought to control her swirling emotions.

Wyatt touched her cheek with his hand, and his thumb gently caught her tears.

She saw his eyes were gentle and contemplative. "I'm sorry Wyatt, I don't know why I told you that."

She turned away from him, not knowing why she'd let her emotions run away on her like that. Wyatt didn't need to know the messy details of her life.

As she started to step away from the truck, Wyatt reached out and placed his hands on her shoulders.

His expression stilled and grew serious. "Listen Abby, I'm sorry Mrs. Hart has treated you so shabbily. But you never need to be sorry for telling me how you feel, all right?"

Wyatt leaned his forehead against hers and wrapped his arms around her. Abby nodded, not trusting herself to speak.

She swallowed hard and bit back tears that threatened to escape.

Being encircled in his arms brought comfort, but also a new awareness of Wyatt as a man. He kissed her forehead lightly. His breath warm and moist against her face, and her heart raced.

He clasped her body more tightly to his, and she relaxed, sinking into his cushioning embrace.

In his arms, she felt protected. She sighed and leaned deeper into his embrace. Just as she was beginning to relax into the comfort of his arms, without warning the loud laughter of children rang through the air nearby.

Abby stiffened and gently pushed against Wyatt's chest and stepped away.

She cleared her throat, still trying to settle her erratic heartbeat. She started to babble like she always did when she was nervous. "I think many folks are having a bite to eat before they settle in for the barn dance tonight. I'm beginning to feel hungry myself."

Abby was relieved when Wyatt's bewildered expression switched to one of mild amusement, as if he guessed she was flustered. He grinned and grabbed her hand. "Well, we wouldn't want you to go hungry. Let's get you fed."

It wasn't long before they found some barbecued beef to eat. The low strains of guitars of the live country band warming up their instruments, drew folks into the large barn they used every year for the barn dance.

Years ago, the stalls and feeders had all been removed, and they had remodelled the massive building. A large wooden stage had been built at the front, complete with a sound system and extra windows added to the side walls.

A new wood floor had been built as well as dining tables added along the sides and back of the barn. Guys and Gals washrooms and a new large kitchen were constructed, and the place bore only a slight resemblance to the misshapen barn it had once been.

As Wyatt and Abby walked toward the barn, they saw a few parents and grandparents driving away with their small children. Some would be back to enjoy dancing without needing to worry about watching their children.

When they entered the barn, people were already dancing to a fast paced polka. Lots of smiles and laughter filled the place. Abby saw Wyatt look around and grinned, raising a hand in greeting.

"I want to introduce you to some folks. Come with me." Wyatt grabbed her hand, and she hurried beside him until they reached a bunch of tables and chairs that were filled with quite a few older ranchers.

"Well, if it isn't Wyatt Callahan." A grey-haired man with broad shoulders, grinned at Wyatt.

Wyatt reached over to shake the man's large, calloused hand. "Bobby Jackson, it's good to see you're still alive and kicking."

"Alive yes, but the kickin' part is slowin' me down some." Wyatt chuckled and the other two men at the table grinned.

Another balding man removed his cowboy hat and set it on the table, looking up at Wyatt. "Sorry to hear about the passing of your father, Wyatt. Mack Callahan was one of the best ranchers in the area. And a good friend."

Abby peered over at Wyatt as he swallowed and spoke. His voice sounded raw. "Thanks for that, Wayne. Yes, Dad will be missed. His shoes were big ones to fill, that's for sure."

The other man seated at the table had dark brown hair streaked with silver while his blue eyes sparkled mischievously. He reached over and squeezed Wyatt's shoulder.

"I'm convinced in this case, the apple doesn't fall far from the tree. You and those six brothers of yours will fill Mack Callahan's shoes well enough. And if I may be so bold as to speak for all of us here, if there is anything you need, just let us know. We'll be happy to do what we can to help."

Wyatt's smile grew thoughtful, and he nodded. "John Peterson, you always did know how to encourage a man. Appreciate it. I might just take you up on that offer."

"Good, good." Abby saw Wyatt's friend look over at her and then back at Wyatt. "Now Wyatt, who's the pretty lady you've got with you?"

Heat crept up her neck, staining her cheeks as all three men looked over at her.

"This lovely lady is my friend and closest neighbor, Mrs. Abby Hart." Wyatt put his hand on her shoulder in a possessive gesture.

Abby offered a slight smile and nodded. "Hello. It's nice to meet you all." She reached out to shake each rancher's hand.

"It's a pleasure meeting, you Mrs. Hart. Is your

husband with you?" Bobby Jackson peered over at her, his eyes searching between her and Wyatt.

She looked at Wyatt and back at the rancher. "No, Tom passed away a few months ago."

Abby looked down at her hands and twisted her wedding band with shaky hands. She really didn't want to go back over the memories of her late husband.

But she reminded herself that she needed the favor of more folks from their small town and getting to know these ranchers was a good place to start.

She swallowed quickly and looked up at Wyatt, who began speaking.

"Abby's late husband was Sergeant Tom Hart. He died unexpectedly not long ago, in a military tour of duty." Wyatt spoke in calm tones. He reached toward Abby, his large hand squeezing her cold one in a gesture of comfort.

A warmth tingled her skin as his touch filled her with an unfamiliar sensation of feeling cared for and protected.

She'd had been in a situation where she had to fend for herself for so many years, that Wyatt's concern for her caused a mixture of unwelcome emotions to flood through her.

Abby recalled the pleasure she felt in the simple touch of his hand, but those feelings scared her. She'd learned early in life, that loving someone caused too much rejection, heartache and loss.

No, she wouldn't let herself rely on Wyatt's protection and care, no matter how well intentioned. She pulled her hand out of Wyatt's grip and with a shaky hand tucked a stray hair behind her ear.

"Sorry, for your loss, ma'am. I hope all is well at your ranch."

"Thank you for your kind words. I'm doing what I can to keep things going." Abby forced a smile, hoping these established ranchers wouldn't see through her words to the lies beneath the surface.

If she were to tell them, she was barely making it from month to month, it would surely shock them.

Wyatt spoke, his low voice soft, clear and determined. "Abby has been doing more than that. She's been busy training horses. Right now she's training four of my two-year-olds and doing a fine job of it."

John Peterson looked at Abby and then back at Wyatt. "Well, I never heard of a woman horse trainer. The man I've always hired every year has been Jeb Williams from out Clear Springs way."

The other ranchers nodded in agreement.

Wyatt spoke again, his tone confident and steady. "Jeb's a good trainer as well. My Dad had him train most of our horses and he always did a fine job. But, Jeb is getting older. When he trained my last horse, I noticed he wasn't as nimble as he once was."

Wyatt looked at her and gave her his confident smile, before turning back to look at each of his friends. "I've seen Abby train my horses. She has a unique ability to understand the innate nature of horses, which is why her work with my two-year-olds have been so effective."

He continued. "So if any of you have a young filly or colt in need of training, I encourage you to give Abby a call. You never know, maybe change will be just what's needed for your ranch."

Bobby Jackson nodded. "Well then Mrs. Hart, since Wyatt praises your skills so highly, how about you train my almost two-year-old mare? I've been thinking about having her trained and was going to call Jeb. But, I trust Wyatt. He knows horses and people. What do you say, Mrs. Hart?"

Abby smiled. "Of course. I'd be happy to work with your mare. I can train her at your ranch if you'd like?"

"That would be good."

"I can start next week." Abby mentally went through her schedule and opted for the first day available.

"Done." Bobby Jackson stood to his feet, reached over and shook her hand. "I look forward to seeing you work, Mrs. Hart."

"Good. I look forward to working with your horse. And Mr. Jackson, please call me Abby."

The other two ranchers chuckled, and John Peterson spoke. "Well, I'll see how Bobby's horse turns out with your training, Mrs. Hart. But if you are as good as Wyatt says, then I suspect I'll be calling you next."

"Yep." Wayne didn't say much, but he was nodding his head with a slight smile at Abby and Wyatt.

Abby nodded. "That's all anyone can ask for." She wanted to be offered work, based on great results she had with horses and not for any other reason.

Wyatt grinned. "Well, it was good seeing you all again. Now, there are a few more folks we wanted to talk to tonight, so we'll be taking our leave. Have a good evening.
"

"You too, Wyatt and Abby." Bobby spoke up and the other men echoed their goodbyes. Wyatt grabbed Abby's hand, and they walked back through the thick crowd towards a drink table.

"Thanks for introducing me to your friends." Abby took the lemonade drink, Wyatt offered her. "I'm grateful to know more ranchers in the area. And I'm excited to train Mr. Jackson's mare. I realize he gave me a chance because he trusts you. So, I wanted to say thank you for your belief in my training abilities. I won't let you down."

Wyatt smiled easily. "Abby, I have complete faith in you. Bobby Jackson will be lucky to have you."

Her lips parted in surprise, and her cheeks blossomed. "Thanks."

They finished their drinks, and Wyatt excused himself to go to the bathroom.

For a moment Abby stood motionless, her gaze searching the room. Some long-time ranchers and their wives were in conversation where they sat on the benches that had been built alongside the barn walls.

Lights were dimmed, and country music filled the air. The simple sounds of acoustic guitar mixed with the western twang of the male lead singer, was familiar and it soothed her.

Someone bumped her shoulder, and she turned. Her best friend, Sierra, wore a big grin. "Abby, you're here." Sierra's blue eyes sparkled, a teasing glint in their depths.

"Yeah. At first I wasn't planning on coming today, but Wyatt talked me into it."

A small smile formed on her friend's face. "Wyatt Callahan, huh? You came tonight with him?"

"Sierra, I know that look on your face. And It's not what you're thinking. We're just two friends who decided to drive together to the Fall Festival." Abby spoke with quiet, but with a desperate firmness almost as if she needed to convince herself of her words. "Are you here with your son?"

"No. I left Cody with his grandparents for the day. I've also been helping my boss today to serve everyone coffee. I'm just on my break." Sierra sighed and tucked a loose strand of strawberry blond hair behind one ear.

Abby noticed the grey haired woman behind a corner counter where there was a small line-up of folks vying for their favorite flavor of coffee.

Ever since they graduated from High School together, Sierra had worked at their small town coffee shop. Abby remembered, her friend had been eight months pregnant those last few weeks of High School. She'd missed getting to her High School prom and also missed out on giving her valedictorian speech because of it.

Since those High School days, Sierra had been living on her grandparents' small farm on the other side of town, working at the coffee shop. Abby and Sierra had continued their friendship.

Since Abby's husband had been away on his tour of duty, she had formed a real close friendship with Sierra. Becoming the sounding board and encouragement they each needed for each other.

Abby had got to know Sierra's son since he was a baby. She loved Sierra and Cody like family.

Even now, her best friend refused to name her son's father.

Well, maybe someday Sierra would tell her, or maybe her son's father would return to Refuge Mountain.

Abby hoped it would be the latter, but she didn't hold out much hope for that happening.

However, she wanted whatever would make her friend happy.

Sierra was the kind of friend that was pure gold, and deserved every happiness. She had helped Abby in more ways than she could count, and Abby was grateful for her.

Abby's brows wrinkled in worry.

She could see dark circles under her friend's weary eyes. "You work too hard, Sierra. You have to make a little time for fun."

"This from the woman who works fourteen hours a day almost every day." Sierra lifted one eyebrow a fraction and smiled.

Abby nodded. "You're right. I'm not the right person to chatter on about relaxing. But the fact remains that I'm worried about you."

Sierra sighed heavily. "I know you do. I do appreciate your concern, but I'll be okay. Granddaddy and Grams really do so much to help me out."

Sierra looked her in the eye. "You should be more concerned about yourself, my friend. I can see you're much too thin, which usually means you're stressing about something. Let it go for tonight. Relax and have fun with Wyatt."

Sierra turned and lifted her hand nodding. "It looks like I need to get back to it. I see my boss waving at me. I'll text you tomorrow, okay?"

Abby nodded with a big smile, but inside she felt momentary panic at the thought of being left alone again. She hugged her friend and Sierra went back to work.

The panic hardly had a chance to set in, before Reno Blackwell stood in front of her.

Abby sucked in a breath and subtly looked around for Wyatt.

A flicker of annoyance and apprehension coursed through her at how he seemed to disappear when she needed him most.

"Abby, you look beautiful, as always." Reno's dark brown eyes held hers, shadowed beneath the brim of his black cowboy hat. He stepped closer before he held her hand in his. "May I have this dance?"

There wasn't any doubt that he was handsome, but there was something about him that grated on her. She'd always thought it was because he was a little too cocky, even though his obvious attention to her was flattering.

She nodded and put her hand in his. She decided tonight she would dance with him once, to be friendly to a neighbor.

Reno led her to the middle of the dance floor, and they began dancing to the male lead singer crooning to a slow country song.

"I'm happy to be dancing with the most beautiful woman here tonight."

Abby merely nodded with a small smile at his compliments, not wanting to encourage him.

"How is your horse doing? She had a problem with her foreleg, didn't she?"

Abby nodded, surprised. "You remembered. Yes, Stocking is doing much better now, thanks for asking."

Reno placed one hand on her waist and pulled her

closer. "I stopped by your place the other morning, but you weren't there."

"In the past couple of weeks, I've been busier. I have four new horses to train now." Abby smiled, pleased with how well the horse training process was going.

"That's great. Are you training for a rancher I know?" Reno questioned, a curious light in his eyes.

"Well, actually yes. I'm training Wyatt Callahan's horses. Which is why I have been gone a lot and missed you when you stopped by." Abby pulled back a little and saw the tightening of his jaw for a moment before he forced a smile.

"That's great, that you're busy training. I'm not surprised, you're real good at working with horses."

"Thanks Reno." Abby could feel his hand on her waist tighten. His dark eyes looked at her for a few moments and she felt disconcerted by his searching gaze.

Abby looked away, past Reno's shoulder. Her eyes widened when she saw Wyatt dancing with Tiffany. She bit down hard on her lower lip. She suddenly felt an unwelcome irritation flood her senses.

She looked again at the source of her exasperation. Why should it matter to her whom Wyatt danced with tonight?

They were both free to dance with other people. She had told him they were here tonight only as neighbors and this was not a date. Then why couldn't she seem to shake her aggravation?

"Are you all right?"

At Reno's question, she laughed a little to cover her annoyance.

"I'm doing great." She forced a smile, hoping if she said it enough, it would become true.

"Good." He expelled a breath as if suddenly coming to a decision. "But I'd like to return to our earlier conversation. I want to ask you to train our newest colt. My brother suggested we should ask Jed, but I'd like you to do it. What do you say?"

Abby raised her eyebrows, surprised by the offer.

She knew Jeb Williams had been training horses for ranchers near Refuge Mountain and in other nearby small towns like Clear Springs for years. She knew he was well respected. But like Wyatt had earlier pointed out, he was also getting older too, and maybe slowing down.

Grateful for more work, she nodded. "Sure. I can make room in my schedule for one more horse. I can start next week if that works for you?"

"Perfect." Reno's dark eyes flashed with satisfaction.

When the singer crooned the last line and the country song faded away, a powerful wave of relief swept through her. As much as Reno's words of admiration flattered her ego, she couldn't escape the increasingly uneasy feeling deep inside.

"I believe this is my dance." Without warning, Wyatt stood there beside her. His voice dipped low as impatience rounded the edges of his tone.

Wyatt slipped his arm around her waist, pulling her close to his side and away from Reno Blackwell.

A shadow of irritation crossed Wyatt's features as he stared at Reno.

Abby felt an odd sense of relief that Wyatt was beside her. But, she wasn't sure how she felt about the fact that

Wyatt seemed to be claiming her in front of Reno and everyone at the dance.

She sighed, realizing she would be happy when this evening was finally over and she could go home.

Reno smirked at Wyatt, but turned to Abby and smiled.

Leaning down, he kissed the back of her hand. "Thank you, Abby. I look forward to seeing you next week."

Abby nodded. "Yes, I'll see you next week." She sent Reno a small smile before she turned, trying to step out of the circle of Wyatt's arms.

But Wyatt only tightened his grip on her waist and pulled her close as the slow paced country song filled the air.

There was a possessiveness in his touch and a fire in his gaze that sent a ripple of awareness through her body.

Her feelings for him were intensifying.

Being so close to him, made her senses spin. She could feel her resolve melting away like snow from the heat of the sun.

Her mind warned her to stay away, while her heart danced with excitement at his nearness.

Pulled in two different directions, which side would win?

# CHAPTER SEVEN

yatt

WYATT PLACED one hand on Abby's waist and held her other hand in his, just as the slow-moving waltz began.

For a moment his gaze swept over her, coming back to rest on her beautiful face.

Her large green eyes held a vague hint of disapproval. The cool watchfulness in her gaze, evidence that she was not amused.

He expelled a slow breath.

He would need to tread carefully and gently. He didn't want anything to ruin this moment. He'd dreamed about holding her in his arms like this for too many years, to mess it up now.

The familiar slow country song the singer crooned was about love and second chances. "This song has always been one of my favorites. I remember when we danced to this song years ago."

He looked at Abby, and she nodded slightly. "I do too." She muttered uneasily. A pensive shimmer hung in the shadows of her large green eyes as she peered up at him.

"I've waited for years to dance with you again."

A rose colored blush blossomed in her cheeks as she took in his meaning. "Wyatt, I want you to know that my being with you this evening..."

He interrupted, finishing the sentence for her. "... is not a date. I understand. But, that doesn't change the fact that I'm happy to be by your side."

"Thank you." She closed her eyes for a moment, but not before Wyatt saw a flash of pain there. If he hadn't been paying close attention, he would have missed it. He wondered what caused her anguish. Every time he got too close she backed away.

He was getting tired of gaining ground with her, only to lose it in the end.

A sudden realization hit him that he needed to do things differently.

Somehow he needed to prove to Abby that she could trust him.

The uncertainty in her eyes made him want to do whatever he could to set her at ease.

So, Wyatt did the only thing that came to mind.

He stepped nearer, moving his large hand toward the center of the small of her back, and pulled her close. His fingers entwined softly with silky long thick hair that fell in waves to her waist.

Abby hesitated for a moment, before relaxing against him.

He smiled. In some small way, it seemed like a victory. Wyatt sensed she was beginning to relax more when she was with him.

Leaning his head close to hers, he breathed in deeply. "Hmm, wildflowers." Unconsciously, the corners of his lips turned up. "The scent in your hair reminds me of you. Sweet, wild and free."

The song was fading and coming to an end, as was their dance.

Abby turned to look at him and her brows creased together. "You might have remembered me that way, Wyatt, but things change... I've changed." She sighed heavily.

Sadness edged it's way into her green eyes. "I don't feel like I'm any of those things. At least, not anymore." The dance ended, and she stepped out of his arms. "Excuse me, please. I need to get some air."

She walked through the crowd of dancers and hurried toward the back door.

His gut clenched. Had he said something to upset her? For a moment Wyatt stood motionless, silently staring at her retreating figure, his thoughts going in every which way as questions filled his mind.

Why did she hurry away from him? He debated for a half-heartbeat if he should follow her.

Tears pricked the back of her eyes as Abby hurried outside.

She half-walked, half-ran towards the back of the building, her quickened steps matching the pent-up emotions that spilled over. Abby ran until she reached the wood fence that stretched around the Agricultural complex.

It was dark outside, except for two yard lights that shone on the outskirts of the buildings.

Leaning up against the fence, she placed her arms on the wooden fence and rested her head on her arms.

Her thoughts rolled back to the evening spent dancing with her handsome neighbor.

Dancing in Wyatt's arms had brought back the wonderful feelings and all the beautiful memories from years ago. His kind words about her — sweet, wild and free — meant as a compliment, had instead triggered all her insecurities and fears.

Abby knew she was different than most of her friends.

She preferred to spend time with animals rather than people. She spoke her mind too plainly and was afraid to love again.

Abby remembered being told many times throughout her childhood to stop adding her two cents worth to the conversation. She'd been told over and over again that her ideas and advice weren't wanted or helpful.

The sad part was that she hadn't only experienced that kind of rejection from her Dad, but the hurt and pain only continued when she married Tom Hart. He'd been fine to live with when he was sober, but when he'd had too much to drink, she had learned quickly not to say too much.

There had been one too many times when Abby had ended up hurt and in pain. Tom would always sober up the next morning, telling her how sorry he was and begging for her forgiveness.

However, the problem was that it happened over and over again. She didn't find any reprieve from the pain and anguish, until the day he joined the military.

As those memories invaded her thoughts, her stomach clenched into a tight ball.

She didn't want to go through that kind of pain again.

Loving someone only meant pain and heartache.

Remembering, she rubbed her arms.

Yet tonight, being held in Wyatt's arms had felt so good that she'd almost forgotten the fact that he had left her all those years ago.

She was conscious of a low, tortured sob that escaped her lips. Quickly, she covered her mouth with one hand, determined not to let her raw emotions get the better of her.

Unexpectedly, a warm hand squeezed her shoulder. She turned with a start. Wyatt stood beside her, his warm gaze studying her.

His tall form was shadowed slightly from the glow of the yard light.

Reaching out, his hand caressed her shoulders as they stood facing each other.

Without warning, anger flew to the surface of her emotions. Lingering memories brought to the forefront all the pain that she had done her best to keep buried.

Abby stepped away from him and out of his reach, leaning against the wood fence.

His grey eyes darkened and glittered, his gaze penetrating hers.

"Abby, I'm sorry if what I said upset you. Talk to me. Help me understand." Wyatt's tone was even and his words were more like a statement than a question, which made her imagine what he must have been like as the Captain of his unit.

He was confident in his words and actions. Sure of who he was. The men under his command must have followed him without question.

She envied him that kind of self-assurance and for a moment really wished she carried that level of confidence in herself.

"It's just..." Her voice wobbled and she couldn't go on.

Abby expelled a heavy sigh. How much did she want to tell him about what was really going on with her? It was embarrassing enough that Wyatt had seen her in tears twice.

Abby swallowed. She breathed in another steadying breath before she raised her eyes to find him watching and waiting for her answer.

*Tell him. At the very least, it will clear the air between you two.*

She spoke quickly, her words sounding stilted to her own ears. "I was upset because your words reminded me of who I was years ago."

She swallowed quickly. "The girl you once knew, hadn't realized yet what hardships real life would bring. How those struggles would change and shape her into a woman who was the opposite of the person you see. As much as I long for it, I am no longer that sweet, wild and free girl you once knew."

Wyatt let out a long, audible breath, his gray eyes steady on hers. "I'm sorry life's been hard on you, Abby."

He took a step toward her, but she held her hand up, a signal she didn't want him to come any closer.

She took a step backwards, her belly clenched tight like a fist.

Her temper flared and she threw words at him like stones.

"Are you, Wyatt? Are you really sorry?" Her words came out clipped and pointed as anger rose to the surface from years of holding it deep inside.

"I am." He replied in a low voice, his tone solemn.

"Then, explain to me why you left seven years ago. You and I were engaged to be married, but suddenly you left town without a word. I was expecting to marry you Wyatt, remember? And without any warning you left me." The harsh words tumbled out, one after another.

Her blood pounded, her face grew hot with humiliation and rejection as she remembered that day years ago and the weeks that followed. "How could you do that to me?" She wrapped both arms around her waist, surrounding herself in a cocoon of anguish.

Abby stared at him, her misery like a steel weight. A nauseating sinking of despair fell over her, as memories and emotions washed over her, a clear reminder of what happened all those years ago.

Wyatt ran a shaky hand through his thick hair. When he spoke, his voice was thick and unsteady. "I *am* sorry, Abby."

He expelled a breath before continuing. "It wasn't my intention to leave without a word. That day, when I asked your father for his permission and blessing to marry you, he told me in no uncertain terms that he wouldn't welcome me as a son-in-law. At least not at that point."

Wyatt rubbed the back of his neck before he continued speaking. "Your dad hinted that if I was willing to wait a few years until I had completed my Veterinary degree and he saw I was somehow good enough for his daughter, the answer might be different. So I returned home."

"I was upset that your Dad put me off, I'll be honest. The next day, however, I tried calling you. When I couldn't get through to you, I looked for you in those places where we usually met. You weren't there."

"So, I wrote you a letter explaining what happened. I dropped the letter off at your house, hoping to see you, but you weren't home. So, I put it in your mailbox." Wyatt sighed heavily.

"After a week, when I didn't hear from you or see you anywhere in the places where we usually met, I wrote another letter and gave you my address at college, hoping you would write back."

A soft gasp escaped her as Abby listened to Wyatt's explanation. "You wrote me?"

"I wrote you fifty two letters. One letter a week for a year." His tone of voice mirrored the look of calm self-confidence in his features.

Abby stood there motionless for a moment, amazed and shaken.

Turning away from him, she started pacing to absorb the news. "I wonder why I didn't get them? I didn't see any letters even after we came back from the two week camping trip that my Mom and Dad surprised us with that summer."

She looked over at Wyatt, and he raised one eyebrow. "Might I suggest it's possible your parents got rid of the letters? If they did that, maybe it's also possible that the surprise camping trip your parents planned, could have been their way of placing some distance between us?"

Abby shook her head, not wanting to believe the worst of her parents. Would they have been so scheming in their plans for her life?

More memories surfaced about that summer.

"I do remember my Mom told Hadley and I not to take our phones or any type of electronics on our camping trip, so I wouldn't have received your call." Her misgivings increased by the minute and she paced faster as if keeping beat with the thoughts swirling in her mind.

Would her mom have planned to hurry her away from Wyatt, and to ensure she had no way to contact him?

Suddenly she stopped, her eyes opening wider and struggling with uncertainty and confusion that grew stronger the more they talked. "I believe you, Wyatt. It seems I'll need to get some answers from my mom."

He nodded, grey eyes wordlessly appraising her.

She thought back to those weeks after Wyatt left. It hadn't been long before her parents had invited her to go with them to a garden party at James and Martha Hart's home. That was the evening she'd seen Tom again. It wasn't until the next year that they began dating.

As she continued to think about what happened years

ago, a pulsing knot within her demanded more answers from Wyatt.

"Still, the fact that you wrote those letters, doesn't explain why you didn't come back home after you finished that last year of college. You could have come back to me, but you didn't." Abby rigidly held her tears in check and swallowed the ache of inner pain lodged in her throat.

Her sorrow from the regret of lost years between them was like a massive hole in her heart that had never been healed.

Wyatt stepped closer, unspoken pain alive and glowing in his grey eyes.

He opened his mouth to speak, but Abby interrupted.

Her words tumbled out before she could stop them. "It was real — you and me — wasn't it? I thought we loved each other. I waited to hear from you. Waited and waited, desperate to hear from you. It... it wasn't over for me." She stuttered, her voice low and tormented with a misery so acute it was worse than physical pain.

Her anguish peaked to shatter the last shreds of her control as a raw primitive grief overwhelmed her. She stared at him, waiting for answers, biting her lips to stop tears from escaping.

He gazed at her, grey eyes blazing in a way that left a burning imprint on her.

His low voice was husky with emotion. "What we had was real. You and I both know it."

Without warning, Wyatt stepped forward and reaching his muscled arms around her waist, he clasped her body tightly to his.

Abby trembled visibly at his touch. His breath was warm against her face and her heart raced. He reached one finger under her chin, urging her to look at him, his steady gaze riveted on hers.

Her belly tingled with warmth at his closeness. Her legs felt like jelly and hesitantly she put her hands on his broad shoulders, to steady herself.

Wyatt's grey eyes darkened to black, his smoldering gaze searching hers. Pain and longing lay naked in his eyes, and the knowledge twisted and turned inside her.

Her mind told her to turn away, but her heart told her to stay. Uncertainly, her gaze searched his.

His eyes moved downward to focus on her lips. Unconsciously, she moistened her lips with her tongue.

"Abby, what we had back then wasn't over for either of us." His forceful words and burning gaze searched her eyes once more. She shivered with awareness at the passion she saw in his eyes. And somewhere deep inside, her traitorous heart agreed.

There was a bold determination in his voice that hadn't been there before. "As I see it, it still isn't over."

Wyatt swooped down and claimed her lips with his own. He moved his mouth over hers with a hunger that belied his outward calm. His demanding lips caressed hers. Give and take.

She was shocked at her own eager response to the touch of his lips on hers.

It was almost as if he had been starving for her kisses for years and just now was able to enjoy them.

The push and pull of his demanding lips on hers nearly stole her breath. Her heartbeat accelerated, and she moved her hands up around his neck to bring him closer to her.

His response to her willing kiss was to crush her to him, smothering her lips with demanding mastery.

Abby felt her knees weaken even more, and she succumbed to the forceful domination of his lips. She was shocked by her own eager response to the touch of his lips.

Suddenly, without warning, his kisses changed and he began a series of slow, shivery kisses.

He placed one hand behind her neck while his other hand held her close to him. His hand moved circles around the small of her back as the gentle massage sent currents of desire through her.

She felt transported on a soft wispy cloud while his lips weaved a series of gentle caresses over hers.

Her senses reeled as if short-circuited. The blood pounded in her brain, leapt from her heart, and made her limbs tremble.

Being held in Wyatt's arms was something she had been convinced would never happen again. Being in his arms in this moment, she was happy she was wrong.

While her mind told her to run far away from this man who had left her years ago, her heart told her to forgive him and give their relationship another chance.

Mixed emotions swirled through her and she trembled. Doubt and fear warred within a heart that craved acceptance and love.

THE FIRST TOUCH of Abby's lips on his sent a shock wave through his entire body.

He had dreamed about holding her in his arms for years.

When she'd married, it had taken all of his control to put thoughts and dreams of Abby out of his mind. She'd been off limits then. But things had changed.

Tonight, the woman he loved for so many years was finally in his arms.

Crushing her to him, he savored every taste of her sweet lips. He coaxed her to relax in his embrace and was rewarded when Abby softly slipped her arms around his neck and opened her mouth to his.

He answered with a slow drugging kiss that explored the recesses of her mouth. She sighed, using her soft fingers, she caressed the back of his neck.

Her response to him sang through his veins.

A seed of hope sprouted inside his heart. Maybe this time around they would finally have their chance.

He moved his lips over hers with a kiss as tender and light as a summer breeze.

Wyatt was enjoying the dreamy intimacy of their kiss, when without warning drops of rain fell on his head, sliding down to his cheeks.

He didn't want to end their kiss, but when loud sounds of thunder rolled in the darkening clouds above and rain began pouring down, reluctantly he pulled his lips from hers.

The corners of his lips turned up in satisfaction. When she looked up at him, he saw the fullness of her red lips. She looked like she'd been thoroughly kissed.

Across her pale and beautiful face, a dim flush raced like a fever.

Her big green eyes darkened with emotion and she swallowed convulsively as she looked at him.

"Honey, I really want to stay and kiss you all evening long, but we should go before you're soaked through from this rain." Wyatt leaned over and placed a light kiss on her forehead.

Awkwardly, she nodded and wrapped her cardigan tightly around her body.

He grabbed her hand, and they ran across the yard towards Wyatt's truck. Country music played loudly as they hurried past the barn dance, but Wyatt was glad they didn't pass many people as they hurried across the yard.

Abby shifted in the truck seat as he started the truck. He reached for the blanket in the back and wrapped it around her shivering shoulders.

"Come sit beside me, sweetheart." He pulled her closer, so she sat beside him on the bench seat of the truck. Gently, he tucked the blanket around her.

Abby turned to him, a tired smile lingering on her lips. "Thank you, Wyatt."

He wrapped one arm around her shoulders and kissed her forehead. She leaned her head against his shoulder as Wyatt drove back to Abby's ranch.

The moment he parked the truck near Abby's ranch house, he leaned close only to see her sound asleep.

Wyatt chuckled softly as he opened the door quietly. He picked her up gingerly and carried her in his arms into the house.

Remembering the layout of the ranch house, he

quickly found Abby's bedroom and lay her down on the bed. Tugging her shoes off, he wrapped the blanket gently around her body.

He stood motionless by the side of the bed for a moment, his gaze settled on hers. He couldn't help but notice she'd lost weight and appeared tired and pale. There had been too many difficulties for her to handle in the past few months.

Wyatt decided he would need to keep a closer eye on her.

His thoughts returned to their evening together, making him smile softly. His blood soared as he recalled their passionate kisses. Things were going to be better between them from here on out.

He decided from now on, he would pursue his best friend — his first love — until she agreed to be his.

Kissing her forehead gently, he closed the bedroom door behind him.

As he drove home, he smiled softly remembering his Dad's letter and his last request.

Maybe Mack Callahan had the right idea after all.

But the question was, could he convince Abby to be his bride by Christmas?

# CHAPTER EIGHT

bby

ABBY'S FINGERS shook the hot cup of latte in her hand as she looked through the side window of *The Little Bean Cafe*.

Outside the large window of the coffee shop, all was quiet. Only one or two vehicles drove by every so often on the main street of their small town of Refuge Mountain.

She envied the stillness on the narrow street, as it was so opposite of the turmoil that swirled inside her own heart.

That confusion was one of the reasons she was here today. She was desperate to talk to her best friend.

As she looked around the cafe, she saw the elder Peabody sisters, sitting a couple of tables over sipping their tea.

Gretchen Peabody looked her way, offering her a thin-lipped smile. After a moment, her twin sister Gertrude also turned to look at Abby, her expression mirroring her sister's.

Abby managed a nod, plastering a happy smile to her lips in return. She looked back down at her coffee cup, feeling unnerved at their stern-faced expression.

Picking up a spoon to stir the dark liquid, she wished folks in their small town wouldn't listen to or spread gossip. She sighed heavily, imagining what they were saying about her, having seen her with Wyatt at the Fall Festival.

She shook her head slightly, trying to dispel the dark thoughts. She decided she wasn't going to think about that right now.

Turning her head at the soothing sound of hot coffee being poured into a coffee cup, she saw her friend Sierra standing beside their table filling her cup. She set the coffee carafe down on the table and mixed cream and sugar into her cup.

Sighing happily, she took a sip. "Just what I needed. And I'm glad you stopped by. You're right on time, too. Mrs. Jenkins decided to give me my lunch break early today." A grin overtook Sierra's features as she sat down across from Abby.

Despite her friend's casualness, her bright blue eyes focused on her with a hawk-like gaze. "Now why don't you tell me why you're really here."

Abby set down her half empty cup and wiped her hands on the napkin before looking at her friend with a deliberately casual smile. "How do you know I'm not here just to spend some time chatting with my best friend?"

"Because, your hands have been shaking a little ever since I sat down and you've got that restless look in your eyes." Sierra held her cup of coffee to her lips and took a sip, her gaze steady and direct. "I know there's something bothering you, so talk to me."

Abby sighed and her expression stilled and grew serious. "I'm just so confused about my feelings for Wyatt."

Sierra set her coffee cup down on the table and leaned closer, her voice low and teasing. "Ah, so you must've had a good time at the Fall Festival, right?"

A slight smile touched her lips as she recalled their evening together. "Yeah."

"I know that dreamy look. Wyatt kissed you, didn't he?" Sierra's eyes narrowed and the corners of her mouth turned up at the corners.

Heat surged up her neck to her face, causing her cheeks to blossom in a rose colored glow. She nodded, remembering Wyatt's passionate kiss.

"Ah, so it's going very well between you two. That's good."

"No, it's not. I'm worried and scared."

Sierra cocked her head to one side, a puzzled look on her face. "Of what? Falling in love is supposed to be a good thing."

"Well, I'm scared of the attraction that seems to be growing between us." Abby's brows crinkled together in worry as memories of past rejection slammed to the forefront of her mind.

"Hmm… is it because of what happened with Tom?"

Sierra grabbed her hand and squeezed lightly, a look of compassion in her big blue eyes.

Abby appreciated the gesture of comfort. She was grateful to have a great friend with whom to share her hurt and pain. "Yeah, I guess. But it's also because of what happened between Wyatt and me years ago."

"You mean because he left without a word not long after he proposed?"

Abby nodded as she remembered her conversation with Wyatt. "Wyatt told me he wrote me letters, once a week for a year. Letters, which I never got."

"One letter a week for a year? Wow, he must have really loved you." Sierra's words caused a warmth to spread throughout her belly. She'd known Wyatt had loved her, but back then she was young and didn't know how to fight for what she wanted. She sighed heavily.

"But about you not getting those letters. Something seems fishy about that. Did you talk to your mom about what happened?"

Abby shook her head. "No, but I need to. And I have to say, I'm not looking forward to that conversation." Abby swallowed and bit down hard on her lower lip. "But maybe it will help clear the air between my Mom and I."

"Yes, it will. It'll be good for the two of you to talk." Sierra's features pinched with painful memories for a moment.

Abby reached over and squeezed her hand. "I'm sorry, I shouldn't have brought up the subject of my mom, when I know you must be missing yours."

"I'm okay. Some days I just really miss her." Sierra shrugged, before she looked at Abby and forced a smile.

"But let's get back to you and Wyatt. So, you're worried. I think it's normal to have those feelings at the beginning of a relationship."

Abby raised an eyebrow. "It's more than that. I'm terrified I'm going to fall in love again with Wyatt and it'll just end in heartache and he'll leave, just like last time. Or maybe he'll turn out to not be the good man I thought he was."

"Abby. Look at me." Sierra grabbed both of her hands, focusing her gaze on her. "I know you fear being in another relationship. I can't help but notice you're obsessing about all the negative 'what ifs'."

Her friend leaned over. "What would happen if you focused instead on the good 'what ifs'? For instance, what if Wyatt is a better man than you thought? What if he's so in love with you, he wants forever with a big family that you've always dreamed about?"

"You're right." Abby sighed, thinking of the past few weeks. "Wyatt has already treated me quite well. In fact, he seems to have gone out of his way to be helpful. He's taken care of my animals, introduced me to ranchers in the area and has protected me from a certain annoying neighbor."

"See?" Sierra gestured with her hands. "If you want my advice, I think instead of worrying, why not just enjoy all the attention he's giving you?"

Abby thought about it and nodded slowly as she set her cup to the side. "Maybe you're right."

"I know I am." Sierra leaned closer and whispered in a half voice. "And consider this: What if Wyatt figures out that he wants more than to simply help you with the ranch land? What if he realizes what he really wants is his beautiful red-haired neighbor?"

"I'd be surprised if that were true. Besides, if he's interested in me, how come I haven't seen him since the Barn Dance a few days ago?"

"I'm sure Wyatt's been busy, same as you."

"Maybe."

Sierra turned her head to see her boss indicating, it was time to get back to work. "I've got to go. But I want you to think about one more thing. Is it possible that Wyatt has his own fears to work through as he thinks of getting into a relationship with you?"

Abby got up from the table to stand beside her friend. "Hmm, maybe."

Sierra wrapped her arms around her. "Just talk to him, Abby. That will help settle a good many things."

"You're right. Thanks, Sierra. You're a good friend."

"Yeah, I know. I'll be calling on you to return the favor sometime." Sierra chuckled and waved as she hurried back to work.

Abby smiled and waved back, slipping her jacket on and walked out into the cool fall air.

As she walked to her truck, she couldn't help but notice that some stores, office buildings and even the Community Library had festive decorations surrounding the edges of the rooftops and around the doors and windows.

Cute little silvery bells hung down from red bows on doors that lent a glow of wonder that only this time of year could bring.

Driving down main street, she couldn't help but sense

that special feeling that seemed to fill the air every Christmas. Like the silver bells that hung on the bell tower at the Community Church, Christmas reminded her of hope, miracles and love.

A knot formed in her belly.

Her experiences from the last few years, didn't give her any reason to believe any of that was for her. So far, it seemed most of what she'd experienced was disappointment, failure and loss.

Sighing, she turned down the highway that took her back to her ranch.

But even though she didn't hold out much hope that things would change for the better in her life, she'd promised Sierra that she would try.

Parking her truck in front of the barn, she hurried to the house to change into her work clothes. She needed to hurry, or she'd be late getting to the Blackwell ranch. She was due there this morning to train Reno's horse.

However, it wasn't seeing Reno and working with his horse that filled her with anxiety.

It was the fact that she was expected to show up at the Callahan ranch afterwards that caused her stomach to twist in turmoil. Would Wyatt talk to her, or would he avoid her like he had been for the past few days?

Memories flooded Abby of their heated kiss the night of the barn dance.

Did Wyatt have good memories of the day they spent together, or did he have regrets?

"MR. CALLAHAN, will you teach me how to ride a horse soon?" Seven-year-old Joey looked up from where he was shovelling the hay into the wheelbarrow.

Those big brown eyes stared at Wyatt, making it difficult for him to resist. His brother Tony walked over to listen in on their conversation.

"I know you don't like cleaning out the stalls, Joey." Wyatt walked over and leaned his shovels against the wooden stall. "It's not much fun, but it's all part of learning to ride a horse. Any cowboy knows that it's not enough just to know how to ride a horse, you have to learn how to take care of one too."

Joey tilted his head to the side, thinking on it. "So, shovelling out the old hay and putting fresh hay down and cleaning the muck out of the barn is part of taking care of a horse?"

"Yep." Wyatt chuckled. "But don't worry. Next time, we'll get to brushing the horse and learning how to take care of the bridle and saddle. When you've learned to do that, you'll be ready to learn to ride."

Tony grinned. "I can't wait, Mr. Callahan."

"I'm glad. I'm convinced both of you boys will learn quickly." Wyatt smiled. "But for now, lets get our work finished for the day." Both boys went back to scooping the old hay into the wheelbarrow.

Wyatt watched them a moment longer, satisfied that both boys were fast learners. He thought of the day he'd first met Joey and Tony a few months ago. They had been with their foster mom, Mrs. Beaseley at the Refuge Mountain Country Fair in the summer.

Seeing their eyes light up as they saw the horses barrel

racing, carriage races and the performing dogs, reminded him of when he was their age.

When he'd talked with their foster mom, she mentioned that was only days ago, she had received the boys as foster kids from parents who were strung out on drugs.

The moment Wyatt heard that and saw the purple and green bruises on each of their thin arms, all the memories that haunted him for years came back to him.

He realized he wanted to do something for these boys that would make a positive difference in their lives. So he offered to teach them to ride horses. Their foster mom was happy for the boys to be learning about the horses they loved.

Wyatt looked at Joey and Tony realizing he was happy to be bringing some joy into their lives.

Memories returned to him of that first week he'd come to live at the ranch as a young boy.

He'd been real scared.

It had only been two years since his Dad went to jail and he'd become a ward of the state. By that time he'd already been in three foster homes, and none of them had been loving or nurturing.

By the time he met Mack and Annie Callahan, he didn't expect to be treated differently. He came into this family with his mind made up and a chip on his shoulder. He came into this family expecting to be treated harshly or to be forgotten.

In the end, it was Annie's gentle, and loving ways that won him over.

Mack on the other hand was patient with him and his

brothers, so they learned quickly how things were done on the ranch.

He remembered his Dad's first lesson had been all about cleaning the barn and learning how to take care of the horse's feed and tack. Very similar to what he was teaching Joey and Tony today.

He was grateful his Dad had wisely taught him the practical steps first. When he and his brothers finally had their chance to learn horseback riding, it had felt more meaningful because of it.

The boys were almost done with their work when he heard the creaking of the barn door.

Wyatt turned to see Abby standing in the middle of the open doors.

For the past few days, his thoughts had been flooded with memories of their time spent together at the Fall Festival.

He'd purposely stayed away from her the past few days. The emotions raging in his heart had scared him.

It seemed like the night of the barn dance had sparked a fire that had spread like wildfire to ignite every part of him.

He wasn't expecting to fall for Abby so hard and so fast. In fact, he wasn't expecting to fall in love at all. He had been trying to avoid it.

How could a man like him — whose life had been chock-full of terrible mistakes — even think he deserved love and happiness with a woman as good and kind as Abby?

For the past few days he'd tried to push aside his growing attraction to her, and it wasn't working.

Wyatt was very much afraid that he was doing the very thing he swore he wouldn't do: *falling in love with his beautiful neighbor.*

If he continued following this path of attraction, she would discover all his grievous past sins and never forgive him.

His brows drew together in an agonized expression for a moment as the weight of that burden hit him. Wyatt closed his eyes for a moment and swallowed convulsively as his thoughts raced, imagining the horrible fallout between them.

Shuddering, he drew in a deep breath, looking down at the barn floor. When he opened his eyes Abby was studying him, her cheeks pale, green eyes wide and round with concern.

Wyatt forced a nonchalance that was so opposite of what he was feeling and leaned against the wooden edge of the stall door. His eyes captured hers.

Abby's cheeks stained with red as she clutched the reins, stepping closer to her mare. Her small hands patted Stocking's neck in a steady rhythm.

"Hello Wyatt." Abby spoke a soft greeting and managed a small tentative smile.

Wyatt nodded, a glint of humor finally returning. "Good afternoon, Abby."

He turned to look at the boys. " As you can see, I have helpers today. You might remember me introducing you to Joey and Tony at the Fall Festival?"

Abby nodded, a warm smile flooded her face. "I do. It's nice to see you boys again."

"It's nice to see you again, Mrs. Hart." Joey spoke

clearly and Tony merely nodded. Joey was the undisputed leader between the two boys. Tony seemed to look to his older brother to speak for both of them much of the time.

To Wyatt's surprise, Tony walked timidly over to Abby's horse to hand the mare a clump of straw he had in his small hand. "Is your horse hungry?"

Abby sat on her haunches and looked at the small boy, her expression thoughtful and warm. "Thank you for offering to feed her. She just galloped from home, so she might want to eat. Let me get the bridle off her first and put her in a stall, then you can feed her. Would that be okay?"

"Sure. She probably eats better that way, right?" Tony reached a tentative hand to Stocking's neck, smiling as he touched the soft horse hair.

"You are really good with horses, Tony. I can tell you have the gentle touch they need."

"Really?"

Wyatt smiled at the hopeful expression on Tony's face, it reminded him of feeling a similar need as a child.

His heartbeat sped up, and warmth flooded him. This was a part of the reason that thoughts of Abby flooded his mind and heart. She was thoughtful and compassionate, gently caring for others around her.

It wasn't only her beautiful features that attracted him, her compassion for others and caring nature also drew him.

From the gentle way she listened and spoke to these boys, he knew Abby would make a wonderful mother to some lucky children someday.

He longed for those children to be his. He wanted to

be the father to her children. He longed for them to be a family.

Quickly, he shoved down the intruding thoughts. That was just wishful thinking.

Shaking off the wayward thoughts, he walked towards Abby.

"If you want, I can take Stocking." He offered, taking the horses' reins from her hands. As soon as he did, his hand touched hers and a familiar shiver of awareness ran up his arm.

Looking into her bright green eyes, a bolt of attraction as sudden as lightning, ripped through him.

She suddenly pulled her hand away, and her cheeks blossomed with that gentle rose color he liked so much.

"I'll put your horse in the corner stall." He nodded and led the horse down the aisle of the barn and into the stall, happy to put some distance between them. What was wrong with him?

His thoughts were filled with Abby as he took off the mare's bridle, saddle and brushed her down. She was so beautiful. This woman was all he'd ever wanted, the woman he dreamed of marrying. He had a difficult time resisting her.

It was a good thing Joey and Tony were with him and Abby in the barn, or he would likely forget his resolve to stay away from her.

The two boys came into the stall and offered Stocking some hay as Abby filled the trough with clean water.

Before long they finished feeding the horse and Joey and Tony's foster mom arrived to take them home.

Wyatt waved to the boys as Mrs. Beaseley drove away.

"They're good boys. That's real good of you to spend time helping them, Wyatt. They look like they are happy to spend time with you. I really admire you for doing that."

A warmth spread from his belly upwards at Abby's words of praise. Each word of appreciation was like a small dart that further chipped away more of the ice block encased around his heart.

He just nodded. "Thanks." He spoke quickly, tamping down emotions that threatened to clog his throat. Not trusting himself to speak, he turned and headed toward the barn.

"I thought maybe you could start with Mustang today? He has had little attention lately and could use a good work out." Wyatt led the way to the black two-year-old stallion's stall in the barn.

Abby nodded and smiled briefly. "Sure."

While she took each of the four horses out one-by-one to train, Wyatt kept busy, checking the other horses that were inside the barn. He watered and fed each one and made notes on how each horse was doing physically.

It was part of his training as a Veterinary doctor to watch for certain signs in an animal's health. So far, all the horses looked fine. He was grateful.

He'd just finished the rounds, when Abby brought back the last mare from training.

"All done?"

"Yep. And they're quick learners."

"Good."

Abby followed him, and as soon as they reached the mare's stall she brushed her down and gave her feed.

They walked out of the stall and Wyatt closed the door, when suddenly she spoke. "Sorry I was a little late today. It took longer than I expected at the Blackwell ranch."

Wyatt leaned against the side of the stall and looked at her from beneath his black cowboy hat. Jealousy suddenly reared up inside him. He expelled a quick breath and forced his shoulders to settle and replied in a calm voice. "How did that go?"

"Good. The horse is good to work with. It's Reno's constant interruptions that are annoying. At least you don't interrupt me when I'm training, for which I'm grateful."

Wyatt shook his head. "Well, I don't need to. I trust that you know what you're doing."

"See? That's the difference. I don't think Reno trusts me to train his horse yet. But the problem is that his questions and comments could've waited until later. It's ridiculous."

Abby put her hands on her hips and he could tell she was irritated.

Wyatt chuckled a little. "Abby, look at me." He put a finger under her chin and lifted up her face so her eyes met his. "I don't think the reason Reno keeps interrupting you has anything to do with the horse you're training. I think it's because he wants your attention."

"That's absurd."

"Is it? Then tell me, did he ask you on a date after you finished training his horse today?"

A rush of pink tinged her cheeks, and she nodded, giving him the answer he expected.

Abby sighed heavily. "Why does he pester me? I just wish he'd let me train his horse and be done with it."

Wyatt stepped close to Abby and put his hands on her shoulders. "Because Abby Meadows Hart, you're a kind, compassionate and beautiful woman. Any man would be thrilled to have you by his side."

A slight smile lit up her face and she turned to look at him.

"Even a man like you?" The stain in her cheeks deepened to crimson. "Forget I said that." She turned away quickly, but Wyatt caught her waist and pulled her close to him.

She lifted her head, her big eyes staring intently at him. At the base of her throat, he saw a pulsing beat that echoed the rapid beats of his own heart.

His arms encircled her, and he whispered into ear. "Especially a man like me."

Wyatt studied her intently before he lowered his head and touched his lips to hers.

Touching her sweet lips sent a shock wave through his entire body. Wyatt's lips parted hers in a soul-reaching massage. To reach the deepest part of her heart was what his own heart desired.

He tried to stay away from her, but he couldn't. He tried to ignore his feelings for her, but he couldn't. He tried to shield his heart from loving her, but he couldn't.

His beautiful friend was the one woman he longed for, and she was also the one woman who was impossible for him to claim as his own.

His lips came coaxingly down on hers, in a need to convince her that he was the man for her.

Her sweet kisses in response were a delicious meal and he savored every moment.

Far back in the deep recesses of his mind, he wondered what would happen to his heart when he had to let her go?

&.

ABBY FELT her knees weaken as his mouth touched hers.

She was shocked at how she returned his kiss with reckless abandon.

Despite her best efforts to not get into a relationship, she had to admit that her handsome best friend was slowly stealing her heart.

Giving herself freely to the passion of his kisses, she slipped her hands around his neck and pulled herself closer to him. He responded by tightening his arms around her and pulling her close to his heart.

She relished being held in his strong arms.

Abby had convinced herself that she was unable to give her heart over to any man ever again.

But her heart swelled with a feeling that she thought long since dead.

She felt protected, valued and loved.

It was an awakening experience that left her reeling.

It was a feeling she didn't think she'd ever experience again.

But those were the very emotions that Wyatt awakened.

His kisses softened, pressing her lips to his, caressing her mouth more than kissing it. She quivered at the tenderness of his touch and began to lose herself in his sweet kisses.

She was relaxing into his arms when, without warning, her cell phone rang.

Dazed at the ringing tone that sounded a second time, she pulled away from him.

"I've got to answer this." Abby smiled weakly at Wyatt. His gray eyes were dark and filled with tenderness and passion from their kisses. He nodded and stepped away so she could answer the phone.

"Hello?" Abby slipped her phone next to her ear, but she needn't have. It was Mrs. Hart on the other end of the line, her voice so loud that Abby had to pull the phone slightly away from her ear.

"I'm coming home now. Be there soon."

Abby expelled a slow breath.

"Was that Mrs. Hart?" Wyatt asked.

"Yes. She's at my ranch, waiting for me. She says we need to talk." Abby's brows creased in worry. "I'm really not looking forward to this."

She tucked her phone in her vest pocket. "But I might as well get it over with."

Abby hurried to Stocking's stall, quickly slipping the bridle and saddle on her mare.

Leading her horse outside, Wyatt followed her.

He placed gentle hands on her shoulders and placed a gentle kiss on her forehead. He looked at her and with a warm voice he spoke. "It'll be okay. You've got this."

"Thanks, Wyatt." Abby sighed. "I needed to hear that."

Wyatt helped her onto the saddle, and she looked at him. "See you later."

"You most definitely will." His confidence caused her to blush. He touched his fingers to his cowboy hat and nodded.

She smiled and spoke to her horse. "Let's go home, Stocking."

Her mare started at a trot, but soon they were galloping across Callahan land towards home.

Thoughts swirled around and around in her head.

Memories circled her as she remembered Wyatt's sweet kisses. She was drawn to him and didn't know how it happened, but each time she saw him the pull was stronger.

She admired his intelligence, his courage and his faithfulness to take over the ranch after his Dad passed away. Wyatt was a good man, and she felt a tiny glow of warmth curl up inside her belly every time she thought of him.

What would happen between the two of them? Should she stop things before they became too attached to one another?

She had a feeling it was already too late. Her heart had already decided whom she would love.

As Abby reached the ranch yard, she saw Mrs. Hart sitting in her car waiting for her.

Abby quickly took off the bridle and saddle off Stocking and set her free to roam in the pasture.

Hurrying to the house, she smiled a friendly welcome to Mrs. Hart, who stepped out of her car.

"Welcome, Mrs. Hart. Let's go into the house and have some tea, shall we?" Abby smiled and led the way into her house. When she found a spot in the sunny kitchen table, she filled the kettle and set it on the stove so the water could boil for tea.

"I don't understand why it took you so long to get home." Mrs. Hart complained as Abby set the teacup in front of her.

Abby forced herself to remain patient as she replied. "I was training Wyatt Callahan's two-year-old horses. Some days the training takes longer than usual. But I came home as soon as you called. I hadn't realized you were coming to the ranch today."

She hadn't expected to see her mother-in-law today otherwise she would've come home earlier.

Mrs. Hart shifted in her chair, her brows pulling together to form a deep groove on her forehead. "I didn't realize I needed an invitation to stop by to visit my son's widow."

Abby cringed a little at the bluntness of her words, but forced a smile. "Of course you don't need an invitation, you can visit anytime. But just so you know, now that I'm training more horses, some days when you show up I might not be at home."

Mrs. Hart expelled a heavy sigh and shifted the conversation. "Well, I just wanted to stop by, to ask you about the money you owe me and my husband. When do you think you'll be ready to get that to us?"

Abby toyed with her teacup. She'd already known that was the reason for her mother-in-law's visit today. She had been making plans to get the money she needed.

"I still have a little over a month before the date we set at the lawyer's office to get that ten thousand dollars to your husband. But don't worry, I'll make sure he receives it in good time." Abby drank the last of her tea and set her cup firmly on the table.

"Good. Don't leave us waiting." Mrs. Hart's stern faced expression, was a familiar one that she'd felt the effects of, ever since she'd married Tom.

Her mother-in-law stood up and was about to leave when she noticed the wedding picture that Abby kept on the counter near the phone.

She watched as Mrs. Hart stared at the picture for a long time, her finger tracing the lines of his body. "He was the one bright light in an otherwise dark life."

Her mother-in-law's eyes was as cold as ice as they met her own. "Yet you took Tom from me — twice. First when you married him, and later on when you let him leave to join the military. It's your fault my son is dead." She walked away and then paused by the door. "The very least you owe us, is that money."

Abby's heart constricted at Mrs. Hart's words, instantly feeling the blood drain from her face.

She shriveled inside at the thin lipped expression on her mother-in-law's face and did her best to hide her inner misery from her probing stare.

As the door closed loudly behind her, Abby's hands started trembling.

The swell of pain in her heart was beyond tears.

A raw primitive grief overwhelmed her. She stumbled into the living room and sagged her body down onto her late husband's favorite couch.

Wrapping her arms around her knees, she recalled her mother-in-law's words. Was Tom's death her fault?

Her husband had been the one to decide that's what he

wanted to do. No, he said it was what he needed. He was struggling with the pressure and was drinking heavily, and he decided to make a clean break of it.

She felt sorry for Mrs. Hart. She was struggling with the loss of her son, but did she have to be so mean spirited? It was true what her friend Sierra said, that family and friends had a way of hurting you the most.

But she would not wallow in her pain and heartache.

It was time to do what she'd been putting off for weeks. She needed to call Refuge Mountain's Agriculture Auction.

It was time to sell both horses. That was the only way she would have enough money to pay back the debt her late husband owed his father.

If she did that, it would mean she only had one more week to spend time with her favorite horse.

Abby didn't know how she could handle it emotionally, but she would sell Stocking.

Her mare was the same horse she first received as a teenager. It was the same horse that had always been there, even through all the losses and pain in her life.

Deep inside, even though it seemed ridiculous to others, her horse had become the one constant source of joy and stability in a life otherwise riddled with troublesome upheaval and loss.

After she sold her horse, she would truly be all alone.

At this point with all her setbacks, Abby was convinced there was a good chance she'd be lonely for the rest of her life.

An inner torment gnawed at her.

She bit her lip, refusing to shed a tear.

Pulling out her phone, she searched for the number to the Agriculture Auction Mart, and dialed the number.

Her hand trembled as she held the phone to her ear, waiting for someone on the other end to answer.

A strange emptiness flooded her soul at the coming loss.

This sacrifice would be her second one in the last six months.

Didn't they say trouble came in threes? Did that mean there was another loss just waiting for her around the corner?

Her hand tightened its grip on her phone and her body trembled as a sense of foreboding filled her senses.

# CHAPTER NINE

yatt

"How's ranching going, Bobby?" Wyatt took a sip of his coffee, peering over the steaming cup at the grey haired cowboy.

Bobby Jackson had been a good friend of his Dad's and they had recently begun their monthly meetings once again. They had continued meeting for coffee together after Mack Callahan passed away.

Since his Dad's death, Wyatt had joined the old-timers hoping to learn from their years of wisdom.

Seated across from him at an old coffee shop located just off the highway between their ranches, were his Dad's friends Bobby, Wayne and John. Lately these three had become his good friends too.

"To be honest, not so good." Bobby rubbed at the grey

hairs on his chin, his lips set in a thin line. "Three days ago, some rustlers scurried off with thirty head of my cattle. I had my son Eli look into it and all he found were tire tracks on the southwest side of the pasture."

"You talked with Sheriff Turnbull?"

"Yep." Bobby removed his cowboy hat for a moment and scratched his head. "I told him, I've never had so many cattle taken from my herd in one day. Seems like whoever is rustling, is becoming a little too confident."

Wyatt nodded, setting his cup on the table. "I agree. The Sheriff has only had false leads ever since rustlers took off with fifty head of my cattle a few weeks ago. I think there might be more to this cattle stealing ring than we realize."

John Peterson nodded. "Well, you have a much larger spread than I do Wyatt. With my five thousand head of cattle, my ranch isn't much of a temptation for thugs who want to steal cattle."

"So you haven't noticed missing cattle?" Wyatt pressed for answers. He intended to get to the bottom of this unsolved criminal activity.

John shook his head. "Not yet. I do have hired hands taking turns watching during the night shift, so who knows what will turn up?"

The other ranchers nodded, each one sipping their coffee deep in thought.

"Hopefully we will know something soon." Wyatt slipped on his coat and stood to shake each rancher's hand. "It was good talking to you all, but I need to get back home. See you later."

He'd just started to walk away when Bobby spoke up.

"Hey Wyatt." He turned to see Bobby wearing a big grin. "Just wanted to let you know that Mrs. Hart is doing a fine job training my two year old. Never seen a new horse obey directions that quickly. She's definitely got a way with horses. You tell her I'll be asking her back when my colt is old enough to be trained."

Wyatt grinned. "I'll tell her, Bobby. Abby will be happy to hear that." He waved and hurried out of the coffee shop and into his truck.

As he drove home all he could think of was that there had to be some missing piece in the search for these cattle rustlers. They needed to get to the bottom of this.

As he drove onto the large ranch yard of the Triple C, Wyatt spotted his foreman Carlson and his two other cowhands Slim and Lennie walking out of the barn. He parked the truck and rushed over to them.

"Just wanted to check in with you boys. Have you noticed any more problems in the northwest pasture?" Wyatt looked at all three of them, hoping one of them had something new to report.

"Nope. Leastways, not yet sir." Carlson spoke up first.

Wyatt nodded at him and looked at Lennie and Slim. Lennie shook his head no, but he couldn't help but notice that Slim wouldn't look him in the eye. His hands fidgeted with the belt loop on his dusty jeans.

"How about you Slim? Have you noticed anything out of the ordinary?" Wyatt was curious about what he had to say.

At his direct question, Slim looked up and mumbled. "No, sir. I haven't seen a thing."

Wyatt wondered why his hired hand seemed to have a

twitch right when he was asked direct questions about the cattle they were supposed to watch over.

In that moment, Wyatt decided he would need to find someone who would keep a close eye on Slim and maybe his other hired hands too.

"Well, alright then."

Carlson stepped forward. "Boss, do you want us to continue taking the night shift watching over that Northwest corner of the pasture?"

Wyatt thought for a moment. "No. Why don't you three take a break for this week? You can start the night shift again next Monday."

"Sure. Sounds good, boss." Carlson nodded and all three cowhands walked back to the log cabins that Mack Callahan had built when he'd first bought the land.

Wyatt was glad they had lots of room for their hired hands. It looked like he would need to ask two other hands to take this week's shift.

He was determined to figure out who was on the wrong side of the law, stealing cattle from hard working ranchers.

He turned to walk to the house, when he spotted Dakota riding his gelding back to the barn.

Wyatt hurried towards him. "You're just the man I need to talk to."

Dakota slipped off his horse while Wyatt followed him into the barn.

"What's up big brother?" Dakota took the saddle and bridle off, his dark eyed gaze studying him.

Wyatt reached for the brush and started brushing

down the gelding before he spoke. "I'm suddenly concerned about one of our hired hands."

"Concerned. Meaning you don't trust him?"

Wyatt cocked his head to one side and shrugged. "I don't know yet."

"Who is it?"

"Slim."

Dakota's dark laser eyes bored holes into his. "Okay. What do you want me to do?"

"I have a favor to ask of you." Wyatt looked over at his tall dark haired brother, whose broad shoulders and muscled arms had won many a physical argument in the past.

However at this moment, there were other less bodily talents that his brother had that would prove useful. "I'm wondering if you could put to use those instinctive skills you inherited of the Native American Lakota warrior and begin tracking Slim?"

"You mean follow him and see what I can learn about who he's meeting and why?"

"Yeah, basically." Wyatt gave him a half grin.

Dakota chuckled. "You came to the right guy. That's right up my alley. It won't take me long to ferret out information."

"I know. You've got the blood of a warrior. Who better to track someone without them knowing it?" Wyatt winked at his brother.

Dakota nodded and grinned. "I'll let you know what I find out."

"Thanks man, I owe you one. See you later." Wyatt

clapped his brother on the shoulder and hurried out of the barn.

Checking his watch, he realized he needed to get going if he wanted to make it to their small town Auction in time. He got in his truck and drove to Refuge Mountain hoping he liked the new cattle that were being offered today.

His good friend Zeke MacCallister, the owner of their small town's Auction mart, called Wyatt a few days ago letting him know there would be a bunch of Black Angus cattle for sale at today's auction.

Wyatt was determined to increase his herd with good breeds. He wanted to do his Dad proud. Taking good care of the ranch and the cattle he left in his son's care was one of the best ways he knew how to make up for all those years that he had been away from home. He owed his father.

Arriving at the Auction mart, he saw rows upon rows of trucks parked outside the large Agri-Complex building. He walked inside the building and was about to go sit up with the other farmers and ranchers up on the grandstand, when he saw Sheriff Turnbull waving him over.

Wyatt hurried toward him. "Hey Sheriff. How are things going?"

"Good."

"Any news about my missing fifty head of cattle?" Wyatt stuck his hands in his jean pockets, bracing himself for the worst.

The Sheriff took off his cowboy hat and ran a hand through his hair as he explained. "Well, it's turning out to be more complicated than we first thought. We found a man who was caught stealing two cows."

He shook his head and sighed. "He figured his boss owed him, because he had just fired him without pay and he needed a way to feed his family. But this man we brought in for questioning, Ned Depplin, we discovered his boss is Gavin Copton, who has a large ranch just south of Clear Springs."

"Why does that matter?"

"Well, I'm hoping we can get this Ned fellow to talk. Maybe he knows something. Perhaps he has connections to others who have been stealing cattle from ranchers in these parts."

Wyatt rubbed his chin and nodded. "Hmm. Seems like you might have a good lead there. Keep me updated on what you find out. There's more than just my ranch at stake in this thing. Other ranchers around here have had unexplained losses."

"True. And I give you my word I'll do everything I can to solve this, Wyatt." Sheriff Turnbull set his jaw with a new determination.

"I know you will. Thanks, Sheriff." Wyatt nodded. One thing he knew about Sheriff Turnbull, he was like a bulldog with a bone.

Once he got his teeth dug into something, he wouldn't let it go until he did everything he could to uncover all the crimes committed against local ranchers.

It wasn't long before the loud speaker rang with the bold voice of the auctioneer, announcing the first set of horses in the lineup.

Wyatt nodded to the Sheriff and hurried over for a closer look at the horses that were for sale.

He watched different horses being bought up by ranchers. None of the horses there interested him as he restlessly waited for the auctioneer to introduce the sale of the cattle.

Wyatt shifted in his seat, when suddenly two horses came into the fenced in area that he immediately recognized.

His mouth dropped open in surprise as Abby's horses came into view. Quickly, he forced his jaw to close as the auctioneer confirmed the two horses were hers.

Questions skittered across his mind. Why would Abby need to sell her horses? He thought she was making enough money now with all the horse training work she was doing for ranchers in the area.

He remembered Abby had mentioned she needed to sell her horses quite a few weeks ago. However, he assumed her finances were fine now that she was earning income elsewhere.

Wyatt's gaze was glued to Abby's favorite horse, Stocking. This mare was a poignant reminder of how much Abby was giving up. She loved all horses, but Abby had always had a special bond with Stocking.

Memories invaded his thoughts of Abby riding this horse in the pasture and on the riding trails where they rode their horses side-by-side. Wyatt couldn't imagine seeing his beautiful neighbor without the horse she adored.

In that moment, he decided he wasn't about to let

Abby lose something else in her life that meant the world to her.

When the auctioneer began the sale of the horses, several ranchers raised their hands to buy them. Wyatt joined them, determined to buy them no matter how much it cost him.

"Sold to Wyatt Callahan." Wyatt smiled widely at the auctioneer's announcement. He'd paid a good sum for the two. But it was worth it.

He would do anything to bring a little happiness back to the woman he adored.

AT THE SOUND OF KNOCKING, Abby hurried to the back door and opened it.

Her friend Sierra stood there with a smile, beside her with a big grin on his face, was her six year old son, Cody.

"Hey you two. I'm glad it worked out for you to come for a short visit this morning. Come on in." Abby stepped back to give the two of them room to enter the house.

Cody had been to her ranch many times before and as he hurried inside, he called for the dog. "Lassie, where are you?"

At the sound of his lilting boyish voice, the long haired dog bounded toward the six year old. Cody reached his arms around the large golden retriever, squeezing the ball of fur with all the strength he could muster.

Abby giggled. "Aww... Cody, that's perfect. Lassie hasn't been hugged so well in a real long time."

"Well, you know Cody, I swear he's got a love for all

animals in his blood." Sierra's tone was wistful for a moment, almost as if she was remembering something, but she quickly switched topics as they walked into the comfortable family room.

"So my friend, how are things going?"

Abby sat down and brought her feet up onto the sofa to get comfortable. Her face closed up in worry as she thought about all the difficulties she'd dealt with in the past few days.

"From the look of that crease on your forehead, I'd say things have been troublesome for you." Sierra spoke in low tones from where she sat on the opposite end of the couch.

Abby nodded slowly, her gaze fixed on Cody, who was busy playing with Lassie and Buttercup in the corner of the room. "Yeah. I've had some difficult conversations I've had lately."

"With Wyatt?" Her friend shifted and leaned her head against the side of the sofa, one hand on her chin and concern in her blue eyes.

Abby sighed heavily and shook her head. "No, with Tom's mom. She stopped by this week." She pulled her knees up to her chest and bit her lip as she remembered their conversation.

"She stopped by about the money Tom owed his folks?"

Abby nodded. Biting her lip, she looked away for a moment as she recalled the bitter and angry words her mother-in-law had spoken.

"Talk to me. What did that woman say this time?"

Sierra touched her hand, squeezing it with a gentle pressure. Her friend leaned closer to look her in the eyes.

Abby swallowed. "Mrs. Hart said the very least I could do was pay back the money Tom owed them. Then she told me that her son had been the one bright light in her life and that I stole him from her twice. First when he married me and then when I encouraged him to go into the military."

Nauseating shame slammed into her like a rising tide as she recalled her mother-in-law's words. "Then she said, it was my fault her son was dead."

Swallowing the sob that rose in her throat she hugged her knees against her chest tightly. A single tear formed a trail down her cheek as a new anguish seared her heart.

Sierra whispered. "I'm so sorry she said that to you. Those are cruel lies." Her friend moved to sit beside her and slipped an arm around her shoulders. Searching Abby's face, she spoke again. "Not a bit of that is true, Abby."

"But, maybe it is my fault. If Tom wouldn't have married me, maybe he would not have chosen to go into the military and therefore to an early grave." Grief and despair tore at her heart as a suffocating sensation tightened in her throat. "Maybe in a roundabout way, I really did cause my husband's death."

Sierra grabbed her gently by the shoulders and with a gentle force turned Abby towards her. "Look at me."

Abby lifted her gaze to look into her friend's blue eyes that were full of the warmth and concern. "You are not responsible for Tom's death. He chose to marry you and later on he decided to join the military, right?"

Abby nodded.

"So, both choices were Tom's, not yours. You are not responsible for his choices." Sierra waited until Abby nodded in agreement, before she continued. "But your mother-in-law shouldn't have said those hurtful words to you, I'm sorry she did. None of her accusations are true."

Abby's clamped lips imprisoned a sob. Shakily she said. "Maybe you're right."

"I am. So you can let go of any notion that you're at fault for your late husband's death." Her friend expelled a frustrated sigh and was silent for a moment.

Abby wiped away moisture from her eyes with the edge of her long-sleeved shirt. "What are you thinking?"

Sierra frowned a little looking out the window before she turned to Abby. "I just remembered something my Grandma told me a few weeks ago. I mentioned to her about Mrs. Hart being unkind to you. She told me something, which might help you understand your mother-in-law a little better."

"I'd like to hear it." Abby had wanted to understand Tom's mother better ever since she first married him years ago, but it seemed Martha Hart was always pushing her away.

Sierra began. "Well, Grandma said that her and Martha were best friends in High School and they talked about everything, especially boyfriends like most gals did."

Her friend took a breath and continued. "At the start of her Junior year Martha had been introduced to a bachelor rancher — Henry Morden — who had recently bought land in the area. As they neared the end of her senior year,

Martha told my Grandma she was desperately in love and wanted to marry Henry."

"What happened?"

"It so happened Martha's parents already had their eye on another man they wanted their only daughter to marry. Mr. James Hart was a young man. Martha's father was grooming him to take over his business one day. So, on the day when Martha announced to her parents the man she wanted to marry was Henry Morden. Her parents demanded that she stop seeing this fellow immediately."

Sierra grimaced and continued with the story. "Martha didn't stop seeing him. In fact, they planned on running away together, only her parents discovered them trying to leave in the middle of the night."

"Martha's parents forced her to stay home and told her to begin planning her wedding to James Hart. Martha didn't plan anything, but a couple months later she found out she was pregnant. Her parents forced her to marry James within the month. And James Hart was glad to marry Martha for the money."

"That's so sad that she went through so much heartache. I didn't know that." Abby was silent for a moment as she thought of what Sierra had told her. "So, Martha Hart was pregnant with Tom..." Abby's thoughts trailed off as she realized what that meant.

Sierra raised both eyebrows and finished that thought. "...when she married James Hart." Sierra nodded.

Abby brows creased together as further insight came to her about what happened to Martha Hart. "Does that mean Tom was really Henry Morden's son?"

"Yes. Grandma told me, that James Hart treated Martha coldly throughout their marriage because she was pregnant when they married." Sierra sighed and looked over at her own son Cody, who was happily playing with the dog and cat. "It's those kinds of hurtful words and actions that have far reaching consequences."

Abby nodded. "That certainly was true for Tom. I remember him telling me that he never felt his Dad loved him. His father favored Will instead, giving Tom's younger brother all the attention and love that Tom longed for from his Dad."

Sierra's blue eyes looked sad. "I'm sorry."

"I'm sorry too, mostly for Tom." Abby sighed heavily. "But I am sorry for Mrs. Hart too. She's had a difficult life. It explains so much." After hearing her mother-in-law's story, Abby felt she understood her a little better. Those hurtful words that she threw at Abby came from a lifetime of pain.

"It does, doesn't it?"

Abby nodded, still reeling from the new awareness she had of Mrs. Hart.

She was interrupted by Cody's excited voice. "Mommy, can I go outside with Lassie and Buttercup?"

Sierra hugged her son and kissed him on the forehead. "Sure, but you need someone out there with you. We'll be right behind you, okay?"

Abby grinned at Cody's eagerness to go outside to play.

"Sure." The small boy tugged on the golden retriever's thick fur. "Let's go Lassie." Cody called and ruffled the dog's hair.

Abby giggled. "Your son is the Pied Piper. The animals follow him wherever he goes." Abby stood to her feet shaking her head and grinning as they both followed the boy outside.

Sierra chuckled, nodding in agreement. "He has a real love for animals, that's for sure."

Cody began chasing the dog and reached the barn when he called out. "Could I pet the horses, Aunt Abby?"

A sudden wave of loss flooded Abby. As much as she didn't want to, she needed to let Sierra and Cody know what happened.

Abby reached Cody and knelt down so she could look him in the eye. "I'm sorry Cody. Aunt Abby had to sell the horses."

She bit her lip hard and swallowed, refusing to let herself get emotional. "Someday I hope to have another horse for you to ride, but for today you'll need to stick to playing with Lassie and Buttercup, okay?"

"It's okay Aunt Abby. Someday, you can get another horse." Cody reached toward her, his small arms wrapping around her waist.

It was the little boy's hug that caused tears to prick at the back of her eyelids.

"You're right. Thank you Cody." The little boy soon scampered out of her embrace and ran back to his friend, the dog.

Abby turned to Sierra, blinking back tears. "Your son is amazing."

"Yeah, I kind of think so too." Sierra grabbed Abby and pulled her into a tight hug. "I'm sorry about the horses."

Abby's voice broke miserably. "Thanks. Me too." She

stepped back and quickly wiped at her eyes. "But, I needed to pay back Tom's parents. Selling those horses was the only way I could do that."

She clenched her jaw in determination. "Getting that debt paid off has been on the top of my list. Now, all I need is a miracle to save the ranch from foreclosure."

"Good thing Christmas is the season of love and miracles. You might just be surprised how things work out for you, my friend." Sierra's voice rang in her heart like a bell of hope.

Problem was, Abby didn't have much hope left. Wasn't it a little too late for her own personal miracle?

# CHAPTER TEN

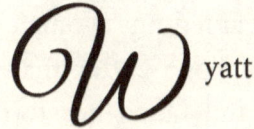yatt

"Mr. McCrae said he was passing by Abby Hart's ranch a couple weeks ago and noticed you were helping with her horses." The subdued smile on his mom's face didn't fool Wyatt.

She set the yarn and crochet needle down on her lap and looked over at him.

The soft glow in her blue eyes was made brighter by the dancing firelight. As was their nightly routine, his mom sat in the den and usually Wyatt or one of his other brothers joined her to talk and just spend time together.

Tonight he sat beside her on the comfortable sofa. So far, from the start of their conversation, Wyatt realized his mom was getting ready to have a serious discussion.

"I see you've been spending more time with Abby." Annie Callahan wasn't known for being subtle.

Wyatt knew she was trying to ask if things were getting serious between them.

"Abby needed someone to take a look at her horses. Stocking's been having a little trouble healing since his foreleg was caught in that thick thorn bush a couple months ago." Wyatt chose to give his mom only the necessary facts about his relationship with Abby.

He didn't want to get her hopes up about his relationship with Abby. Wyatt could admit to himself however, that deep down he'd never gotten over his first love.

He wanted Abby more than he'd wanted any woman. But, he also believed she deserved someone better than him. He'd made too many mistakes and failed her too many times.

Perhaps, Abby's father had been right years ago when he'd told her: *Wyatt may be a Callahan now, but he comes from bad blood. I don't want you getting mixed up with someone like him, and I definitely don't want you marrying him.*

As far as Wyatt could tell, all of it was true. Vivid memories of anger, rejection and abuse still haunted him from his childhood. One of his fears had always been that he'd end up like his birth father.

Maybe it was only a matter of time.

Maybe there were certain failures and mistakes that really couldn't be forgiven.

Wyatt expelled a long breath and did his best to shake off the downward spiral of thoughts.

Forcing a smile, his gaze met hers.

Annie Callahan's beautiful face was shining with a steadfast and serene peace. It was almost as if she knew more than she was letting on.

His mom was a little hard to shake once she got her mind set on something.

The last thing he wanted to do was to get his Mom's hopes up only to disappoint her.

So, he did the only thing he knew to do, and down-played his relationship with Abby.

"Mom, I'm simply helping Abby with the animals at her ranch. She helps me too by coming to our ranch to train our horses." He leaned back, studying his Mom's features, trying to figure out what she was thinking about.

His mom swivelled slowly towards him, her stitching forgotten. There was a calm but purposeful look to her gaze that made him uneasy. "I know you and Abby are good friends, Wyatt. It seems you always have been. But, I also remember that day seven years ago when you told me you'd found the woman you loved and wanted to marry."

"That was years ago…" Wyatt began, but his mom kept talking.

"I know, son. It has been a lot of years and a lot of water under the bridge." She reached for his hand and squeezed it, holding his large powerful hand in hers for a moment before she continued. "But, I can't help but feel the same way as your father did, that you two are meant to be together."

Wyatt sighed heavily, unsure of what to say to that.

"I know there is so much pain inside you. And in fact compared to some you've had it the hardest with all that you had to face as a little boy. So much pain, heartache and trauma you've gone through."

She continued. "But from the many years I've lived on this earth, I've come to realize that sometimes you have to risk losing love to gain it. That's the risk I took, when your Dad came back into my life all those years ago. My mind argued against it and told me I was foolish to risk my heart to love a second time. I thought love and marriage were over for me."

"But, Mack Callahan kept loving me until he won me over." A brightening of pride lit her blue eyes as her steady gaze held his. "Don't let fear hold you back from opening your heart to love, son. Instead, take the risk. It'll be worth it, I promise you."

Wyatt shifted uncomfortably, aware that his mom had just uncovered his deepest heartaches and biggest fears.

He sat there in silence absorbing her words, unsure of what to say. Annie Callahan was a master at understanding each of her children and she had him pegged.

She stood to her feet and walked over to the mantle that sat above the roaring fireplace.

She picked up two engraved bells that the Refuge Mountain town council had made for the Callahan family.

They were silver bells to represent hope for every person who came to their small town. On one bell was engraved the word, *love.* On the other bell was engraved the word, *miracles.*

"Your father donated the large bells that sit in Bell Tower of the community church before he died. During the dedication service, you remember he asked Reverend Jon to ring these bells once a year at Christmas."

His mom gentled traced the engravings on the bells. "It was to be a reminder for the people of our small town of Refuge Mountain that hope, love and miracles are available for us all. People just need to believe."

Wyatt stared at the bells his mom held in her hand, smiling at the warm memory. "I remember. Folks told me that Dad donating those bells was a very meaningful gift for our town."

"It was." His mom ran a finger over the inscribed words on each bell a peaceful smile on her face before she put the ornaments back on the mantle.

Slowly, she walked over to him and kissed him on the cheek. "Wyatt, I believe there is a reason you came back home when you did." A gentle smile turned up the corners of her mouth. "I'll leave it to you to figure out what that reason is."

With that, Annie Callahan walked out of the den and off to bed.

As usual, Wyatt was left reeling from one of his heart to heart talks with his Mom. Annie Callahan had a way of getting down to the heart of the matter and as usual it left him feeling uncomfortable.

He moved restlessly, his thoughts spinning in a circle. As usual, his Mom words hit far too close to home.

The truth was, pain and fear held him back from truly being vulnerable. He was attracted to Abby. He loved being with her but in his heart of hearts he was afraid to risk telling Abby that he loved her.

He was very much afraid once he told her the truth of what happened to her late husband, she would reject him.

Wyatt sighed heavily and stood to his feet, his thoughts still swirling.

He had just started to dampen the fire, when his brother hurried into the den.

Turning, Wyatt smiled in amusement as he glanced at Dakota's unusual choice of clothes. He was dressed in dark baggy clothes with a ball cap on his head.

Wyatt recalled these were normal clothes for Dakota when he was tracking someone and was doing his best to stay anonymous.

"Here you are. I'm glad I caught you. I've got some news you'll find interesting." Dakota's mouth turned up in a smile that hinted at the fact that he was very pleased with himself.

"I'm listening." Wyatt finished dampening the fire before turning to face his brother.

Dakota sat on the long couch and put his feet up, a satisfied smile on his face. "Well, it turns out you were right to be suspicious of Slim."

"I figured. What did you overhear?" Wyatt slipped his hands in his pockets, disliking the fact that some of his hired hands would be deceptive.

Dakota took off the ball cap and toyed with it in his hands as he told the tale. "I followed Slim at a distance when he left the ranch earlier tonight. He drove to Benny's Bar and Grill in Clear Springs. I went inside, doing my best to stay undercover but still close enough so that I could hear what was going on."

Wyatt started pacing as he listened.

"Slim sat down at the bar and ordered a beer. Before long, a guy in a Cowboy hat and expensive looking cowboy boots, joined him there." Dakota stroked his chin for a moment.

"I might have seen this guy before at the local rodeo. But anyway, I digress." He grinned and continued telling the story. "Slim spoke up and said 'there you are.' Then, I overheard Gavin ask Slim if he was ready for the upcoming delivery."

"Hmm, an upcoming delivery. I wonder what that means?"

"Just wait a minute, I'm getting to that." Dakota chuckled. "Slim said, 'I'm ready, but circumstances have changed a little.' To which Gavin asked in low angry tones, 'what could possibly have changed our schedule? You're hired by me to get a job done.' At that, Slim turned a little pale. His hand shook the beer he held in his hand as he replied, 'I know and I'm sorry but we'll have to put the job back a week. I'll let you know when we're back on and can take care of the delivery.'

The furrow between Wyatt's brows grew deeper as he thought about the conversation his brother was retelling.

Dakota continued. "At that point, Gavin quickly gulped back the rest of his beer and spoke harshly. "This better happen soon. To make sure it does, I'm going to have a chat with my partner. He's been a little too careless about his duties lately."

"I think it's that red haired beauty he's got his eye on. I'll need to take care of that situation. But as for you, make sure you let me know when you can handle that delivery.' That's when Gavin stormed out of the bar. Slim stayed a little longer until he was halfway drunk. And later, I followed him back to the ranch."

Wyatt ran a hand through his thick dark brown hair, and spoke with a bridled anger in his voice. "Gavin huh? That must be the same rancher Sheriff was talking about that lives just outside Clear Springs. Gavin Copton I think was his name."

"Sounds about right." Dakota stood to his feet and looked at him with a glint in his dark eyes. "Seems to me, like there's something fishy going on with at least one of our hired hands."

"Yeah. I kind of thought something wasn't quite right." Wyatt shook his head and rubbed the back of his neck. "I'm convinced the delivery they are talking about is rustling our cattle."

At Dakota's nod, Wyatt continued. "And I'm fairly certain Slim told Gavin they needed to put the job back a week, because I told all three of those hired hands — Slim, Carlson and Lennie — to take the next week off from working the nightshift."

"That tells me, they are planning to round up and steal a bunch more of our cattle. We'll need to set up people we trust to watch the night shift for the next few weeks."

"Might be a good idea to let the Sheriff in on the plan." Dakota grinned. "I know we Callahan boys are tough mavericks and can handle our own, but in this case it might be a good idea to also have the law looking out for our best interests."

"Yeah, you're right. I'll talk to Sheriff Turnbull tomorrow first thing." Wyatt walked up to his brother and slapped him on the shoulder. "We might just get this small problem of rustlers stealing our cattle solved after all."

Dakota nodded. "There wasn't any doubt in my mind. Good night brother."

As Wyatt stood and watched Dakota walk down the hallway, set his chin in determination. They were going to get to the bottom of all the cattle rustling once and for all.

There was no way he had worked this hard to grow his Dad's ranch, only to have the land and cattle his father loved, dwindle down to nothing.

Tomorrow couldn't come soon enough.

He was looking forward to having that chat with the Sheriff.

ABBY HURRIED across the field so she would arrive at Reno Blackwell's ranch on time.

Her thoughts twisted in pain in remembrance of the loss of her beloved horses.

It was a wound that cut deep.

In fact, it didn't feel right to be training horses now that she didn't own horses of her own.

But, the bigger loss was that her horses had become so much a part of her. It was like losing close companions or friends.

To most people, that sentiment would sound strange, but that's how she felt. With each passing day, she missed them more and more.

Arriving at the Blackwell ranch, she shook her head quickly in an effort to rid herself of the downward spiral of her thoughts. She couldn't dwell on it instead she needed to focus today on doing her job.

Abby walked through the open barn door, walking towards the stalls where the younger horses were kept. Several horses whinnied at the sound of her footsteps. She turned to see three new horses in the stalls beside the mare she was training.

She touched her hand to the velvety tip on each nose as she passed them.

A new curiosity swirled around in her mind.

Reno and his brother seemed to have picked up a bunch of extra money lately. She recalled a conversation with Reno only last year. He'd told her he didn't know if they would be able to continue ranching with all the money they had lost.

Well, they must have figured out a way, because not only were there new horses in the barn, but as she looked around she discovered new supplies. New saddles, bridles and halters were strung up in the barn's tack room.

Setting aside all the questions that surfaced, she focused on walking the mare to the fenced training area and began the day's training.

Time always seemed to fly by when she was working with a horse. A contentment and joy filled her as she taught the mare how to listen quickly to commands.

Working with horses, she'd learned that trust went hand in hand with how she cared for each one as she trained them.

For Abby, it made sense. It was something she'd also noticed in her relationships with people. Sadly, not many of the people in her life understood how caring for someone and trust were necessary for two people to grow closer.

Abby had just finished training the horse when Reno showed up. He was talking to a man who wore dusty jeans and an orange and blue ball cap.

She realized the man must be someone new that Reno hired. Another new hired hand, that was interesting.

Taking the rope and gripping the mare's halter, she started walking toward the gate.

Leaning his arms on the wooden fence he called out. "Finished?"

"Yep." She led the two year old out of the training area and Reno walked up to her.

"She's taking well to her training?"

"Yes. Your mare is a quick learner. She's a pleasure to work with."

"Glad to hear it." Reno walked with her into the barn as Abby brushed the horse down and gave her fresh water and food. "Since you've finished for the day, why don't you come inside and have a cup of coffee?"

Abby was surprised by his offer, but wanting to be nice she replied. "Sure. That would be a nice break."

They walked together to the house with the crisp air blowing against her cheeks. A chill invaded her body matching the unease she felt around Reno.

Once inside, Reno led Abby towards a breakfast nook with table and chairs. "I'll get the coffee going. Be right back."

"Sure. Thanks." Abby nodded at him offering a friendly smile. After he left, Abby looked around at the walls, hoping to see pictures.

There were only two paintings of landscapes on the

walls. No pictures of friends or family adorned the walls to give their home a friendly atmosphere.

It felt quite empty and lonely. Abby was intrigued.

She was still thinking about it, when Reno walked back to the table with a steaming cup of coffee in each hand.

"I'm glad you decided to have a coffee with me." Reno sat across from her, his dark eyed stare making her nervous. She shifted in her chair, and toyed with the spoon beside her cup.

"It seemed like it was the neighborly thing to do." Abby offered a quick smile, doing her best to stick to normal topics that they shared an interest in. "Looks like ranch life is treating you and your brother well."

"It is. Things have been going good." Reno leaned forward slightly. "But I will admit that it does get lonely. I would be much happier if I had someone to share all of this with."

The pointed way he studied her alongside the meaning behind his words, caused Abby to squirm in her seat. They had only gone to the movies once and since then Reno treated her like he owned her.

She didn't belong to him, but it had been difficult to help him see that.

"I'm sure someday you'll find a woman who is perfect for you." Abby hoped she was getting her point across. But maybe she would have to spell it out.

Reno sipped his coffee, his eyes narrowing. "I think the perfect woman is sitting across the table from me right now."

Abby shook her head and started to speak but Reno interrupted her.

"You are perfect for me, Abby. Think about it." He leaned closer and his eyes zeroed in on hers. "You are newly widowed, and I could be there for you. You have a love for this land and animals, which is something we have in common."

He paused, a glint of confidence shining in his dark eyes. "But, the greatest benefit as I see it, is that our land borders one another. We could combine our ranches into one, share the creek and the waterfall and buy even more cattle and horses. We would become the greatest ranchers in the area."

Abby stared at Reno, unable to believe his bold words. Well, on second thought, she could believe it.

She recalled other times in the past — when Tom was still alive — that Reno had asked to buy that portion of her land that had the greatest access to water. That included the plot of her land that held the waterfalls and the largest access to the creek.

She did her best to keep her expression neutral as she responded. "I understand what you're saying, Reno. But, as I've told you before I'm not ready for a serious relationship, not with my husband's passing only a few months ago."

"I understand you're a grieving widow Abby, but I can't help but hope to change your mind, and soon." He seemed very pleased with himself and she suddenly saw him with abrupt clarity.

Reno wasn't going to give up until he married her and had her land as his own. She wasn't fooled. It wasn't her

Reno wanted, it was the land and the water rights he was after.

A loud ring abruptly filled the room, shattering the silence. She was grateful for the interruption. It would give her time to cool down.

He started talking on the phone and stood to his feet before he whispered. "I've got to take this. Be right back."

Abby watched Reno walk into the next room in a deep discussion with whoever was on the other end of the phone line. When he was gone from her sight, she stood up to look for the bathroom.

Walking out of the breakfast nook she found a long hallway that led toward some rooms. She hoped to find it there. As she walked, peered into each room. She passed two bedrooms before she saw a room that looked like an office.

She stood motionless for a moment, but curiosity urged her feet quietly into the room. One glimpse of the maps on the walls and the two computer desks convinced her to look inside the room.

With a quick glance behind her, and seeing no one there, she hurried inside.

Her gaze scanned the room, taking note of what was there.

Filing cabinets were in the corner and the room was large enough to hold two large office desks. Yellow notepads, pens and pencils were placed neatly to the side with pens and pencils stacked in large penholders.

Looking up at the walls, Abby saw a large map with a bunch of red pushpins located on specific sections.

She stepped closer and saw that the map had a zoomed in look of the Refuge Mountain and Clear Springs area.

The map filled up the entire wall and included the ranch land that surrounded both towns.

Curious, Abby leaned closer, noticing that red circles were drawn around specific spots on the map and there were yellow sticky notes with short notes at each location.

Looking closer, she could see Reno had circled his own ranch land in green. As she studied the map, she was surprised to see her land as well as the Callahan ranch land circled in red.

There were other ranches in the area circled as well. One of them looked like Bobby Jackson's ranch where Abby had been going weekly to train horses.

Small yellow sticky notes that had each ranchers name and a number printed on it was attached near to the ranch land they owned.

Puzzled, she continued to look further out and saw a few ranches outside Clear Springs had circles on them as well. One of the largest ranches there was circled in green.

Written on the yellow sticky note attached to the ranch land was the name Copton. The rest of the land surrounding the area was circled in red.

A flicker of apprehension coursed through her.

What was going on? Something bothered her about this map.

Without thinking it over, she quickly reached in her back pocket and grabbed her phone. She took a bunch of pictures of the map with some close ups as well as pictures taken at a distance.

Abby would show these photos to Wyatt and maybe he would have a better idea of what this was all about.

Tucking her phone back into her back pocket, she hurried out of the room and walked back down the hallway.

"Abby?" Reno called and stopped suddenly when he saw her walking toward him.

"Hi. I just needed the bathroom." Her heart thudded loudly in her chest and fear formed a tight knot in her belly. She hoped Reno wouldn't sense the fear that wrapped around her like a cloak.

"Good. Since I'm finished on the phone, can I offer you another coffee?" His voice held a coaxing tone.

She ignored it and responded with a forced calm she wasn't feeling. "You know Reno, I really need to get back home. There is a long list of things I need to get done today. But thanks for the offer."

He nodded and tried again. "Are you sure?"

"Yes, I'm sure. Thanks Reno." Abby began to walk toward the door. Slipping on her light jacket and her cowboy hat and boots, she nodded at Reno. "Thanks again Reno. I'll see you next week at the usual training time."

"Sure." He ripped out the word impatiently.

She could tell he was annoyed with her, but she wasn't going to respond to that.

Abby waved and hurried out of the house and down the trail that took her across the Blackwell ranch land, thankful when she finally reached her land. As she approached she saw a man playing with her dog outside the barn.

Wyatt. What was he doing here?

He stood to his feet when he saw her, a satisfied expression on his face.

"Hey Wyatt. Did you decide to stop by and play with Lassie?" Abby teased, and the corners of her mouth turned up into a grin. She was surprised but glad he was at her ranch. It was strangely comforting that he seemed to always show up just when she needed him the most.

"Just wanted to see you." Wyatt looked past her shoulder, looking towards the Blackwell ranch in the distance. "How did the horse training at Reno's ranch go today?"

She didn't fail to catch the note of hardened steel in his voice. Was he jealous of Reno Blackwell? Abby thought she had made it clear in her words and actions that she had no interest in her neighbor.

Yet, if she was honest with herself, a part of her revelled in Wyatt's open admiration of her.

For a moment, the anxiety she'd been feeling since being at the Blackwell ranch lifted.

She smiled. "Yes. I just finished up and glad to be home."

"Good. I'm glad you're back home too." Wyatt stepped closer to her and touched the long braid that hung over her shoulder.

She caught her breath. He was doing crazy things to her heart again.

Every time she saw Wyatt, she felt his care for her and a little more of her heart opened up to him.

A nervousness skittered over her whole body. And she hurried to change the subject. "I have something I want to show you, Wyatt."

Amusement flickered in the gray eyes that met hers.

"Good. I have something to show you too. But you go first."

Abby reached for the phone tucked in the back pocket of her jeans.

She searched for the photos and then showed them to Wyatt.

"What's this?" Wyatt touched the phone's screen to make each photo larger.

"When I finished training Reno's horse today, he invited me to his home for coffee."

Wyatt creased his brow and nodded his head for her to continue. "Go on."

"Yes, well, we had coffee and then Reno had an unexpected phone call. So I took that opportunity to explore a bit of the house." He tilted his head, gray eyes filled with concern.

"I found a room that seemed to be Reno and Leonard's office." Abby pointed to the photos on her phone. "These maps are what I saw on their office wall."

Wyatt spoke with a bridled anger in his voice. "I wonder why so many ranches in this area circled in red? These include yours, mine and Bobby Jackson's ranch."

"I don't know, but it looks like something shady is going on." Abby replied in a low voice and looked over at him watching his reaction.

"Yeah, it sure does." His jaw locked with a new determination. "I'm not sure why these specific ranchers in Refuge Mountain and Clear Springs have been targeted, but I'll bring this new information to Sheriff Turnbull. It may be a lead that will help to find those behind the cattle rustling in these parts."

Biting her lip, she nodded and looked away. She paused to catch her breath, as anxious thoughts swirled round and round like a hamster wheel without any stopping place.

He handed her the phone and her hands shook as she tucked it into her back pocket. "Look at me." Wyatt put one hand under her chin and lifted it, forcing her to look at him." Don't worry Abby, we'll investigate and figure out what's going on."

She swallowed back fear, nodded and agreed, whispering. "Yes."

His gaze moved from her eyes to her lips. Her heart jolted and her pulse pounded. Leaning forward, his lips almost touched hers, when suddenly she heard a loud thumping noise.

Startled, she stepped back. "I need to check on that." Abby hurried to open up the barn doors.

"Actually, that's what I wanted to talk to you about." Wyatt followed and her pace quickened.

She reached the horses stalls and staring, a soft gasp escaped her. "My horses are back."

Abby turned, her gaze focused intently on him. "You brought my horses back?"

He nodded, staring at her wordlessly.

"But I was already paid for the sale of the horses." A realization dawned on her that Wyatt had bought her horses and then gave them back. Who was this man who would take time out of his own busy schedule to help her with her animals and then later buy them back?

Tears of pleasure found their way to her eyes and

without thinking she walked toward him. "Why would you do that for me?"

"Abby, you should know by now that I'd do anything for you." Wyatt stood there motionless, his gray eyes shadowed under his cowboy hat.

She stepped closer and putting both hands on either side of his face, stood on tiptoe and touched her lips to his and whispered. "Thank you, Wyatt."

Suddenly, he swept her into the cradle of his arms, his warm lips touching hers in a hungry kiss. Abby recognized the perfect harmony between them, how comfortable she felt in his arms — *as though they belonged together.*

He pulled his lips away from hers only for a moment, a surprised look on his face. Only an instant later he reclaimed her lips with unerring ease. A moan of welcome spilled from her throat as she began to tremble. An unfamiliar awakening unfolded slowly within her like the petals of a hothouse flower.

That sensation was followed immediately by confusion and an all too familiar fear. She pulled away from Wyatt and buried her face in his neck. Her arms trembled.

"Do I frighten you, Abby?"

"No, it's not you." Abby looked at him, uncertain of how much to tell him. "It's just that it's been so long since a man has held me close in his arms like this. I tried desperately to convince myself that I didn't want to feel this way ever again, but as you can tell, that hasn't worked too well."

"So, you like it when I kiss you and hold you in my arms?"

Abby bit her lip and nodded.

He pulled her close to him, intent on kissing her again, when the roaring of a car engine rang in her ears.

Heat burned her cheeks and she looked at him with a greater awareness of the depth of her emotions than she ever had before. "I'll go see who that is."

Wyatt nodded, a small smile turned up the corners of his mouth, a look of satisfaction on his face.

Abby swivelled, walking toward the barn doors, her happiness growing as her thoughts remained on Wyatt.

Peering outside, she saw her mother's car parked near the house.

"Hi Mom. I'm over here." She hurried toward her mom, who was walking up the steps to the door of the house. As usual, her mom wore dress pants, with a silk blouse and a matching jacket.

Abby had always felt like she wore old tattered clothes whenever she stood next to her mom. It had always seemed like she didn't quite measure up to her mom's expectations. Hadley had always pleased her mother more than she did.

Her mother turned and frowned. "There you are, Abby. I see you've been working in the barn again." Her mom wrinkled her nose at her.

Abby sighed in exasperation. She wasn't in any mood for her mom's usual criticisms. "Why are you here?"

"Because I..." Her mother stopped as she looked over her shoulder. "What is he doing at your ranch, Abby?"

Abby turned to see Wyatt walking out of the barn. "Wyatt is helping me. The better question is what are you doing here?"

"I came to check on you and to see how you are

doing. I wanted to talk, but it looks like you're busy." Her mom clammed up as soon as Wyatt walked up to them.

Wyatt touched his fingers to his cowboy hat and smiled, nodding at the two of them. "Hello, Mrs. Meadows." Her mother only gave him the smallest hint of a nod and Wyatt turned towards Abby. "I was just leaving. See you later, Abby."

"Thank you, Wyatt for everything. I'll see you later." A hint of a blush stained her cheeks. She looked over at him and smiled.

He grinned and then turned and politely nodded again at her mom. "Mrs. Meadows."

With long strides he crossed the ranch yard quickly, and finding his horse, he was soon galloping in the direction of his ranch.

Her mom huffed and expelled a long sigh. "Well, it certainly looks like you two have been getting fairly cozy."

"We've been renewing our friendship, Mom."

Mom nodded. "Well, from the way he looks at you, I think he believes your relationship to be a lot more than friends. Be careful not to get too close to that man, Abigail. I don't like it."

Abby opened up the door to her house and her mom followed her inside. She turned on the kettle to boil water so she could make her mom tea. Her mom sat at the kitchen table as she waited.

"I know you don't like Wyatt mom, but I believe you're mistaken about him." Abby added the tea bags and poured the hot water into the china cups. "Actually, I think you've been mistaken about him for years."

"What do you mean?" Her mom's brows furrowed together.

"He's a good man. If you knew how much he has helped me in the past six months since he's been home, you would be amazed." Abby set the teacups on the table and sat down.

"I'll admit, I haven't seen that side of him."

Abby's jaw set in determination. "Well, you should look harder, Mom."

There was a silence between them for a moment before Abby spoke again. "The fact is, when Wyatt asked me to marry him years ago, Dad refused him."

"I remember." Her mom sighed heavily. "Why do you bring this up now? That was years ago, it's all water under the bridge."

Abby shook her head silently. "No mom, it's not. Because something has bothered me about what happened seven years ago. And I'm asking for some answers from you."

"Oh." Her mom straightened in her chair as if realizing it was time to get down to the real truth of the matter. "All right."

Abby could tell this conversation might not be pleasant, but she was determined to get the truth out once and for all.

"After Wyatt asked to marry me and Dad refused him, did you and Dad take our family camping, with the intention to take me away from Wyatt?" Abby's eyes focused on her mom.

Her mom's hand shook slightly and a red stain bloomed on her cheeks. "Yes. Your father and I thought it was best at the time. You were so young and we thought it would be a mistake for you to marry Wyatt Callahan."

Abby could hardly believe what she was hearing. Well, she might as well get this over with, as she was certain the next question would have the same answer. "After we got back from camping trip, did you hide letters Wyatt wrote to me?"

Red stained her mother's cheeks and she nodded. "Yes."

Abby couldn't believe it. All these years, she had believed the lie that Wyatt had left without a word. "Wyatt told me he wrote one letter a week for a year before he stopped. And you kept those letters secret all these years. You let me believe that Wyatt had just left without a word. That he suddenly didn't care about me."

Tears shone in her mom's eyes. "I'm sorry Abby. Your father thought you were too young to marry, and he insisted Wyatt Callahan wasn't good enough for you."

"Well, I must not have been too young to marry, since you and Dad were excited for me to marry Tom only a year later."

Her mom had the grace to look sheepish. "You're right. Both of us were not in favor of you marrying Wyatt. But we thought we were protecting you, Abigail."

Abby bit her lip, to hold back tears from streaming down her cheeks.

"I feel so betrayed by you and dad. That's a lot of wasted years, believing a lie and not knowing the real truth." Her voice broke miserably. "Wyatt really did love me." She whispered more to herself than her mother.

For years her life had become a bitter battle. It felt as if her sense of loss was beyond tears. The only things left were the raw sores of an aching heart, still longing for the kind of love she once knew.

Her mom had become silent and remote.

"I think I need some time to think this over on my own, mom." Abby stood to her feet, indicating her need to be alone.

Her mom's face was pale and tears hung on her lashes. "I'm so sorry, Abby. Maybe, keeping Wyatt from you wasn't the right thing to do. I'm sorry if we made a mistake all those years ago."

"I know, Mom. I appreciate you saying that." Abby led her mom to the door.

Her mom turned, "Will I still see you at Refuge Mountain's annual Christmas Banquet on Saturday?"

Abby knew these community events had always been important to her mom and she would come, but she would have Wyatt by her side.

"Yes, I'll be coming with Wyatt."

Her mom pinched her lips tightly together and nodded. "I'll see you later, then." She gave her a wobbly smile before walking to her car.

Abby's stomach grew sour from everything she'd learned today.

All these years she had believed Wyatt had been uncaring and selfish and that he'd left her without a word. When really it had been her parents who had planned and schemed behind her back.

At some point, when her anger simmered down, she would need to forgive her mom.

And she especially needed to apologize to Wyatt for how she'd been so wrong about him for all these years.

# CHAPTER ELEVEN

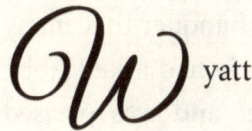yatt

WYATT POURED himself a cup of coffee, while peering out at the streaks of orange-red of morning sun surfacing along the distant horizon.

His thoughts all night — and if he were honest, for the past week — were focused on the beautiful red haired girl-next-door.

Wyatt even had a dream last night that they married.

Sipping his coffee, he realized that his dream might have been the reason he woke up so early this morning. He had decided to take his Mom's advice.

He was going to push back his fears to risk loving the one woman who meant the world to him.

Last week, when Abby had kissed him in the barn, was the first time he'd truly felt her heart opening up to him.

He couldn't really explain it, but he had sensed a new vulnerability to receive love.

He knew that was a big step for her.

Abby had been hurt in the past, and he prayed she would find it in her heart to forgive him for leaving seven years ago.

There was also a sense he had that not everything had been perfect in her marriage to Tom Hart.

It wasn't any of his business, but he hoped someday Abby would trust him enough to share more personal details of her life. He would need to do the same, which didn't come easy for him.

Tonight was the annual Christmas Banquet that many folks from their small town attended. He had asked Abby a few weeks ago if he could take her and was pleased when she said yes.

Eager for the day to begin, he gulped down the last of his coffee.

He had just stood to his feet, when Dakota hurried into the room. His brother's brows creased together and his jaw was set in determination. "You're not going to believe this."

"What?" Chilling tingles travelled up Wyatt's arm as a sense of foreboding rushed through him.

"Three of our hired hands are gone." Dakota announced. "I have to admit I didn't see this coming."

"Who is missing?" Wyatt grabbed his jacket and hurried outside with Dakota.

"Slim, Carlson and Lennie." Dakota pointed to the cabin where they had bunked together. They went inside and saw that all the clothes and all extras were gone.

As they walked outside, Wyatt rubbed a hand through his hair as he considered this new problem.

"Let's go talk to a few of our other hired hands and ask if they know anything." Wyatt hurried toward one of the other bunkhouses and knocked briskly on the door.

A dark head popped out. "Yeah. What's up?"

"Dal, we've got a problem. Looks like Carlson, Slim and Lennie are missing. Do you know where they might have gone?" Wyatt looked at the man who must have just crawled out of bed.

"Never heard anything about that, boss. Although they did say you had asked them to take over the night shift to watch for cattle rustlers last night."

Wyatt turned to Dakota, his eyes wide with surprise, before he turned back to Dal. "Let me get this straight. Carlson said that I had asked the three of them to take over the night shift?"

"Yep. That's what he said. It's why you found me here so early in the morning." Dal tucked his shirt into his pants. "But, I wouldn't have any idea where they went to, unless it's to Benny's bar where Slim likes to go. I don't know much else about those three."

Wyatt nodded. "Okay. Thanks Dal."

They started to cut across the yard, contemplating their next move.

Dakota piped up. "We need to check the cattle count in all the pastures again."

Wyatt nodded and spoke on his two-way radio. He grinned at Dakota. "Everyone is up now."

Not a minute later, his five brothers stumbled out of the ranch house.

"Why are we up so early?" Cole rubbed sleep out of his eyes, staring at Wyatt and Dakota.

"Here's what's happened." Wyatt explained that their three hired hands were missing. "So, I believe we'll find missing cattle as a result of those three hired hands leaving. So we'd like you all to go to each of our pastures and do a cattle count. We'll meet back here."

By noon, all seven brothers met back at the barn.

After checking with each brother, it turned out that only the northwest pasture had missing cattle.

Dakota had counted that corner of the ranch. "I counted a hundred head of cattle missing. And I noticed the tire tracks took a different direction than last time."

Wyatt expelled a breath and spoke with a new resolve. "I'll call Sheriff Turnbull and ask him to come take a look. We need to get this settled once and for all."

"We will, big brother. No worries." Denver clasped Wyatt on the shoulder before turning and heading back to the house with his other brothers.

The afternoon flew by quickly and all too soon it was time to leave for the Christmas Banquet.

He straightened his red tie, combed through his wavy hair one last time and hurried out the door. Arriving at Abby's ranch, his heart pounded like a beating drum as he walked up to her door.

Abby opened the door and walked outside looking dazzling in a tea length jade green dress. Her dark auburn hair hung loosely around her shoulders and only enhanced her beautiful wide green eyes.

"You're stunning." Wyatt couldn't take his eyes off her. This woman made him breathless and eager as a man falling in love for the first time. Her cheeks blossomed pink at his compliment.

"Thank you, Wyatt. You look quite handsome yourself." Abby's teasing smile made his insides jangle with anticipation for a wonderful evening together.

Wyatt leaned down and kissed her cheek gently. "I picked up these wrist flowers for you."

He gently slid the band of flowers onto her wrist.

Abby fingered the flowers. "Oh Wyatt. These red roses with the green leaves and dainty white baby's breath around them are beautiful. And they match the Christmas colors tonight." She looked up at him and sighed. "Thank you."

Wyatt grinned as he opened the truck door and helped her inside. Soon they were driving toward their small town.

Looking over at Abby, he couldn't believe how lucky he was to have this beautiful woman by his side.

She turned to look over at him and asked. "How have you been? It's been a few days since we last saw each other."

Memories of their kiss flooded his senses as he glanced over at her. "I've been good, waiting to see you again."

Abby smiled. "And how's the ranch?"

He expelled a breath. "Not so good. Just found out this morning that three of our ranch hands went missing along with a hundred head of our cattle."

"Oh no." Abby gasped.

"I've already called the Sheriff and he and his men are looking into it. We should hear something in the next few days, I imagine." Wyatt clenched his jaw. "I'm determined to get to the bottom of this cattle rustling. This has got to stop."

Abby nodded. "It does. Hmm, I'm curious what the Sheriff will discover when he looks deeper into the problem."

"Yeah. I'm sure we'll be surprised when all the thugs are finally rounded up." Wyatt smiled as he parked his truck in the parking lot of the Community building where the large Christmas Banquet was being held.

He walked around to the passenger side and opened up her door. He held out his arm and she slipped her hand in the crook of his elbow.

Leaning down, he whispered. "But let's think about better things than capturing cattle thieves. Looking at your captivating face tonight, I can think of much better thoughts to focus on."

Her green eyes danced at his compliment.

Drawing her hand closer to his side, Wyatt put his hand over hers protectively.

A warm glow flooded him, thrilled to have Abby at his side this evening.

&.

HER HEART DANCED with a strange excitement to be at Wyatt's side tonight.

As they entered the double doors of the Community Center the Christmas decorations and bright lights, were made all the brighter from the glow of happiness she felt inside.

The place was filled almost to capacity with folks from their small town.

Father Tim and Reverend Jon stood together with the Peabody twins over by the Christmas tree.

Abby assumed they were in another one of their debates over the merits of too many Christmas decorations.

She remembered that Gertrude and Gretchen Peabody had always been very frugal with their money and even in their own business, they only put one wreath on their door each year — the same one they used every year for the Christmas season.

She smiled to herself at the differences found in the folks across their small community. Yet, at the same time, their differences were what made their small town interesting and unique.

Abby glanced at the long table filled with different drinks.

"Can I bring you a cup of hot apple cider?" Wyatt asked thoughtfully.

"Yes, please. You always seem to remember what I like. Thanks Wyatt." Her face creased into a sudden smile at his thoughtfulness. Looking around the room, her gaze landed on her Mom and Hadley.

They walked toward her, giving Abby a quick hug.

Her sister spoke first. "So, you came with Wyatt. I remember you showed up at the Fall Festival with him. At that time, you said you were only friends. Tonight you're with him again. Does that mean the two of you are an item?"

Abby clamped her jaw tight and stared at Hadley for a

moment, telling herself not to get angry with her. "Yes I came with Wyatt tonight. And no we're not an item as you put it. We simply appreciate each other's friendship."

Hadley hissed. "Maybe on your part it's friendship. For him — with the way he looks at you — it looks like he wants a whole lot more."

Abby sighed and didn't bother responding to her sister's comment. Maybe things were getting a little more serious between her and Wyatt, but she certainly wasn't about to let her sister know that.

All she knew was that the walls around her heart had begun to collapse and in its place was a new awareness of him. A tangible bond had begun to develop between them that surprised her.

However, she wasn't about to let Hadley or her Mom know what was happening in her heart. They hadn't treated her feelings carefully in the past and until she saw a change in them, she wasn't going to risk revealing too much of herself to them.

Her mom stepped toward her and grabbed her hands lightly.

"Abby, I'm glad you've come tonight." Her mom smiled tentatively as if remembering their last conversation.

"Thanks, Mom. I'm glad to be here too. You are looking very festive." Abby's gaze took in the green skirt and matching blazer that was accented by a crimson colored blouse.

"Thank you. You know how much I adore dressing up for the Holidays. It makes me happy." For the first time since her dad passed away, her mom had a warm glow about her.

"I'm glad." Even though she was still irritated at her mom for hiding Wyatt's letters years ago, in her heart she still wanted her mom to be happy. "I don't see James and Martha Hart here tonight. For years, they've been one of the first couples to arrive."

Her mom put a hand on her heart and mouth dropped open. "You didn't hear the news?"

Warning spasms of alarm erupted within her. "No. Did something happen?"

"Oh my dear." Her mom's hand was still on her heart and she lowered her voice. "James Hart had a heart attack late last night and passed away just this morning."

Her mouth dropped open in surprise. "Oh my goodness. I didn't know. I'll need to stop by and pay my respects to Mrs. Hart and Will."

Early last week, she had dropped by her mother-in-law's home to give her the money she owed them. Martha Hart had given her no indication that her husband was feeling poorly. She rubbed her arm as a chill passed over her skin.

"Yes. Do that. She will appreciate the visit." Her mom and sister soon turned to talk to someone else.

Abby was still pondering the sad news, when Joey and Tony hurried up to her. Mrs. Beaseley eyed them from a distance. The boys hugged Abby and she grinned.

"Hey Joey and Tony." Both boys were all dressed up with dress pants and white shirts with a red bow tie. "You two look great."

Joey sighed in frustration. "I don't like to dress up like this. But, we are singing with the children's choir tonight so we had to."

Abby smiled at the disappointment in his voice. "Well I think you both look great and I'm looking forward to hearing you sing."

"We have a secret surprise after we're done singing." Tony spoke up shyly.

Abby's eyes widened. "Oh, how exciting. I really look forward to seeing it." She said as she gave them both a gentle smile.

Tony grinned widely and Joey grabbed his little brother's hand. "Come on Tony, it's time for us to get back."

Mrs. Lynda Goode stood up and spoke into the microphone. Lynda Goode was a widow in her mid-twenties who owned the yarn store on Main street which she had cleverly called *A Goode Yarn.*

Since her husband died three years ago, she had put her heart and soul into her business and had weekly events for ladies so they would feel included.

Already, she'd had a great deal of impact on making their small town a friendly and warm hearted place many folks wanted to come to.

"Hello everyone and Merry Christmas. If you will all find your seats, we will begin to get everyone sorted and started on lining up for food. Later on we'll have a short Christmas program by the children."

Wyatt walked to her side carrying the hot apple cider drinks. "Let's go find somewhere to sit."

"Why don't we sit at the table with your mom and brothers?" Abby suggested. Wyatt nodded and pulled out her chair so she was seated beside Annie Callahan.

"Hello, Abby. How nice that you are joining us."

Wyatt's mom reached over and squeezed her hand. "How have things been going with you and your ranch?"

"Keeping busy and staying out of trouble, I guess. I've been having fun training four of your horses." Abby realized she tended to babble when nervous. Being near Wyatt's mom had always had that effect on her for some reason.

"Yes, and Wyatt has told me what a great job you're doing." Annie's smile was sincere. "You've always had a real understanding of those great big creatures, Abby. I admire you, I really do. Horses have always been one of the animals I've struggled to get along with."

Abby chuckled. "I'm surprised. You've been ranching for years and have been around horses probably most of your life."

"It's true, but give me a chicken or a dog to take care of any day of the week, rather than a horse." She leaned over and whispered. "To tell you the truth, they still make me a little nervous."

Abby pondered that for a moment. "Well, Mrs. Callahan, if the day comes when you would like someone to go riding with you or just to help you understand your horse better, I would love to do that with you."

"Oh Abby, you are a sweetie. You know what? I think I'll take you up on that." Mrs. Callahan squeezed her hand once more before turning to talk to everyone around the table.

Wyatt looked at Abby, a light shining in his eyes. "I don't know how you do it, but you always seem to make my mom happier just by being beside her. My two best girls, side by side. I could get used to that."

Heat rose from her neck to her cheeks and felt a warm glow flow through her. His suggestion that he could get used to that sent warm tingles in her belly. What would it be like to be by Wyatt's side and in his life everyday?

It was the first time she'd seriously thought about that, since their engagement had ended suddenly seven years ago. She was surprised that the usual fears didn't accompany that thought.

Throughout their meal, Abby enjoyed a little happy banter with Wyatt's brothers — only three of whom had come to the Christmas Banquet. And all too soon it was time for the children to sing.

Seeing Joey and Tony with a dozen children singing her favorite Christmas carols, caused her own heart to sing with delight. They ended their selection of songs with a new song about miracles and love at Christmas.

Joey and Tony as well as a few other children rang silver bells during different parts of the song.

As soon as they were finished, the choir leader announced that the children had special gifts they wanted to give people. Joey and Tony walked up to Wyatt and Abby, each carrying a silver bell with a red bow on it.

"This is for you both. Thank you for being so nice to my brother and me. Merry Christmas." Joey hugged Wyatt and Abby and Tony followed his lead.

Tears pricked the back of Abby's eyelids. "Thank you, boys for the wonderful Christmas gift. I will treasure the gift and the memory of you two, always." The boys grinned at them both before hurrying back to their seats.

She looked at her bell, which was engraved with the

word *miracles*. Glancing over at Wyatt's bell, she saw his engraved with the word *love*.

"Those two boys are pretty special." Abby turned to Wyatt her eyes shining with unshed tears.

Wyatt nodded. "Yeah. I hope some nice couple comes along and adopts them soon, so they don't have to be shifted from one foster home to another." Wyatt studied the boys as if in deep thought.

Abby wondered at his statement. She knew Wyatt had been adopted, but didn't know much else about his childhood. Maybe he'd experienced a similar home situation to what Joey and Tony had. She would need to ask him about that sometime soon.

Before long, the evening was over.

Abby stood to her feet. They said their goodbyes to Mrs. Callahan and Wyatt's brothers. Wyatt was waylaid by another rancher who wanted to talk to him. Abby picked up her purse and was turning, when her sister Hadley walked up to her.

"You won't believe who I just talked with." She began and pointed over to the Christmas tree. "Look over that way. Do you see that man standing near Mrs. Goode?"

Abby nodded, unsure of where this conversation was going.

"Well, I was just talking with him and learned that he's a soldier, just returned home. Guess whose unit he was a part of?" Hadley questioned and Abby shrugged her shoulders.

"Wyatt Callahan's special ops unit."

Abby nodded slowly, but wasn't surprised. She knew Wyatt had been in charge of a bunch of people in the military. It probably explained why he was a good leader of people.

"So?"

"Well, Sergeant Drew Standish was in Wyatt Callahan's military unit, along with your husband Tom." Hadley paused before continuing. "Sergeant Standish said that it was Wyatt who was in charge of their special unit of five soldiers. It was Wyatt's fault that your husband Tom is dead."

Abby stood motionless, stunned at what she was hearing.

It was Wyatt's fault her husband Tom died in that mission?

The pain in her heart became like a sick and fiery gnawing. Icy fingers began to seep into every pore of her skin.

Why hadn't Wyatt hadn't said a word?

Her throat was raw with unuttered shouts and protests as anger built inside of her.

She needed to talk to him.

"Excuse me, Hadley. I need to go." With a curt nod to her sister, Abby found Wyatt waiting for her near the door.

"Read to go home?"

"Yes." Abby walked straight ahead and was silent for the ride home.

It wasn't until Wyatt drove onto her ranch, that he asked. "What happened Abby? Is everything all right?"

"No everything is not all right." Abby admitted, her voice rasped out. "I just found out that you were the

Captain in charge of the Special ops unit. One of your the soldiers on your team was my husband Tom."

"Yes. But…" Wyatt began to explain but Abby cut him off.

"You were in charge. You didn't save him. It's your fault, that my husband died." A new anguish seared her heart and the words erupted from her voice in a half-choked, desperate cry.

"Let me explain…"

"No Wyatt. There is no explanation for this. This is too big for even you to fix, no matter how sorry you are." Her misery was so acute that it was a physical pain.

She slammed the truck door and hurried into her house.

Leaning her head against the back door, sobs burst out of her like a dam that had been held back way too long. Her legs weakened and she slumped to the floor cradling her legs in a flood of tears.

She cried for the loss of her husband. She cried for the loss of her friend Wyatt. She cried for the loss of love that would never return to her again.

Now, she would need to let go of Wyatt. They could never be anything ever again.

She didn't know how her heart was going to handle so big a loss.

# CHAPTER TWELVE

bby

Abby had only been asleep for a short while when she was startled by a deafening blast coming from the yard.

Sitting up quickly, she hurried to her bedroom window and looked outside.

The sky was beginning to darken. She looked at her night clock and realized she had slept for an hour.

She remembered coming home from the Christmas Banquet while it was still early evening.

Memories of her evening and what she'd learned about Wyatt's involvement in her husband's death had stunned her. But she wasn't going to think about that right now.

First, she needed to figure out what was happening on her ranch.

She shivered, wondering if some neighbors were hunting nearby. It almost sounded like a gunshot.

Without warning, another sudden boom exploded in the air.

Abby scrambled to pull on her jeans and slipped her warm hoodie over her head.

Slipping on her boots, she grabbed her dad's old rifle by the door and hurried out of house and across the yard.

At the distinct sound of a horse galloping, she turned and in the distance she saw a man riding away. She couldn't see what the man looked like. She could barely make out the ball cap he wore on his head.

What was he doing on her ranch land?

Clenching her teeth in anger, she ran to the barn. Hurrying through the barn, she was relieved to see nothing had been disturbed.

Opening the sliding barn door that led to the pasture she looked for her horses. She had placed Stocking and Blackie in the pasture before she left for the Christmas Banquet as the weather had been warm.

Peering outside, she looked in the direction of the pasture and stopped, her eyes growing big and round.

Shock flew through her as she stared at the dreadful sight. Her horse Stocking lay there on the cold ground, unmoving.

Abby dropped the rifle in her hand and rushed over to her. Kneeling by her mare's head, she saw blood pooling on the ground. Once more she looked at her horse's eyes, which were wide and staring, vacant and lifeless.

Her breath caught in her lungs.

For a moment she was too stunned to move and too stunned to cry.

Desperate, she reached trembling hands along her mare's neck, stomach and chest, searching to find the wound. Finally, she found two bullet holes, both near her horse's heart.

She could feel blood drain away from her face as the reality of what happened set in.

Her favorite horse was dead.

Stocking, her one faithful companion since she was a teenager, was gone.

To make matters worse, her mare didn't die of natural causes.

Someone, the man who galloped away on his horse, had deliberately shot and killed her horse.

Clenching her teeth, a sudden anger coursed through her veins. Who was this man? Who would do such a horrible thing? Who would boldly come onto her property and cruelly kill her horse?

Standing on shaky legs she swallowed, blinking back tears. She couldn't give in to tears now that would have to wait. There was something she needed to do first.

Pulling out her phone, Abby searched her contacts and dialled the Sheriff's number.

She wasn't sure exactly who to call, since her horse was already dead. But she assumed calling the sheriff's office was a step in the right direction.

Determination welled up inside of her to see the thug who was responsible for this crime, be caught and put in jail.

With a rush of words, she explained to Deputy Sheriff Jason Hardy what happened.

"I'm sorry about what happened to your horse, Mrs. Hart. We'll be out to your ranch as soon as we can. Sheriff Turnbull is on another case at the moment, but hang on because we're on our way." Deputy Hardy's resolved tone was oddly comforting.

"Thanks." The phone shook in her hand and she disconnected the call.

Turning her head, Abby stared at her horse, swallowing the despair in her throat. Her misery was so acute that it was like a physical pain. *I can't do this right now. I can't stay here. Right now, I need to get as far away as I can from this horrible sight.*

She remembered the cave up the mountain near the waterfall. It was the same place she'd ran to as a little girl the day that her father came home drunk.

Abby had tried to stand up to him so he wouldn't hurt her mom, but received bruises on her face and arms for trying. Hurting all over, she had run as fast as her feet could carry her to the place she felt safe from the world.

This was the place she needed now more than ever.

Without thinking, Abby began to run towards the mountain that stood tall and majestic at the end of the pasture on her ranch. The simple act of running, helped clear her mind.

By the time she reached the waterfall, she was panting and out of breath. She walked down the well worn path that led to an outcropping that overlooked the waterfall.

A cool mist from the waterfall touched her skin and she shivered.

Finally she reached the large rock that had become like a familiar friend.

Memories came back to her of sitting in this very spot. When she'd been hurt by her father, Wyatt had found her sitting here sobbing. Even back then, he had held her close and let her cry on his shoulder.

He had been the one to reassure her that she would be all right.

Now here she was once again, her emotions in chaos from so much pain and loss.

A raw and primitive grief overwhelmed her as she thought about all that had happened this past year.

First was her husband Tom's sudden death six months ago, followed by a realization that she was going to lose her ranch by the end of the year if she didn't pay off the mortgage.

Now, someone had finished off her horse — the one horse that she loved for so long.

Pulling her knees to her chest, she closed her eyes as tears slipped down her cheeks. Her heart ached with pain for all she had lost.

With her head bowed and her body slumped in despair, she sobbed.

Letting go of tightly held emotions she softly wept, rocking back and forth.

She was so wrapped up in her own emotions, the world faded into the background.

When there was a scraping sound beside her, she hardly noticed. It was only when a tall form stretched his long legs beside her that she jerked in surprise.

"What are you doing here?" Terse words rolled off her

tongue at the shock of seeing Wyatt beside her. She hurried to wipe away the tears with the sleeves of her hoodie before looking at him again.

"Your mom came to find me."

"My mom?"

Wyatt explained, his voice stoic and calm. "Yes, apparently your mom stopped by your ranch and found you gone. She was worried, so she stopped by the Triple C to find me. She asked if I'd search for you."

"How did you know where to find me?"

An intense but secret expression was in the upturn of his lips. "Because, my dear Abby, where else would you go when something hurtful happens in your life?" His smile was gentle as he turned to look at her. "Ever since I found you here the first time all those years ago, this has become one of my favorite places."

Abby was glad that the sun was beginning to set and hoped it hid the flush on her cheeks. Wyatt had a way of breaking down her walls. But this time, they weren't going to come down so easily.

"I do come here often. And yes, it's usually when I'm in pain." She looked at him pointedly.

The words erupted from her lips, clipped and cold. She was desperate to keep the walls up around her heart. In an attempt to veer him off the subject that most tormented her thoughts, she blurted out what happened.

"Someone shot my horse Stocking tonight." At Wyatt's look of shocked surprise, she quickly said. "I already called the Sheriff's office and talked with the Deputy Sheriff. They told me they would be over to the ranch soon."

"I can't believe someone would do anything that terrible. I'm glad you called the Sheriff. He will find whoever is responsible for this." His voice was firm and determined. The way he quickly came to her defense shouldn't have surprised her.

She nodded, finding comfort in that fact. "I couldn't stay. I needed to get away for awhile to think."

"I understand." He peered over at her. "For what it's worth, I'm real sorry. Stocking was a great horse."

Trying to hide her inner misery from his probing stare, Abby looked down at her hands tucking them into the arm sleeves of her hoodie. "I'll definitely miss my mare." She swallowed. "It's not easy to lose something or someone that means a lot to you."

Her words held a depth of meaning and she could see by the distress on Wyatt's face that he understood what she was getting at.

"No it's not." He admitted softly. A pained look began to spread over his face, matching her own. His gray eyes seemed tormented.

At his expression, an unexpected compassion tore at her soul and for the first time she questioned what actually happened on that military mission.

Wyatt leaned closer and whispered. "I'm sorry Abby. I should have told you sooner that Tom was in my Unit."

"Yes, you should have." She released a shuddering sigh.

Wyatt turned to look at her, his gray eyes filled with sadness. "But I am truly sorry that your husband died."

His voice shook with emotion and his face went pale as if reliving the event. He covered his shaking hand with the other one.

"I believe you." Turning to him, she asked quietly. "What really happened that day, Wyatt?"

Wyatt creased his brows together in misery, pausing before he spoke. "I'll start at the beginning. It was right after I finished Veterinary College that I went to Boot Camp."

He turned to her with an intensity that surprised her. "With your upcoming marriage to Tom Hart, I didn't want to stick around home."

The pained expression on his face caught her off guard. Had he loved her more than she realized?

He swallowed quickly before continuing. "As I finished my training, a spot opened up in a Special Ops unit and we were sent to Afghanistan. The higher ups in the chain of command told us our mission was to uncover a big terrorist cell there."

Wyatt expelled a breath. "It was found out later through different sources, that this terrorist cell was controlling at least a dozen cells on American soil, and they were getting ready to trigger a big planned attack."

Wyatt continued. "According to command, it was critical to take out this terrorist group to accomplish the mission. And we did, but the victory was hard won."

She saw him shudder and he drew in a sharp breath. "We found the terrorist cell. They were hiding in a cave compound and we demolished it from the ground. It was when my team and I were on our way back to the checkpoint, that another terrorist cell group surrounded us. They took my team to a secret location and tortured us."

He set his jaw in determination as he recalled what happened.

"I'm so sorry that happened to you and Tom and the rest of your unit, Wyatt." Abby closed her eyes feeling utterly miserable now that she learned all that he'd gone through. "It's a miracle any of you survived."

A vein throbbed in Wyatt's neck and he nodded, his expression one of rigid control with no room for surrender. "It is. It took a few weeks, but one day we escaped. That day had started out as another day of torture, until the guard who had been set to watch us, left suddenly."

"I remember the guards were careful not to let us know where they held us — part of their strategy was to make us feel completely isolated and hopeless, like we were never going to escape. Their goal was to break us. Their goal was to get information by whatever means necessary. But when you're trained as a Special Ops soldier, it's near to impossible to break us. We were trained not to break."

Abby listened, her thoughts going crazy, imagining the horror Wyatt, Tom and his men had been through.

"When the guard left that day, I knew it was our chance — perhaps our only chance — to escape. We reached the end of the tunnel in the cave. By this time, we each had a gun. At the end of that tunnel, was an open desert and to the right was a village."

His voice shook as he continued and a tear slipped down his cheek. "As the five of us ran, we skirted around some buildings, doing our best to stay hidden, but shots were fired at us. We returned fire and killed the men shooting at us until no one was shooting at us any longer."

Wyatt ran a shaky hand through his hair and paused a moment before continuing. "We were about to leave when

I noticed Tom had been wounded. He was bleeding from his stomach and I knew he wouldn't make it much longer."

"He wanted us to keep going, but I said *only if you come with us*. The four of us carried him until we found a thick bush of trees near the mountains.

We stopped and lay Tom down on the ground, covering his shivering body with the tarp we grabbed when we picked up the guns. Tom was shivering so badly by this time, his body going into shock. I kept reassuring him that he'd be okay. Only a few minutes passed before he spoke."

"At that point I think he realized he wasn't going to make it because he whispered to me. 'Tell Abby I'm sorry for all my mistakes. Tell her I loved her the best I knew how.' He took a breath and whispered one last time: 'Promise me you'll take care of Abby, Wyatt.' I promised him I would. Tom died only a few minutes later. We buried him right there beside those trees." Wyatt's cheeks were wet with tears as he turned his gaze toward her.

His eyes were haunted and filled with pain. Abby couldn't imagine the pain the both Tom and Wyatt went through.

Soft tears rolled down her cheeks and she gulped, her voice tortured. "Thank you for telling me, Wyatt. It means a lot to know you were with Tom at the end."

He nodded quietly and wiped away tears and looking toward the waterfall.

Thoughts swirled round and round in her mind of what Wyatt had revealed about Tom's death.

She pulled her knees to her chest, biting her lip to

control the sobs that wanted to escape. She missed her husband, but if she were honest with herself, she also felt guilt for those last few weeks together and how they'd argued before Tom left for the military. Yet, her husband's last words to her were comforting and she was grateful Wyatt had been there for him.

"I'm sorry Wyatt. I shouldn't have lashed out at you like I did. Tom's death wasn't your fault." Abby closed her eyes for a moment, her heart aching in pain and regret.

"It's okay, Abby, I understand I really do. The truth is, it should have been me that died that day, not him." Wyatt's voice was shaky and raw. She reached for his hand and squeezed it as she peered into his tormented eyes.

A stab of guilt lay buried in her breast. She thought of Wyatt and how she had blamed him so harshly for Tom's death.

The fact was, he had been doing the best job he could for all his men and tried to get them to safety. And right now, he was condemning himself for being the one that survived. She couldn't stay silent and let him believe that lie.

"I don't pretend to understand why some people die and some people live." Abby hesitated for a moment before speaking again. "But, I do believe your life was preserved for a reason, Wyatt."

"Maybe." Releasing a heavy sigh, he rubbed a shaky hand through his hair. "When I think of my life, I'll always wonder, was it worth it that I lived while others died?"

Abby turned to face Wyatt and saw that his face was bleak with sorrow. The effect on her was shattering and her heart opened up a little further to him.

"I believe you are here for a reason Wyatt, never doubt that. You're alive today, because there are things still left for you to do on this earth." Abby was surprised at how strongly she believed that. "It's up to you to figure out what that is."

He sat motionless for a moment, his gaze traveled over her face and searched her eyes. "Maybe I already have a good idea about one of the reasons I'm still here." His nearness was making her senses spin. It was too easy to get lost in the way he looked at her.

Wyatt lifted a hand to touch her hair, lifting his other hand to caress her cheek. He leaned closer, his eyes moving downward to focus on her lips. He was so attractive and compelling to her, but she had to resist.

There were too many emotions raging through her and she felt confused. Proof of her turmoil on the inside was in the fact that she too readily believed how her sister skewed the truth about Wyatt being at fault for Tom's death.

Now, that she heard Wyatt's story, she believed he was telling the truth of what happened. But, somewhere deep inside, Abby struggled to let go of all the hurt and pain that Wyatt had caused when he walked away from her years ago.

The truth was, right now she was struggling to free herself from those negative emotions and truly forgive him.

She pulled away from him, fighting back tears.

He removed his hands from her cheek and let her go.

"I'm sorry, Wyatt. I can't do this. I'm so confused and feel like I need some space to think. Right now, I need a break from whatever this is between us." She felt as hollow as her voice sounded. His gray eyes studied her intently, pain flickering in their depths.

Regret clung to her like an unwanted blemish. The silence between them, unbearable.

"I understand." He nodded after a long hesitation.

Abby stood to her feet, desperate for some space between them. She had to go. "The sun is setting, I should probably be getting back to the ranch."

Wyatt stood as well. "Let me go with you. It doesn't seem safe right now, and I want to see to it that you get home safely."

"I'm sure I'll be fine Wyatt. I know this mountain like the back of my hand. Besides, I'm sure your family is expecting you back home." She had walked a little ahead, her voice thick from the raw sores of an aching heart.

"Abby, I'm not leaving you alone. I will see you home. I know you don't like me much right now and probably want me to leave. But, that doesn't change the fact that I will do the right thing and see you home safely." Wyatt caught up to her and she looked at the fierceness in his gray eyes and the set of his jaw.

"All right then. Thanks." Abby nodded. She was annoyed that there was a part of her that was relieved by his protectiveness. She walked faster, hoping it wouldn't take them long to reach the bottom of the mountain.

If she didn't hurry, Abby was afraid she would turn and tell Wyatt she changed her mind. She would tell him that she didn't want a break between them and needed his love more than ever.

She marched ahead, fighting her own battle of personal restraint.

A terrible loss filled her aching heart and she was fairly certain she might have just made the biggest mistake of her life.

# CHAPTER THIRTEEN

yatt

WYATT FOLLOWED Abby down the mountain, his heart aching.

His spirits sank lower as stinging regrets battered his thoughts. Abby's request that they take a break in their relationship was no less than he deserved.

Tugging on the reins of his gelding, he walked alongside his horse keeping an eye on the beautiful woman in front of him.

His throat ached with defeat.

As his gaze followed her slim form hurrying down the mountain, his arms ached to hold her close one last time.

That wasn't going to happen any time soon. Maybe it wouldn't happen ever again.

Remembering their conversation, he recalled with clarity the resolve and determination in her voice.

Was Abby holding back from him because he had led the team of soldiers, which ultimately led to the loss of her husband's life? He clearly remembered her saying she was sorry that she'd blamed him.

Then what was the impenetrable wall that stood between them? Did she deny him, because of something else from his past?

Maybe he was too broken inside to have a deep and lasting relationship with a woman. Maybe those childhood years of being forced to hide his real feelings had well and truly encased his heart in a crypt of stone.

Maybe Abby saw through his outer shell to the defective and weak small boy on the inside and was trying to let him down as gently as she could.

Watching her, he didn't know what to do, except continue to be committed to protect her and to be her friend. He needed to do that.

Perhaps, he would earn her trust in time.

Wyatt was convinced he'd be waiting a long time because it didn't look like that sort of trust would be earned anytime soon.

Abby suddenly stopped in front of him. He walked behind her and she held a finger to her lips, the universal sign to be silent.

"Do you hear the sound of cattle nearby?" Abby whispered as she looked through the crisscrossing light of the fading sun into the tree line beyond.

Wyatt listened closely and sure enough, he heard low

moos and the occasional huffing and scratching noise that he heard everyday from his cattle.

"I do. That's strange. Isn't this still your land on this part of the mountain?"

Abby nodded. "It is. I don't understand what's going on."

Wyatt released his horse's reins, letting them hang down to the ground. His gelding had been trained to stand in one area when the reins were grounded.

"Let's go take a look around." Quietly Wyatt grabbed her hand and they moved forward, stepping carefully in between the thick trees. They continued walking until they came to an area that dipped downward into a large flat area.

Peering behind some trees, they saw a large herd of cattle in the small outcropping below. He could see two large cowsheds that had been built next to large trees, with a small section of each building reserved for hay. Around the perimeter was a makeshift fence to keep the cows from wandering off.

Abby gasped and her body stiffened in shock at the sight.

"What are all these cattle doing here on my land? Where did they come from?" She whispered, an edge to her voice.

As he stared wordlessly at the herd of Black Angus cattle, questions flooded his mind that echoed hers.

"Maybe we should get closer and check it out. Whoever is responsible for bringing these cattle here, is trespassing on your land after all." Wyatt turned toward Abby, his gaze searching hers.

A hint of fear lingered in the large green eyes that met his.

She set her jawline in determination and nodded. "Yes, let's go see what we can find out."

With a quick nod, he grabbed her hand and they ran behind one of the sheds. He couldn't see anyone around, but Wyatt was sure someone came here daily to feed the cattle and to keep watch on their investment.

"All right, here's our chance. I see a few cattle nearby. Let's go check them out. Maybe we can see if they've been branded." Wyatt whispered in a low voice, keeping an eye on the perimeter of the area.

"I'm ready."

They walked toward the cattle, doing their best to keep their pace slow so the cattle wouldn't be scared and run away.

Wyatt reached the first cow that stood at the hay feeder. He ran a hand across the thick black cow hide checking for branding marks.

He quickly noticed the ear tags had been removed. Moving his hand across the shoulders, he felt a bump in the thick skin.

Looking closely, he lifted his brows in surprise as he saw the brand. It was labelled with the Triple C brand.

A steely quality could be heard in his voice as he whispered to Abby. "These are Callahan cattle. Someone has stolen our cattle and placed them on your land."

Abby stared wordlessly shaking her head, giving him a sidelong glance of utter disbelief. "That's crazy. I'd like to give whoever did this a piece of my mind."

A slow smile spread his mouth wide at hearing Abby get riled up. It was good to hear her spunky side again.

Wyatt stepped toward the next cow and again found the Triple C brand. He was about to turn to Abby when a shotgun blast filled the air.

"Get down, Abby." Wyatt grabbed her hand and pulled her towards him protectively. "We've got to get out of here."

Ducking their heads, they ran behind the cow shed they'd just come from.

"What do you two think you're doing here? Stay away from my cattle!" A man yelled at them, his voice getting closer.

His lips thinned in anger and he raised one eyebrow and turned to Abby and whispered, his words cold and brittle. "His cattle? Right."

Wyatt took a couple of deep breaths to calm his raging emotions and looked around at the mountain. He needed to find a spot where they could run that would protect them against this new danger.

"Let's get to higher ground. I remember seeing a large boulder higher up that is well hidden. It will give us the cover we need." Wyatt pointed to a spot near a thick row of trees.

She nodded, shivering. "Okay. I trust you, Wyatt. Let's make a run for it."

"Okay. Here we go." Wyatt surged forward with Abby by his side. When they were almost near the big rock, he heard Abby cry out.

Wyatt turned to see Abby had fallen to the ground.

He raced over to her and picking her up, carried her

bridal style the rest of the way. The sound of a bullet flew by them, but didn't reach them. He ducked them both behind the large rock, just as another shot was fired.

"Oh, my leg hurts." Abby rigidly held her tears in check and grabbed her leg with one hand.

Wyatt scrambled to look at her leg and saw blood seeping through her jeans. He grabbed his pocketknife and cut open a portion of her jeans directly above the wound. It was bleeding steadily and he knew he'd have to do something.

He ripped off the bottom section of his t-shirt and pressed the cotton cloth to the wound. Holding his hand there, he called on his two-way radio.

When his brother Denver answered, Wyatt spoke in a rush. "Denver, call for an ambulance to meet us at Abby's ranch. She's been shot in the leg. We'll be there soon. Also, call Sheriff Turnbull and see if he's arrived at Abby's ranch and ask him to bring a police squad up the mountain. Let them know we found our stolen cattle, but there's a man shooting at us and we could use some help."

"Calling for help now. Stay safe brother." Denver replied and Wyatt turned off the radio.

She sighed and whispered. "How fun that you carry a two-way radio with you."

"Abby, trust you to be lying here in pain and still able to talk about things like they're fun." He swallowed his worry. "Now I'm convinced you're going to be okay. I need you to hold still so I can fasten a tourniquet."

She nodded and Wyatt could see her breathing was becoming rapid and her skin was clammy to his touch.

Without warning, memories of a similar trauma from his childhood hit him and he pushed them away.

He swallowed worry that tried to crowd his thoughts and breathed a prayer heavenward. *Please don't let her die. Help her live. I love her.*

Wyatt continued to work.

He remembered practicing the tourniquet procedure both in Veterinary college and as part of his training in the Military.

Taking off the belt from his jeans, he wrapped the belt two inches above the wounded area in her thigh. Watching her leg closely, he saw that the bleeding was slowing down.

He hoped the Sheriff and his police officers would arrive soon.

Abby whispered in a shaky voice as he studied her leg. "The man with the gun had an orange and blue ball cap. It might be the same man I saw at Reno Blackwell's ranch."

Wyatt raised an eyebrow. "I'll need to let the Sheriff know. Maybe we've figured out who has been behind the cattle rustling this entire time."

She closed her eyes for a moment. Her breathing sounded shallow to him.

He would need to keep an eye on her.

As he observed her leg, it seemed like it would be all right for the moment. From his first aid courses, he knew the longest recommended time to leave a tourniquet on was two hours. He was counting on his brother to have people coming to help soon.

Looking down at Abby, he noticed her skin glistened with perspiration and her green eyes were anxious.

"Sweetheart, you'll be okay. I'll see to it." He leaned down and touched his lips to her forehead. "I'm going to get you safely out of here."

Her face was pale and pinched. With the semi-dark sky of the sunset hovering above them, he could see the shadows deepening under her eyes.

She sighed lightly, looking up at him with exhausted eyes. "I know you will. I'm sorry for being so much trouble, Wyatt."

When she shivered, Wyatt stretched out close to her, holding her gently in his arms. "You are no trouble, Abby Meadows Hart. You are perfect just as you are. And I'm going to do everything in my power to see to it you get well. Now, you just rest and I'll try to keep you warm."

"All right." He could barely hear her soft whisper.

The sky had darkened a little more, when he heard a couple shots fired and then the welcoming voice of Sheriff Turnbull.

He could hear the sounds of footsteps headed up the mountain ridge where they were.

Sheriff's voice called out. "Wyatt, are you and Abby there?"

"Over here Sheriff." Wyatt got up and quickly checked the wound on Abby's leg. Relieved that her leg still looked okay he carried her out of their hiding place.

"There you are." Sheriff Turnbull looked at her pale face. "Well, let's get Abby quickly off this mountain. The ambulance is waiting at Abby's ranch, but we can take her in the Jeep. The medics are here to help."

He was relieved to see two men carrying a stretcher.

He laid Abby gently on the canvas and explained to them that he'd placed a tourniquet around her leg.

They took in the information about the gunshot wound, checked Abby's wounded leg. One of them adjusted the tourniquet and then they carried her to the Jeep.

Wyatt whistled for his gelding and the horse trotted toward him and turned to the Sheriff. "Just wanted to let you know, Abby recognized the man with the orange and blue ball cap as the man who shot her. She mentioned seeing him once before at Reno Blackwell's ranch."

"Yeah, I recognized the man when we put him in handcuffs tonight. He's wanted for more than just cattle rustling." Looking around the perimeter the Sheriff added. "If I'm not mistaken, these are your Black Angus cattle?"

Wyatt nodded. "Yep. I didn't get a chance to do a head count, but it looks like there are close to a hundred head of cattle. Ironically, it's the same head count that went missing from my ranch."

Sheriff nodded. "Well, don't worry. The Sheriff's department in Clear Springs county have already brought Reno's partner to jail. Also, they are closing in on the whereabouts of your missing ranch hands, about to make an arrest."

"And as we speak, my men are about to arrest Reno Blackwell. I can't believe I let that man pull the wool over my eyes." Sheriff Turnbull shook his head and grimaced.

"Well, at least we discovered it sooner rather than later. Thanks, Sheriff." Wyatt called out.

Sheriff Turnbull waved back at him. "Just doing my duty, Wyatt."

Wyatt got on his horse, following the Jeep down the mountain. His gelding was winded and sweating by the time they reached the barn on Abby's ranch. With hurried steps, he put his horse in the barn and gave him water and feed.

Racing out of the barn, he saw the ambulance had already left. Sheriff Turnbull was about to get into his cruiser, when he spotted Wyatt.

"Looking for a ride to the Hospital Wyatt?"

Wyatt nodded. "Yeah. Thanks."

"I can get you there in a hurry." Sheriff Turnbull turned on the flashing lights and raced down the highway toward Refuge Mountain's hospital. True to his word, the Sheriff got him there fast and they arrived just after the ambulance did.

Arriving at the hospital, Wyatt hurried out of the police cruiser and into the hospital.

After asking about Abby, the nurse asked him to wait outside. The Doctor would come to talk to him after he was finished. Wyatt called Abby's mom and told her what happened. He also called Abby's best friend, Sierra.

Wyatt paced back and forth in the hallway and it seemed hours before the Doctor walked outside Abby's room. By this time Abby's mom and sister had joined him in the waiting room.

The Doctor's voice was calm and cerebral. "I was able to clean and sew up Abby's leg. I don't foresee any problems, but I want to keep her in the hospital for a few more days to make sure. You all can go in her room and see her for a short time. She might not be awake."

Mrs. Meadows hugged Hadley and they both cried

tears of relief.

"That's good to hear, Doctor. Thank you." Wyatt breathed easier hearing those words.

He was about to walk away when the Doctor spoke again. "Were you the guy that put a tourniquet around her leg?"

Wyatt turned back, wondering at the question. "Yes."

"You did a great job. As far as I can tell, you saved her life today." The Doctor clasped his shoulder and left the room.

He felt a bottomless sense of peace and satisfaction at the Doctor's words. Even though he appreciated hearing the good Doctor's words, he wasn't looking for approval. He was simply grateful Abby was alive.

Wyatt sank into a chair in the waiting room until Mrs. Meadows and Hadley had been to see her.

When they had finally finished seeing Abby, he went into her hospital room.

Not knowing what to expect, a new anguish seared his heart when he saw her lying on the hospital bed, silent and still.

As he pulled up a chair close to her bedside, he reached for her hand.

He was still for a moment, staring at Abby's beautiful face laying there so pale and lifeless. It hit him full force how close he'd come to losing her. He covered her hands with both of his and leaned down to kiss her soft skin.

The heavy feeling in the pit of his stomach only grew and Wyatt closed his eyes at the vivid memory of seeing Abby falling to the ground from that gunshot wound to her leg.

He moaned out loud and kissed her hand. In a hoarse whisper all his pent up feelings spilled out. "Abby, I'm so sorry you were wounded. You could have died today."

Swallowing another wave of fear, Wyatt's voice was raw and hoarse. "It's my fault. I should have done more to protect you. I don't know why, but I seem to fail the people I care for the most. When I saw you lying there on that ground with blood oozing out of your leg, for a moment I was paralyzed by fear."

Wyatt's chest tightened as the initial shock of seeing Abby shot, replayed in his memory. Anger and fear flooded him and thoughts swirled, recapturing painful memories that took him back in time to his childhood.

He sucked in a deep breath and spoke, his low voice raw and vulnerable. "I remember when I was only a child of seven years old, living in a one-room apartment with my dad and mom. One night, my dad had come home drunk again. He started getting angry with my mom and began to hit her. I tried to defend her, but my dad threw me to the floor and continued terrorizing my mother."

Wyatt hesitated, swallowing back the fear that clawed at his throat as memories surfaced from that moment. "I don't remember how it happened, but my dad got so mad that he picked up the gun and shot my mom in the leg. She fell to the floor crying in pain. Not long after that my father passed out. I didn't know what to do, but I wrapped her bleeding leg in a towel and rushed over to tell our neighbor Mrs. Grainey."

"She hurried over and seeing all the blood she called the ambulance. They took my mom to the hospital, but they couldn't save her. And I... I never saw her again. The police arrested my dad and took him to jail and I became a ward of the state and went to a foster home."

A suffocating sensation tightened his throat.

"There are too many mistakes and failures from my past that I don't think can ever be made right. I failed to protect my mother and today I failed to protect you. Maybe I'm too much like my birth dad to deserve a second chance. Maybe, when I asked your dad's blessing to marry you years ago, he refused knowing marriage to me would only bring you pain."

Grief and despair tore at his heart. "Maybe I'm too broken and have made too many mistakes to be forgiven or loved by a women as lovely and good as you, Abby."

Leaning his forehead on her hand, he moaned. "And yet, I can't help it. I love you Abby. Please, hurry and come back to me. I'm desperate for another chance to look into your beautiful green eyes."

He captured her hand in his and pressed his warm lips to her skin. He released a long sigh, his whole body shivering, trembling, quaking.

He couldn't stop thinking about how much he needed her forgiveness.

He couldn't stop thinking about how much he needed her friendship.

He couldn't stop thinking about how much he needed her love.

Would Abby ever find it in her heart to forgive him and give them a second chance at love?

"DAD, *please don't hurt mom. You're drunk, don't you see? You don't really want to hurt her. You'll feel sorry in the morning like you always do." Her twelve year old body trembled with fear and anger.*

*"Abigail, you need to move out of the way when I tell you to." Her dad staggered closer to where she stood in front of her mom trying to protect her.*

*His voice was rough with no sympathy etched in its hardness. "Why can't you be more like your sister, quiet and obedient? You're always barging in where you're not wanted. Maybe this time you'll finally listen." Her dad's voice grated harshly and he swung the empty beer bottle in his hand with all his might to where it landed with a thud on her arm.*

*Yelling out in pain, she heard the cracking of a bone and clutched her arm. Her dad shoved her to the floor and stepped toward her mom. She sobbed as the sound of her mother's cries filled their small kitchen. Carefully she stood and clutching her arm she ran outside and toward the mountains, desperate to be somewhere where no one could hurt her.*

Abby moaned, tossing her head back and forth on the pillow from the terror of the nightmare. She heard more voices and was soon dragged back into another horrible dream...

*"Tom, I can smell the alcohol on your breath. Why haven't you stopped drinking, like you promised me you would?" She watched her husband stumble towards her, grabbing the kitchen counter as he walked closer.*

*His dark eyes looked hollow as a bloodshot gaze met hers. "I promised many things, dearest wife. I can't seem to keep my promises. My dad has told me that all my life, so I've come to believe it's true."*

*"Please try harder to stay away from drinking at the bar every evening. It's not good for your focus at work and it's definitely not good for our marriage. I really wish you'd stop."* She moved to the corner of the kitchen near the sink, standing there with her arms folded across her chest.

He mocked her, repeating her words in a high-pitched tone of voice. *"I really wish you'd stop. I really wish you'd stop."* He finally stopped and stood in front of her. *"Abby Hart, the perfect woman and wife would like me to stop drinking."*

She interrupted him. *"I'm not the perfect woman or wife. I make mistakes everyday..."*

He placed a hand over her mouth to stop her words, before his cold voice continued. *"Someone like you, could never understand what it feels like to grow up in a family where everything you do is never quite good enough. Where everyday you are rejected simply because you were born. Where everyday you're shown how much you're not wanted. Where everyday you are sure that your mistakes will never be forgiven."*

Backing away from him, she spoke with a voice edged in fear. *"Don't tell me I don't understand, because I do. My own dad only barely tolerated me and never truly accepted or loved me for who I was. I know what it's like to feel unwanted. I know what it's like to feel unloved."*

Tom followed her and grabbed her by the shoulders gripping her so tightly she knew she'd have bruises in the morning.

His voice hardened ruthlessly. *"No you don't know what it's really like, because if you did you would show more acceptance and love. And most of all you would be forgiving of others' mistakes..."*

Abby's head jerked on the pillow as she tried to put a stop to the man's voice she heard from her past... but the voice continued, only this time it was different, yet familiar somehow.

A low voice sounded in her ears, hoarse with emotion.

As he finished sharing his heart he said. "Maybe I'm too broken and have made too many mistakes to be forgiven or loved by a women as lovely and good as you, Abby."

He held onto her hand like he'd never let her go.

As the familiar voice continued to pour out his heart to her, she knew it was Wyatt. Memories of Wyatt and all that they had been through together returned.

She remembered all the pain and heartache, but she remembered all the good things that had only come into her life because of him. The details came back to her in vivid color.

A gnawing began in her belly and Abby realized with stark clarity, she hadn't shown him acceptance, love and forgiveness. All this time she'd thought everything wrong about their relationship was his fault.

In her mind's eye, it was almost as if she had placed a scoreboard over Wyatt's head and added an X for those times he made mistakes or failed her somehow.

The check marks were reserved for times he had done something that pleased her. As she saw the scoreboard in her mind, almost all of it was marked with an X.

Listening to his self-condemning words of failure and mistakes, forced her to face the truth that she had judged him too harshly.

Wyatt was a good man.

He didn't deserve how harshly she had viewed him. Maybe it was her own fears from a lifetime of hurt that skewed her vision of him, but that wasn't any excuse for being unkind.

It was time she saw the truth about him. In fact, the true score board would show almost all the check marks in Wyatt's favor with hardly any X's on it at all.

She stirred and moved her hand a little to touch his cheek. It was time to tell him the truth.

"Abby?" Wyatt's low voice sounded surprised and hopeful. "Are you awake?"

She nodded, her lips tilting upwards in a small smile as she stared into his handsome face. "Yeah."

He released a slow sigh of relief. "You're going to be okay."

Wyatt rubbed a hand along her arm and watched her, concern in his eyes.

"I am." Abby reached for his hand. He opened his mouth to speak, but she placed her fingers over his lips. "Shh... please, let me say what I need to say first."

He nodded and regarded her with somber curiosity. "Of course."

"As I began waking up a few minutes ago, I heard you talking to me." She watched him shudder, drawing in a deep breath.

His eyes looked down at their hands joined together. She could sense he was uncomfortable with all that he had shared. "It's okay Wyatt. I'm glad you said what you did."

He looked up at her and his gray eyes widened, revealing the tortured dullness of disbelief. "You are?"

Nodding, she squeezed his hand and began sharing her heart. "I need to tell you, I was so very wrong about you. And I'm truly sorry."

"Wrong? You don't have anything to be sorry about Abby."

Abby nodded and held up her hand. "Yes, I do."

She continued speaking the force of her conviction wouldn't release her until she said all that was on her heart. "I'll explain."

"When I listened to the painful story of your childhood and heard you share that you felt you'd made too many mistakes and failures in your past to be truly forgiven and loved, I knew I needed to tell you the truth."

"About what?"

"The truth that I've been so wrong. I haven't been accepting of who you are — including mistakes and failures — as I should be. I want to tell you I'm sorry. *Truly sorry.*"

Tears moistened her eyes. "I've held my own anger and fears in a tight grip for so long, that it has begun to make me bitter. I don't want to be that person who sees every person through a warped lens. Condemning people around me, without having a real understanding of the truth."

Abby recalled the hurtful conversations from the past with her mother-in-law. "I don't want to become an old woman whose heart is so hardened that she can't forgive others."

Expelling an unsteady breath she continued. "So, I want to say I am truly sorry for holding a grudge, for being angry and for every time I've judged you harshly or been unkind to you. And now, I'm asking from the depths of my heart, will you forgive me Wyatt?"

He stared wordlessly at her for a moment, deeply

touched by her words. "I have to admit I'm surprised that you feel the need to ask my forgiveness, Abby. But, I want you to know with all my heart, I *do* forgive you."

"Thank you."

He kissed her hand. "But, on a similar note, I want to say sorry too."

"For what?"

"For leaving you seven years ago, without trying harder to understand what was really going on."

Abby shook her head. "My mom admitted that she and dad did everything they could to put a stop to our marriage."

"I know. But, I'm still sorry for all the times I've been angry, unkind or failed you in any way, Abby. Will you forgive me?" His heart was in his gaze and as their eyes met, her heart swelled with a feeling she had thought long dead.

"Yes. I do forgive you Wyatt."

He sighed in relief, swallowing back emotions.

Shifting his body, he sat on the edge of her hospital bed and pulled her into a tender hug, leaning his forehead against hers.

Wyatt's chest heaved and his eyes closed tightly.

His hands stroked her auburn hair that lay in waves against the white pillow. Abby heard him release a jagged breath and loved the tender kiss he placed on her forehead.

Feeling his arms around her, she felt treasured and loved.

"Heaven help me Abby, I thought I might lose you when I saw all that blood on your leg. I had vivid images of losing you, just like I lost my birth mom." Wyatt's eyes looked deeply into her own and expelling a shaky breath, he squeezed his eyes shut for a brief moment.

As the emotions of the day flooded her senses, Abby cried softly onto Wyatt's shoulder, her arms encircling his neck.

His large hands moved in gentle circles along her shoulders.

"You pulled me away from that madman with the gun, Wyatt. You saved my life today and didn't leave me alone." Abby whispered and a sudden sob escaped as she imagined what would have happened to her if she'd encountered the man with the gun alone.

"I won't ever leave you again, not if I can help it sweetheart." Wyatt kissed the top of her head and cradled her close to his heart.

Wyatt," Abby whispered softly, her mouth so close to his that their breath mingled. "Thank you for saving my life."

She pulled slightly back so she could see Wyatt. Reaching a hand to his cheek, she stared into his haunted gray eyes.

Wyatt nodded, unspoken pain alive and glowing in eyes that refused to leave hers. Then, ever so slowly — almost as if he expected her to pull away — he moved his lips closer to hers. "I can't stand the thought of losing you. I'd rather die myself."

Abby turned her face to accept his kiss, unable to deny him anything.

Trembling hands tangled suddenly in her thick auburn

hair, holding her captive. His lips ravaged hers with an intensity that made her senses spin.

Nothing else mattered in this moment except the warmth of Wyatt's touch. A fierce tenderness rose up inside as Abby passionately fed his need.

Wyatt's heartfelt whisper caused her to come undone. "My sweet Abby, I love you. I can't bear to lose you."

"You won't. I'm here… I'm here." Her body clung to his and she offered her lips to his loving mastery. He rained kisses on her eyelids and cheeks, kissing her over and over again until she was breathless.

Leaving her fears and inhibitions behind, Abby's arms reached up encircling his neck and drawing him closer.

Unexpectedly, she was reminded of the love she had for Wyatt years ago as a young girl of eighteen.

The love that was opening in her heart for him now, went far beyond a simple schoolgirl's crush. It was this deep devotion that she had longed for all her life. Her heart over-flowed with joy in the realization that Wyatt needed her.

Wyatt pulled his lips from hers with a low moan as if unwilling to part from her even for a moment. His strong arms cradled her close to his chest, and she heard the rapid beating of his heart.

A deep sense of contentment and happiness flooded her.

He continued to caress her hair and Abby snuggled closer to his heart.

She loved being held by her best friend, but there was something even more powerful about the tender way he held her now.

Abby sensed a deeper bond with Wyatt, it was almost like their souls joined in a way they hadn't before.

He had told her, he needed her, but it was only now that her heart opened up enough to finally believe him. Abby swallowed back the wave of emotions that flooded her senses.

He held her in his arms and they sat together in the stillness of the moment for a long time. Abby cherished being close to him.

Wyatt's gruff whisper broke through the quiet moment. "I'm sorry for all the times I pulled away from you. I was scared of being rejected and of making myself vulnerable to love. My heart was on the line and I was afraid."

"I understand, Wyatt. I heard what you said about your painful childhood." Abby didn't want him to feel like he needed to relive those difficult emotions again.

"I know, but what I didn't tell you was that I've finally realized that the trauma of rejection and heartache made me too afraid to love. And a big part of that pain has been my fear of losing someone I love again."

The weight of Wyatt's sorrow was in his voice.

"I'm sorry. It's okay, Wyatt." Abby tightened her grip on him, pulling him closer, aware of how difficult it must be for him to speak of the trauma of his past.

Wyatt's body tensed and pulled back, his gaze meeting hers. "No, it's not okay. Don't you see? I don't want to hide from love. I failed to protect my mom and later on I failed to protect Tom in the way they needed me to. What if I fail you too? My heart couldn't take it if I lost you too."

Abby placed gentle hands on his cheeks, looking him

in the eye. "Listen to me. It wasn't your fault your mom was shot, and it wasn't your fault she died. You were a child, who had no control over the situation."

"And Tom's death wasn't your fault either. Your whole team was literally running for their lives. It really was a miracle any of you made it out of there alive. Tom's death wasn't your responsibility. You need to understand that." Abby moved slightly back so she could look deeply into Wyatt's eyes, her own clouded with unshed tears.

"I will try, Abby. But, their deaths continue to weigh heavily on me. I've always felt responsible for them both." He squeezed his eyes shut, a harsh groan released from his lips.

"For years the weight of my birth mom's death — and later Tom's death — has all but crushed me. I'm terrified that somehow I'll repeat the same mistakes with you. I love you so much that it scares me to live in a world without you in it."

Wyatt released a strained breath. "And that is why I'm going to do everything I can to grow, change and make things right between us. But, I'll admit, I might need your help and your grace when I make mistakes. I want to be vulnerable and close to you. I long to spend a lifetime learning how to love you, Abby."

A single tear slipped down her cheek. The corners of Wyatt's mouth turned up, he reached over and with his thumb, wiped away her tears.

She turned to look into her best friend's eyes and the smoldering flame she saw there, convinced her of the truth of his words.

"You really love me?"

Words spilled out of his mouth, sharing the deepest feelings of his heart. "I fell in love with you that summer years ago. I saw you in the pasture, worried that your horse had gone lame." Wyatt smiled tenderly.

"You were so beautiful and charming and I was smitten. It's why I tried my best to not get too close to you until the summer you turned eighteen. It was the toughest thing I've done. You were far too captivating." He expelled a long sigh.

"It's also why I've been so bad tempered these past few months, trying my best to keep my distance and to ignore these feelings." He ran a shaky hand through his hair and grimaced. "I'm sorry for doing that."

Abby was overjoyed to hear Wyatt's words of love. "I forgive you. And I want you to know, I too have struggled to let go of my fears."

She continued, her voice thick and raw. "Tom struggled with being rejected by his dad all his life, and instead of finding healing he turned on himself by drinking most nights and on me by treating me harshly. He told me he couldn't stop his addiction of drinking and gambling, so he said he was joining the military."

Her body visibly shook as memories flooded her mind. "Even though toward the end we weren't very happy, I never wanted him to die. But, I do forgive him for the painful moments we had in our marriage. I'm just sad, that I never had a chance to tell him that, or to ask Tom to forgive me for any part I played in causing him pain."

Tears glistened in her eyes and she ached with an inner pain. It was like a permanent sorrow that weighed her down everyday.

"Thank you for telling me that. I'm sorry that you and Tom struggled in your marriage. I'm sorry he hurt you." Wyatt clenched his mouth tighter in irritation. "But, even though we can't undo the past, we can forgive others and ourselves and begin to heal so we can have a fresh start."

She drew in a deep breath and nodded her agreement, swallowing the emotions that clogged her throat.

"I want that fresh start with you, Abby." Wyatt put his hands on her cheeks, his gaze searing hers. "I've been drawn to you from the first… all those years ago."

"You are my soul mate. You are the woman I long for. You're also someone who also happens to be selfless, beautiful and very… captivating. And I love you." Wyatt faltered on the last word, as his eyes darkened and moved down to focus on her lips.

With a giddy sense of pleasure she let her happiness show and with a shaky voice declared. "I love you too, Wyatt, with all my heart."

A dizzying current raced through her at the passion she saw in his eyes.

His whispered words, mingled close to her lips. He kissed both her eyelids, cheeks and nose before he spoke in a throaty voice. "I want to ask you something."

Her heart jolted and her pulse pounded and she asked, breathless. "What?"

"We started as friends, but now our relationship has shifted into much more." Wyatt tilted her chin up, his gray eyes searing hers.

She nodded her agreement and searched his eyes, curious at the change in his face.

"I love you, Abby Meadows Hart. Would you do me the

great honor of becoming my wife?" There was a slight hesitation in his voice, as if he was unsure if she'd agree.

Abby let out the breath she'd been holding while the corners of her mouth turned up, an invitation on her lips.

Wyatt's fierce love for her, coupled with his need to make her his wife was the most compelling reason for her to marry him.

"Wyatt, I love you. You've saved me, you've trusted me with the most vulnerable part of yourself, and you've honored me by loving me. So, the answer is yes. More than anything I would be happy to be your wife."

The tender passion in his eyes made her heart hammer against her ribs.

Wyatt's mouth swooped down to capture hers with a sweet reckless abandon. His arms tightened around her, pulling her close.

Abby reached her arms around his neck and brushed her lips against his, her kisses saying much more than words ever could.

He groaned and folded her in his arms, kissing her with the hunger of a starved man. "Abby, I'm thrilled to make you mine forever."

His lips recaptured hers, in a slow drugging kiss and her heart raced at the dreamy intimacy to their kisses now.

Her emotions swirled and skidded on the inside while her heart overflowed with love.

This familiar love for Wyatt felt as right and true as it always had.

Abby's heart soared, grateful that at last her dreams of *forever* with her cowboy best friend had come true.

# EPILOGUE

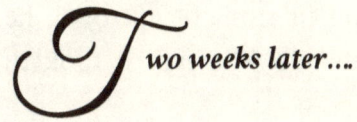*wo weeks later....*

THE JOYFUL RINGING of Church Bells in the bell tower of the Community Church, pealed through the air, the sound making its way toward heaven.

Wyatt could feel the vibration of the bells shoot up from the wooden floor of the church and up through the soles of his shoes.

His body shook, not only from the sound of the bells, but from the reason he was here today.

Loosening the tie of his three-piece suit, he shifted his feet and glanced at the large crowd seated inside Refuge Mountain's Community Church.

They were all waiting for one person: *His bride.*

As the Church Bells continued ringing, he remembered his Dad's last letter and dying request that he give himself a second chance for love.

Wyatt glanced heavenward, a thoughtful smile curving his mouth. *I guess you had the right idea after all, Dad. Abby is my first and only love and today she becomes my wife. I'm grateful for that second chance. If you can hear me from up there, I just want to say thanks.*

His expression stilled and his lips quivered with a smile.

Reverend Jon stood on his other side, standing still as a source of calm serenity — something he desperately needed today.

The extra pressure of being in front of a crowd, he could do without, but he would do whatever it took to make Abby his wife.

An easy smile played at the corners of his mouth as memories rose to the surface of the day he took Abby home to announce their engagement.

Abby had just been released from the Hospital, when they went to tell Annie Callahan the good news. His mom was thrilled and gave Abby an enthusiastic hug.

His fiancé listened as his mom shared the story of how she had married Mack fifty-one years ago on Christmas Eve at the Community Church in their small town.

She had talked about how wonderful a Christmas wedding would be. It was the season of hope, miracles and love and what better way to show that, but for Wyatt and Abby to marry on Christmas Eve?

A look of surprise had come across Abby's face that made him chuckle. She didn't think they would have the wedding organized that quickly. His mom said she had helpers that would get it all done in time.

To his surprise, Abby agreed. They had only two weeks to plan their wedding, but it was done in plenty of time.

Once his fiancé said yes to marry him by Christmas, Wyatt had been free to tell her about the last letter his Dad had written.

When he'd explained about his Dad's request that Wyatt help on her ranch, at first she didn't like it too much. Wyatt explained that even without his dad's letter, he had planned on doing all he could to serve her anyway.

Abby knew the truth of his words and said all that mattered was that they loved each other.

She was surprised by the inheritance Wyatt received from Mack Callahan. And was excited to help Wyatt to build his dream of helping orphaned and struggling boys and girls.

He was grateful to be marrying a wife who had so much compassion and love to give to others.

Flowers lined the front of the church and on the corner of every pew. Wyatt smiled warmly at his mom whose wide smile indicated she was well pleased to be here at her son's wedding on Christmas Eve.

His five younger brothers sat beside their mom, all of them eager to do what they could to keep that look of joy on their mother's face. Seated nearby, was Father Tim. He'd told them he was happy to just sit back and enjoy their wedding.

Wyatt was pleased to see ranchers and other folks he knew from the community. It gave him joy that so many of his friends and neighbors came to celebrate with them on their wedding day.

Hearing a low chuckle next to him, Wyatt turned.

He flashed an annoyed look at his brother Denver standing at his side as best man, a wide grin on his face.

Wyatt mumbled. "What are you grinning at?"

"You. I can't remember the last time I saw you this nervous." Denver whispered, his voice teasing, a common character trait among all his brothers.

"Yeah? Well, just wait. I'm sure it won't be long before it's your turn." Wyatt broke into a mischievous grin that hinted at what was to come.

Denver's brows drew together in an agonized expression.

Wyatt's mouth twitched and it was all he could do to stop himself from laughing.

Breathing deeply, he tried to calm his nerves, when all of a sudden the music changed. He stood up straighter, realizing this was the moment he'd been waiting for.

Joey and his brother Tony appeared at the double doors at the back of the church, walking down the middle aisle, carrying a heart shaped pillow layered with ribbons that were tied to their wedding rings.

Abby had asked the boys to be part of their wedding. Their foster mom, Mrs. Beaseley had been happy for them to participate.

When Abby suggested to him that they adopt those two boys, Wyatt agreed, but only if they could have a long honeymoon first. The boys had agreed enthusiastically, eager to be part of their family.

The boys stood near him and faced the crowd, big

smiles on their faces.

When suddenly the music changed again, Wyatt couldn't help but grin at Denver whose eyes were riveted on the maid of honor that walked toward them.

Sierra looked beautiful in a tea length burgundy colored dress. Her long blond hair hung down her back in waves and the tiny splash of baby's breath by her right ear, only enhanced her beauty.

At this moment however, he was anxiously awaiting the first glimpse of his bride.

In the next moment, he saw her.

Abby stood at the double doors, her hand rested on top of old Sam's arm.

She had known Sam all her life and many times had stopped to talk to him and help him when she came to the Triple C ranch. Since both Abby's and his father had passed away, Sam seemed the perfect choice to walk his bride down the aisle.

His bride was dressed in an ivory colored long wedding dress that rippled behind her as she walked down the aisle.

Long auburn hair cascaded in waves to Abby's waist like a waterfall, making her look lovelier than he'd ever seen her.

Held in her hands, were red and white roses, scattered with baby's breath. Encircling the crown of her head were also delicate red and white flowers.

Seeing her walk gracefully toward him now, a happy smile on her lips, felt like he was looking at a little bit of heaven on earth.

She was beautiful.

Looking at her now, nobody would be able to guess that she'd lain broken and wounded in the hospital only two weeks ago. The Doctor had done a good job fixing up the gunshot wound in her leg and she continued to heal.

She still walked cautiously, but the doctor had assured her it would heal in time.

He was so thankful that her injury hadn't been a lot worse. He was simply grateful she was alive.

As Abby reached his side, Wyatt took her hand gently placing it inside his. Leaning towards her, he whispered. "You are simply gorgeous today, Abby."

His fiancé's cheeks blossomed with pink.

Reverend Jon spoke for a few minutes on the blessings of marriage before he asked them to repeat their vows to one another.

Looking into his bride's beautiful green eyes, he poured his heart into the words that would bind them together forever.

"The first time I saw you, you were a young girl riding across your dad's ranch. You enjoyed life and I saw in you a picture of all that was good, sweet and free. But there have been other times when I've seen you wounded and in pain, and life has thrown you obstacles that have been difficult to find your way through. As I've seen you go through the best and the worst times, I realized something. It's your courage, determination and compassion that won me over since the first day I saw you."

Wyatt's words were passionate and strong. "Now, you are a beautiful woman with a compassionate heart. We've shared many memories over the years, some good and some not so good."

"But we made it through to this moment today. I wasn't sure we would make it to the place where you would agree to become my bride. I'm sad to say, my own fears and insecurities held me back from accepting your forgiveness for a long time." Wyatt paused as deep regrets invaded his emotions.

He continued in a raw voice. "Abby, it was your acceptance, forgiveness and love that saved me and helped me see for the first time the real treasure of who you are. I am thankful for you — for the past, present and future we'll share together — I love you."

Tears glistened on his bride's lashes and on her beautiful face. Squeezing his hands, she released a long sigh and her gaze met his staring deeply into his soul.

When he'd first seen Abby, at her late husband's funeral months ago, he had been convinced that she would never forgive him, never accept him and never love him.

However, in the past few months all that had changed. He'd fallen in love with his best friend.

Starting today, they would have a real marriage based on forgiveness, commitment and love.

With gentle hands he reached for his bride. Gathering her into his arms, he held her snugly against him.

Lowering his head, his lips slowly descended to meet hers.

Her sweet lips intoxicated him. He breathed deeply of the scent of roses that surrounded her, loving the way her arms tightened around his waist.

Holding Abby in his arms, he'd finally found home.

❦

THE MOMENT she felt Wyatt's lips touch hers, blood pounded in her brain, leapt from her heart, and her knees began to tremble.

She was shocked at her own eager response to his kisses.

Slipping her arms around his neck, she returned his kiss, lingering, savoring every moment.

True love had melted all her fears and deep inside Abby knew she'd found the place where she belonged.

It had been a long, painful road she'd taken to find a husband who would love her like this. This kind of love — filled with acceptance, forgiveness and love — had been what she dreamed of as a little girl.

She never thought this kind of love would happen for her.

After years of being told she was either in the way or unwanted, she'd come to believe she wasn't worthy to be loved. But those words and actions from people in her life had all been lies. Those lies had created wounds in her heart and she'd responded by building thick walls around her heart.

Abby saw things with more clarity today, than she ever had before.

Her parents hadn't trusted her to choose the man she loved all those years ago, and had steered her in the wrong direction. She had just accepted their decision, because of her own fears and insecurities.

As soon as Abby had been released from the Hospital,

her mother had returned all those letters Wyatt had written.

Her mom had told her she overheard the Doctor say that Wyatt had saved her life and that's when her mom realized he was a good man and had been a good man all these years.

Her mom finally apologized and asked for Abby's forgiveness, which she gave freely. She finally understood that they had been wrong about Wyatt and was sorry they had stopped Abby from marrying him years ago.

Hadley had come to the ranch with her mom and apologized for all the years of anger and bitterness.

Her sister confessed that she had always been jealous of Abby, because she was beautiful and men had always been interested in her. Hadley felt like she had always been the odd one out, with no boyfriend or husband.

They had hugged and Abby said she was sorry for not understanding how her sister had felt all these years. Their relationship was beginning to heal, for which Abby was grateful.

After they had left, Abby had read through Wyatt's letters until late at night. She realized that he had loved her far more than she ever understood. She'd been so wrong to be angry and to lash out at him. But again, it had been her own insecurities and fears that had made her push him away.

Wyatt really did love her. He didn't feel sorry for her. He had helped her with the ranch, he had bought her horses and given them back to her. Later on, when she got the gunshot wound to the leg, Wyatt had saved her life.

He did it all because he loved her.

Now that she was Wyatt's wife, they would be a family. Her dream of having a family was coming true after all.

They would start by adopting the two boys, Joey and Tony, and hopefully more children would come. For so long she had felt alone, like she didn't really belong and had told herself that would never change.

With her marriage to Wyatt, all the lies she'd come to believe were proven to be false.

As of today, not only were she and Wyatt a family, but she also became a member of the large Callahan family. It was the most wonderful feeling in the world.

Abby's heart spilled over with contentment and joy.

Her new husband ended the kiss, his gray eyes flickering with tenderness.

The wedding guests clapped and Reverend Jon introduced them as husband and wife.

Wyatt turned to her with a heart-stopping grin and tucking her hand in the crook of his elbow, they hurried toward the back of the Church.

They had decided they would greet everyone and thank them for coming to their Christmas Eve wedding. Folks had their own family plans, and they were grateful to share this day with friends.

Sheriff Turnbull walked up to them shaking their hands. His voice was gruff as usual. "It's good to see you two have joined forces. I always thought you two would make a good team."

Abby smiled at the Sheriff's words. She knew he wasn't one to let his emotions show, and she appreciated that he came to their wedding at all.

"We appreciate you making time to join our celebration today, Sheriff." Abby nodded, her eyes flickering with warmth.

"Well, you and Wyatt saved the day a couple of weeks ago. Now that we have your ranch hands, Reno hired hand, and Reno and his partner in jail awaiting trial, I feel like I owe you that." Sheriff shook his head, a grimace on her face.

He sighed heavily as he continued. "Reno confessed. He admitted he wanted Abby's land and water rights, with a goal to become the greatest rancher in the area. All those red circles you saw on Reno's map, were the ranchers in the area he was determined to ruin."

The Sheriff spoke pointedly. "Those circles included you and Wyatt. Which is why Reno hired a man to kill your horse, Abby. He was counting on scaring you enough so you'd decide to sell your place and move on."

Wyatt tightened his fingers around Abby's waist. "Well, he didn't know my wife very well, if he believed that. She is stubborn and doesn't get scared off very easily."

Even though hearing about Reno's plans shook her up, she was pleased to hear Wyatt's words of belief in her.

"I've always known that about you, Mrs. Callahan." Sheriff winked at her and grinned as his gaze shifted between the two of them. "It's good to see you smiling again." He touched the tip of his cowboy hat and shook Wyatt's hand again before he walked away.

Abby released a sigh. She was relieved that all those people who had been involved in the crimes of killing her horse and rustling cattle had been arrested.

"You okay?" Wyatt pulled her close, whispering in her ear.

She turned and looked at him, a wide smile turning up the corners of her mouth. "Never better."

"Good." He kissed the top of her head. "Because your mom and sister are on their way over here."

Abby turned to see them hurrying in their direction. She was thankful her relationship with the two of them was beginning to heal.

They stopped and embraced both her and Wyatt.

Whispering in Hadley's ear, she said. "I see Wyatt's friend Drew Standish over by the door, looking in your direction."

"Oh I see how it is. Now that you're happily married, you want everyone you know to enjoy married bliss too." Abby nodded, giggling.

Hadley whispered. "But, I think you might be onto something. I'll talk to Drew and get to know him better. Who knows, maybe there will be wedding bells ringing in my future."

Abby still had a smile on her face as she hugged everyone in her new family.

Annie Callahan pulled her into a long embrace and gently kissed her cheeks. "Darling girl, I've waited so long for this day. Now you are truly my daughter. It makes me so happy that you're a part of our family now."

Wyatt's mom glanced beside Abby to where Joey and Tony stood, with smiles on their faces. She leaned down and kissed their foreheads. "And you boys are going to be part of our family too. I'm glad."

"Me and my brother are happy too. Does that mean we get to call you Grandma now?" Tony asked, eyes wide and innocent.

"You sure can." Annie Callahan opened her arms and pulled them into a gentle hug. Tears glistened on her lashes as she released them. A wide smile hovered on her lips as she hugged Wyatt.

"I only wish your Dad were here to see this day. He would have loved seeing you married and welcoming all the new family members today."

"I think he's been seeing it all today and is smiling from heaven, Mom." Wyatt hugged her close and kissed her cheek. Annie Callahan had a new light in her eyes as she walked over to talk to her friends.

A warm welcome awaited Abby when Wyatt's six brothers walked over. Each one gave their new sister-in-law a big hug.

"I think I need to tell that brother of mine, to take a break from all his work and treat you to a proper honeymoon." Denver winked at Abby who blushed at the topic.

Wyatt cleared his throat. "I'm changing my workaholic ways Denver, don't you worry. Abby is making a new man out of me."

Abby giggled. She liked listening to them sparring back and forth. Being in the middle of it, made her feel truly like she was part of the Callahan family and she loved every minute of it.

Many of the other guests stopped to talk to them and Abby and Wyatt thanked each one of them for coming.

Suddenly, she saw Mrs. Hart walking toward her. They had talked only last week, when Tom's mom had stopped by and said she was sorry for all the mean things she'd said to Abby through the years.

Mrs. Hart had asked for Abby's forgiveness, which she

had given. It would still take time to heal all the hurt between them, but at least healing had begun.

Much to Abby's surprise, Mrs. Hart had returned the ten thousand dollars. She said with her husband's death, she realized how selfish they had been to demand money from Abby. Martha Hart had apologized that they had asked for it in the first place.

Their relationship was on a path toward healing, but they still had many wounds to overcome. As Mrs. Hart walked toward her now, Abby's hands fidgeted at her side, uncertain and a little worried about what she would say.

A man stood by her side as Martha Hart came to greet her.

"Abby, I wanted to tell you I'm happy you found love again. As much as I miss my son, it's not fair that you remain single. I knew a woman as kind and beautiful as you wouldn't stay a widow for long." Hearing her former mother-in-law give her such high praise surprised Abby.

"Thank you." The quiet words were all she could think to say in response. Abby's eyes drifted to the older man who stood beside Martha Hart.

"I want you to meet my friend from years ago, Henry Morden." Mrs. Hart wore a big smile and her eyes were as bright as Abby had ever seen them.

This was the man that Sierra had mentioned as Mrs. Hart's first love from years ago. Abby could see the happy glow on both of their faces. She smiled. "Nice to meet you, Mr. Morden. Thank you both for coming to our wedding."

"Of course. And I hope you'll be very happy, Abby. You deserve it." Mrs. Hart kissed her cheek. Watching them walk away to join their friends, Abby felt as if a heavy burden had been lifted.

Abby was bewildered but pleased at the change in Tom's mom. Seeing her today with Henry Morden, she hoped Mrs. Hart would have a second chance at love.

One of the last people to offer their congratulations was the Callahan family's lawyer, Mr. McCrae.

He handed Wyatt an envelope and spoke to them both, an enigmatic smile on his face. "This is one gift I'm quite happy to give to you both. Wyatt, you did all that your Dad asked of you and more. I believe he's looking down on you right about now as pleased as any proud father would be. I'm excited to see you both get started on those dreams... and I wish the very best on your marriage."

Mr. McCrae nodded and walked away, mingling with other guests.

After many of the wedding guests left, Abby and Wyatt went outside the church doors, standing side by side at the top of the wood steps.

The Church Bells filled the air, the sound echoing throughout their small town.

"Those bells echo what's in my heart. Being loved by you is a miracle I never thought possible when I first came back home. Now look at us."

"That's beautiful, husband of mine. Now we have something to tell our children and grandchildren." A gentle smile hovered over Abby's lips as she looked up into the sky.

Snowflakes began falling softly, covering everything in a soft white blanket.

Wyatt took off his suit jacket, slipping it over his new

wife's slender shoulders. He pulled her close, his arm around her waist, and kissed the top of her head gently.

"I couldn't have asked for a better wedding day." He murmured as his cheek rested against her hair.

"Yes. It's been wonderful."

"Thank you for agreeing to be my wife, Abby Callahan."

Abby smiled, gazing into her husband's eyes. "I love the sound of my new name. And I'm very happy to be your wife, Wyatt. We have both been on a journey of learning to let go of our fears. Thank you for how you have stuck by me, accepting me as I am, despite my confusion, anger and fear."

Wyatt pulled her close. "We've both had fears and misconceptions. I'm grateful we've chosen to accept and love each other instead."

Her husband shifted, placing both hands on her cheeks, looking deeply into her eyes. "I've waited for this day for so many years. I'm standing here today still amazed that we are now husband and wife. I'm so thankful to have you as my bride. I love you."

A single tear rolled down her cheek at his words. Her husband honored, accepted and most of all loved her for who she was.

She would never get tired of hearing his words of love.

"And I love you. I look forward to being by your side... *forever.*"

**Excited for the Next Book?**

**Don't Wait! Start Reading Denver's Story in *The Redeemed Cowboy's Secret Baby* Today!**

*She's his first love and the one woman he could never forget. He's the Cowboy she fell in love with... and the same man who left her at the altar years ago.*

**Sierra Baxter's life was thrown into turmoil when the man she loved bolted out of her life years ago.**

**Since the day he left, she has worked hard to give her son the security and love he needs. An unexpected and welcome gift was the acceptance and love they both were given among family and friends of their small town.**

**When the town council volunteers her to be the host of Refuge Mountain's Christmas Fair, she agrees.**

But, the day her ex-fiancé suddenly returns to their small town, the town council eagerly chooses him to be her co-host.

Sierra worries knowing the secret she's kept from him for the past six years is about to be uncovered.

Denver Callahan didn't start out with plans to be a famous Country Music Singer.

He'd just written songs on the side, pouring himself into his music, when one day — just before his wedding day — his talent was discovered.

Years ago, he chose the love of music over his first love. But, he'd never forgotten her — the scent of her or her beautiful smile.

Now that he'd returned, it looked like they would be forced together, co-hosting their small town's Christmas Fair.

Seeing Sierra again, his attraction for her is stronger than ever. But, years of neglect and abandonment sit between them like unbreakable walls.

*Will Denver pick up his cowboy hat and return home to stay? Can he convince Sierra that he will choose her this time... his first and forever love?*

## ALSO BY MELODY ARCHER

**Clean Billionaire Fake Marriage Romance Series**

Book 1: The Billionaire's Marriage Bargain

Book 2: The Billionaire's Marriage Contract

Book 3: The Billionaire's Marriage Promise

Book 4: The Billionaire's Marriage Barter

Book 5: The Billionaire's Marriage Pledge

**7 Brides for 7 Cowboys, Small Town Sweet Western Romance Series**

Book 1: The Forgiven Cowboy's Best Friend

Book 2: The Redeemed Cowboy's Secret Baby

Book 3: The Honorable Cowboy's Convenient Marriage

Book 4: The Wounded Cowboy's Beauty Bride

Books 5, 6 & 7 are still to be released.

**Grab the next book in your favorite series when you visit my Author Website below:**

**www.memorablefictionbooks.com**

# ABOUT THE AUTHOR

Melody Archer lives in Southern Alberta with her husband and their five young adults.

Recently, her oldest son married his wife from Brazil and the whole family is really loving spending time together getting to know their new daughter-in-love. ;)

She loves new and classic romantic movies, green smoothies and going on adventures with her family.

*Melody would love to connect with you :)*

# ACKNOWLEDGMENTS

Thank you to all the wonderful people who helped me with this book.

To my cover designer, Wilette from Red Leaf Book Design, thank you for designing this gorgeous book cover.

Thank you also, to my proofreader Cathy who patiently read through each chapter, helping me make this story so much better.

A big thanks to all my wonderful Advanced Readers (my ARC reading team), who faithfully read and left reviews of this book.

Lastly, a huge thanks to three of my young adult children who read through the manuscript, giving me all kinds of great suggestions on how to make this a better story.

Thank you everyone. I really appreciate you!:)

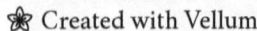 Created with Vellum

www.ingramcontent.com/pod-product-compliance
Lightning Source LLC
Chambersburg PA
CBHW051126190726
48290CB00006B/1702